AM I GOOD ENOUGH TO LOVE?

BRIANN DANAE
DOMINIQUE THOMAS

AM I GOOD ENOUGH TO LOVE?

Written by
BriAnn Danae & Dominique Thomas

Copyrighted Material

Copyright © 2018 BriAnn Danae & Dominique Thomas
All rights reserved. No part of this book may be reproduced in any form without written consent of the publisher, except brief quotations in review form.
This is a work of fiction. Any characters, places, objects, references or similarities to actual events, real people, living or dead, or to real locals are intended to give the novel a sense of reality. Any similarity in other names, characters, places, and incidents are entirely coincidental and are solely of the Author's imagination.

MESSAGE TO THE READERS

Hi, ladies! I first have to thank the Lord for blessing me with this amazing talent. I was so excited to write this story with my uber talented friend BriAnn. I love that we can come together once again on a book and make magic happen! This story really took us through every emotion and we put our all into the Flint sisters. We missed out on sleep and nearly lost our edges lol. Seriously though, this book is everything. These characters are real, their story is and we're sure so many of you can relate to it. So, if you like the book hit us up to let us know and don't forget to leave a REVIEW.
-Dominique Thomas

Ladies! Hey! Here we are again with another collab. I absolutely loved peening this book with Dominque, and I hope you all enjoy it. Like she said, we lost sleep and I'm still

securing my edges as I type this. Lol. I pray you enjoy it and the gems we dropped within the pages as well. These sisters are everything! Let us know your thoughts in a review if that's your thing. Thank you so much for the support. Enjoy!
-BriAnn

PROLOGUE

Detroit MI, 1992

Megan sat on her cream leather sectional with a smile on her face. The liquor had her tipsy. She was a light drinker, and her man knew that shit still he insisted on giving her glass after glass. She bopped her head to the Ice Cube track as she watched Deron shoot dice in the dining room. Friday was their party night, so while her mom kept Logan, they kicked back and had some adult fun.

Megan couldn't stop staring at him as she absentmindedly fiddled with her gold doorknockers. She wanted the earrings with her name in them and Deron being Deron purchased her all the hoops that the jeweler pulled out. Her almond shaped eyes admired Deron's tall, stocky frame and she licked her lips. He was wearing jeans with a leather and suede brown sweater while a large Mercedes chain hung from his neck.

He talked shit and kicked it back with his boys while Megan eyed him. Almost like he could feel her staring at him their eyes connected and he winked at her before going back to his dice game. His dirty red low fade was parted on the side and lined to perfection while rings adorned every finger that he had. Her baby was one fresh ass nigga, and that had been why she'd fallen for him in the first place. They were six years in, and she loved him with all her heart.

Megan stood up and decided to relieve her bladder before she laughed too hard at something and pissed on herself. Never had she had those kinds of issues until she had Logan. That damn daughter of hers had weakened the hell out of her bladder. Now all Megan had to do was snicker, and a tinkle of pee would leak out of her. The shit was embarrassing to her, but she wouldn't complain. For Logan, this would be her first and last baby because she didn't want any more kids. It was all worth it, though.

Megan quickly handled her business and washed her hands. She looked at herself in the mirror and smiled. She was rocking a blue jean dress with ankle heels, and her hair was done up just like Vanity who many people swore she resembled.

As she exited the bathroom and bent the corner, she overheard Deron talking with some of his friends that he hung with. Taking a step back, she eavesdropped on their conversation.

"You talked to Tasia since you been back?" One man asked Deron.

Deron shook his head. He glanced around for Megan before replying.

"Yeah, baby girl is good. This shit so crazy man. You don't even understand," he replied.

Megan's heartbeat increased as she listened to them talk.

"I mean you got it all. Two fine ass baby mommas' and you getting money. How did Megan take the news about Kolbee?"

Megan felt her chest tighten. Slowly, she slipped off her $1000 door knockers. She tossed them onto the ground gentle enough to not bring attention her way.

Deron sighed. Every time he thought of telling Megan, he bitched up. He would never regret his daughter. That was his blood. His legacy. He loved Kolbee already, and she was only an infant. It was what she represented to his main, to the woman he had been with for six years that had him keeping her a secret.

Deron wasn't perfect. He did the best he could, but at times he fucked up. While out of town handling business in Kansas City he met a beautiful woman by the name of Tasia. She was cool, they immediately clicked and before he knew it an affair had begun. Tasia knew nothing of Megan and felt they were exclusive up until she told him she was pregnant. Then shit got real, and Deron had to show his cards. He was living foul, but the nigga in him couldn't let either of them go so now he was trying to find a way to tell his woman about his newest blessing.

"I love Megan. That's been my bitch for a while now.

Ya'll niggas know that, but Tasia is cool. We got a baby together now, and I'm trying to figure this shit out. Megan not gone take this with a smile, you know?"

Deron's friends nodded until their eyes grew wide in shock. Deron turned to see what they were staring at and dropped his beer. Megan ran up to him with the largest knife that she had in the kitchen, and the sharp cutting object immediately pierced his umber toned brown skin.

Deron's face shifted in pain as he gripped her wrist as tightly as he could.

"Shit, baby! Calm down!" He yelled fearing she would kill him.

Megan had the devil in her eyes as she moved fast trying to break his hold. She kneed him, spit on his handsome face and once she saw he still wouldn't ease up his grip she head butted him.

"Megan calm down!" Mary, her best friend, yelled running into the room after hearing the commotion.

"Let me go you trifling ass motherfucka!" Megan yelled through gritted teeth.

Deron shook his head. This was why he hadn't told her. They rarely fought, and now she was trying to harm him. Possibly kill his ass if she could. He'd done this to her, to them and he felt fucked up behind it.

"Baby, please calm down! I'm sorry. I'm so fucking sorry, beautiful," he apologized in his most sincere voice.

Megan shook her head not wanting to hear that *sorry* shit. She let go of the knife and everyone in the room exhaled. Deron let her wrist go and eyed her carefully as she started to smooth down her auburn hair that had fallen out of place in their scuffle.

"I need for all of you motherfucka's to leave my shit right fucking now. I'm about to kill this nigga," Megan stated in an eerily calm tone and left back out of the room.

People started to spread like roaches out of the large room. Deron and Mary followed Megan to the back of the large home and Mary's heart dropped when she watched her best friend pull out her favorite shotgun.

Deron stood tall not letting his worry show on his handsome face or his stance. He stood in front of Mary and looked at Megan. Megan aimed the shotgun at him as he stared her down.

"I'm sorry. I'm man enough to admit that I fucked up, but the baby is here, and I don't regret her. I love my daughter, and I pray that one day you can forgive me and learn to love her too. You can't shoot me, and you know that shit. Put the gun down Megan," Deron told her.

Megan's hand shook as she held the weapon. Tears clouded her vision, and before she could pull the trigger, Deron was snatching the shotgun from her small clammy hands.

Mary sighed with relief and left them alone for some privacy as Megan began to cry hysterically. Deron held her as tightly as he could. Tomorrow wasn't promised but what he did know was that he couldn't walk away from Megan and he refused to let her walk away from him. He kissed her forehead lovingly as she wept into his sweater.

"Her name is Kolbee, and she's so beautiful. She looks like

Logan did when she was a baby. I'm sorry. I'll say that shit until the day that I die, but I won't apologize for having my daughter. You'll learn to love her and forgive me," he told her confidently.

Megan cried harder. He talked about his betrayal with such ease. As if he'd forgotten to pay a bill or mow the lawn. Not at all like he'd birthed a child, had an affair. She was so heartbroken that she couldn't do anything but cry. Deron had never hurt her like that before. He had her questioning everything about their love.

"Please calm down. I will make this right," he promised rubbing her back.

Megan shook her head while pulling back from him. She looked at him. The man that she loved with all her heart and wiped her wet face.

"There is nothing you can do to fix this, and *that child* of yours will never step foot in my fucking home," she said bitterly and raised up off the bed.

If Deron wanted his family in KC, then Megan was positive he wouldn't have the family that was in Detroit.

1

PRESENT DAY

THE HOUSE WAS A MESS. THERE WASN'T ANY OTHER WAY to look at it. However, it was the thought behind it that made Logan smile. She walked around her living room grinning. Jordyn studied her closely with her hand under the bottom of her pointed chin.

"So, do you like it?"

Logan slowly nodded. Her living room had been transformed into a Barbie Doll's playground. Toys were everywhere and while Logan had no energy to clean she also didn't have it in her to yell at her baby.

"Mommy loves it! It's like Barbie moved in and dropped something down on the rent."

Jordyn laughed. She plopped down on the ground and picked up her favorite doll. A tattered, matted hair Frozen doll that her father had given her a year ago.

"Well let's play silly," Jordyn said in only a way that she could, and Logan looked down at her.

Jordyn was a small version of her walking around only her skin was much lighter. Jordyn even had the red hair. On her pale skin were her freckles and on her cute round face were a pair of the prettiest bright eyes one would ever see. Jordyn was gorgeous, and Logan dreaded the day some little nigga knocked on her door looking to take her daughter out.

"Silly? What mommy say about that?"

Jordyn shrugged. Her slanted eyes peering up at Logan in a way that made her smile. A weaker person would have caved immediately at how innocent Jordyn was looking.

"I'm sorry. Can we play?"

Logan smiled. She was dead ass tired. She worked in a salon doing lash extensions, and after being on her feet all day the first thing she wanted to do was wash her ass, but mommy duty was always calling. Because Jordyn had a wishy-washy ass dad, Logan was forced to carry the load for both of them, so if she didn't give Jordyn play time, then she just wouldn't receive it.

"Okay, my name is Jordyn-Elsa-Princess. You just stole Anna's necklace so right now you're on trial for murder," Jordyn said and tossed a white Barbie at Logan.

Logan pushed her red strands away from her face and laughed.

"What? I'm dying because I stole a necklace?"

Jordyn nodded making her own red hair bounce that sat on her head in a large curly afro.

"You stole something mommy and when I was watching the news with granny earlier some crazy looking man had stolen something too. He was on trial for murder, and now you are too. Stealing is bad," Jordyn told her.

Logan smiled although she made a mental note to tell her mom about that news mess. Jordyn was too smart to be watching that tainted bullshit.

"Okay well I'm sorry, and I don't wanna die. Please don't kill me Jordyn- Elsa-Princess," Logan pleaded.

Jordyn laughed.

"You have to raise your left hand and promise to not do it again," she told Logan.

Logan arched her brow.

"You mean my right hand?"

Jordyn's pretty face fell into a scowl.

"I'm five. I make mistakes mommy," she replied, and Logan laughed.

She raised the doll's right hand and looked at her daughter.

"I, Barbie with the missing top and shaved head promise to not steal anymore. Stealing is bad-"

"And will get you killed," Jordyn butted in, and Logan narrowed her eyes at her. Jordyn quickly nodded. "Sorry but I guess you're free to go," she replied.

Logan stood up and glanced around her living room.

"While mommy washes up you clean up and put all of your barbies back in the top boxes. Okay?"

Jordyn's eyes did a slight roll, but she was smart enough to nod. One thing she didn't like was whooping's, so she did her best to avoid getting them.

"Okayyy," she drawled with a drag of her words and

slowly stood up. In her pink pajamas, she began to gather up her toys.

Logan retreated to the back of the apartment and into her bedroom. She took off her clothes and before she could go to her bathroom her cell phone rung. Logan snatched it up off her nightstand and looked at the name that slid across the screen. Her first thought was to decline the call, but out of loyalty to the little-animated life inside of the living room, she answered.

"What?"

Rome smacked his lips.

"Damn hi to you too. Your attitude is all fucked up. That's why we couldn't make this shit work," he expressed in his usual deep voice.

Logan smiled. His words, his actions used to hurt her so much. Now all they did was piss her off. However, what he did to Jordyn did bring her to tears many nights.

"Rome I'm tired. I just got home from work to provide for the child you barely see. Don't call me like you're going to be greeted with some sweet little nothings. I hate you."

Rome sighed.

"You should be tired of saying that shit, Logan."

Logan shook her head as she eyed the door not wanting Jordyn to hear her talking with him.

"And you should be tired of being a sorry ass nigga."

Rome chuckled.

"You got that one. If you wouldn't have left a nigga high and dry a year ago, we could be a family."

Logan shook her head.

"Regardless of if I'm with you or not, you need to care for

your child. Us, you and I will never be. We don't mesh well. You're lazy in and out of the bedroom. I wish I would have known that beforehand, but I don't regret my baby. Now, why are you calling me?"

Rome cleared his throat.

"That money that you wanted for her dance class gone be short. I had to have some shit done on my car and buy my ticket to Miami for my birthday. If I would have waited any longer, then tickets would have been high as fuck."

Rome didn't pay child support. He didn't buy clothes or even do daycare. Logan's mother watched Jordyn and her father although she rarely talked to him sent her money to help with Jordyn as well. Logan couldn't think of a time when she could ever depend on Rome, and that angered her. Her caramel colored skin grew hot as she sat down on the edge of her bed.

"I hate you. Like I really fucking hate your sorry ass. It was only $580, and you couldn't do that? You have a job. You stay with your brother, and you don't have any real fucking bills. Man, the fuck up nigga!"

Jordyn ran into the bedroom as Logan's eyes watered. Rome hung up in her face like the pussy ass nigga that he was, and Jordyn blocked him. He wasn't needed in her daughter's life anyway. Just another way for the devil to bring darkness into her life. Until he got his shit together, he wouldn't be getting through to either of them.

"What's wrong? Did my daddy make you mad or was it grandma or oohhh did auntie Jerricka do it?"

Logan smiled weakly at her daughter. Whenever she lost her cool around her, she felt bad. She kissed her forehead and touched her soft hair that still smelled like her strawberry shampoo.

"No that was mommy shouting out to the world how much she loves you now can you finish cleaning up? You just in here staring at all mommy's goodies," Logan teased because she was still wearing her underwear.

Jordyn smiled and waved her hand in the air.

"Mommy, please. We are both girls. I have that already," she replied making Logan fall back on the bed and laugh.

"Damn Logan. Throw that pussy back," Uriah grunted and slapped Logan on the ass.

It had been six months and four days since she'd had some long pipe up in her. Logan's eyes were shut tightly as her body welcomed the pleasure. She needed it. Her body craved it, and she was praising the Lord above for blessing Uriah with a meaty, long tool. His dick was hung, and he knew how to work it. He'd always been her backup plan, but after going off on Rome the previous night, she knew she needed something to take the edge off.

Since she didn't smoke sex would do.

Logan was glad with her decision.

"Ugh! I'm cumming," she whimpered like that was a problem.

Uriah sunk his teeth into his bottom lip and fucked her through her release. Once she was done he flipped her over and slid back inside of her. He looked down at her pretty ass face, and his dick got harder. Logan's dark red hair was sweated out at the edges. Her lips were slightly parted, and those big ass breast of her's were bouncing with every thrust that he gave her.

"Damn you so pretty. I been waiting for this," he exclaimed, and before Logan could respond, he was shooting off inside of the condom.

Immediately once he pulled out Logan was ready to go. She sat up on the bed ran her hands through her wet strands. Uriah discarded the condom and cleaned off his dick before joining her on the hotel bed. He kissed her back, the rose tattoo going down the center before trailing his tongue up to her shoulder that had another rose that was bleeding. The tattoos were kind of dark, but he liked them, and the artwork was legit. Clean as hell with no messy lines. Uriah pulled Logan back down on the bed and forced her to look at him.

"Why do you do that?

Logan frowned at him. Her heart was still beating wildly, and she was anxious to climb into her own bed to go to sleep.

"Do what?"

"Anytime some deep shit happens with us you check out," he replied.

Logan gave him a small smile.

"Uriah, we have never even had sex before. What are you talking about?"

Uriah shrugged. Logan was more like a nigga then a bitch. She was so detached that he feared he would never know the real her. He'd been surprised as shit when she called asking him to meet up with her. Like the nigga he was he did, and now he was regretting that shit.

"Forget it. We fuck buddies now? You weren't trying to give a nigga a real chance," he said bitterly.

Logan laid back and stared up at the ceiling. Rome had hurt her, but he wasn't the first man to do it. No, it was her father. Still, she'd given the pretty boy with the basketball scholarship a chance. Rome had put her through it and even dropped out of school in between doing all of that. He wasted his time and her's. She refused to let another nigga hurt her.

"Uriah its late and I'm tired. That was good, but I need to get home. I'll call you," she said and placed a quick kiss on his lips.

Uriah mean mugged her as she quickly got dressed. Logan hastily left out of the hotel room and went to her car. As she put on her seatbelt, she received a call from her father, Deron. Her teeth gritted as she accepted it.

"Hi."

Deron hated how nasty she had become towards him, and he blamed a lot of that on her mom that had filled her head up with lies.

"How is my granddaughter doing?"

Logan started up her car and pulled out of the lot.

"Fine."

Deron sighed.

"And, how are you? You never call me anymore. You act like you don't fucking know me when I'm the man that raised you."

Yeah me and your other child. Logan shook off her thoughts.

"I've been busy with work and Jordyn. You know I have no support from her dad."

"He a sorry ass nigga," Deron replied, and Logan snorted.

"He's not the only one," she mumbled, and Deron's brows bunched together.

"Fuck is that supposed to mean? Logan, you got something to say to me?" He asked getting angry. He started to cough, and Logan's shoulders slumped.

"No, I don't. Look you know why I'm upset. You left Detroit, and I feel like it was because you wanted to be closer to her."

Deron shook his head. He was ashamed that he had let his family fall apart the way that it had.

"I moved to Atlanta years ago because your mom put me out. You know that, and still, I took good care of you. You didn't want for shit. Your sister stays in KC, and it's nothing wrong with me being close to her. Unfortunately, she treats me the same way that you do," he replied.

Logan rolled her eyes. She didn't understand how you could be family with someone that you didn't even know.

"My sister. Okay. Look I have to go."

"No! I need you to come visit me. It's something really important that we need to discuss, and it will be in person. Your sister will be here as well. This isn't an option Logan. I already got the ticket and bring my granddaughter with you. I emailed you everything, and I want you to know that I love you. I wasn't the perfect daddy, but I love you girls, and I will die loving you all," he said before ending the call.

Logan sat her phone in the cup holder while frowning. The last thing she wanted to do was see her father and a sister she had no connection to.

2

I SHOULD HAVE IGNORED THIS DAMN CALL. With her bottom lip tucked between her teeth, Kolbee's amber colored eyes rolled to the top of her head. For the life of her, she couldn't understand how bill collectors were able to contact her when she had a block list that was a mile long. Her mind had been elsewhere when swiping her phone screen, and now she was regretting it.

"Ms. Flint, are you able to make a payment today?" the collections lady spoke softly. Her voice wasn't demanding, but that didn't stop the burn in Kolbee's throat or her eyes from misting.

Scattered across her wood dining room table was a stack of bills she had fallen behind on far past their due dates. If it wasn't her college calling and emailing about late payments, it was the loan company's she had gone through to pay for school. Not to mention her past due credit card bill. She was close to thirty-thousand dollars in debt and was sick to her stomach about it.

"I'm sorry, not today. Can I take your information down and call when I can?" she asked politely.

"Of course. Just try to get on top of this. Interest will be added each month. Are you ready for my information?"

Nodding, Kolbee mumbled a yes, but she wasn't writing a thing down. There was no need to knowing she wouldn't be able to pay off any bill any time soon. She needed a miracle to come through for her.

"Or a damn sugar daddy," she huffed once she was off the phone.

At the tender age of twenty-six, Kolbee didn't imagine her life being like this. Looking back on the fun she had in college, and the education she did receive in those three years before she had to withdraw; Kolbee was wondering if that degree she was working so hard towards was worth the stress it had been causing her for the last two years. Dropping out so close to the finish line devastated her. Not only that, but it had placed her under a deep depression for months after.

"They'll get their money when I get some extra money. Whenever the hell that'll be. Mama!" she called out while standing to her feet.

"I'm in my room," her mother, Tasia yelled back.

The two lived together. Though Kolbee wanted to be on her own, she didn't have the proper funds to cover her means of living. Staying with her mama was okay with her. She had been her entire life and didn't see a thing wrong with it. Tasia, on the other hand, wanted her daughter to move the hell out. Not because she didn't want her there, but because she wanted Kolbee to grow through her struggle and learn responsibility.

"What's up, ma," Kolbee grinned as she stepped into her mother's bedroom door.

"Nothing. What's up with you?"

Kolbee chuckled at her reply. Tasia and her daughter were thick as thieves. When Tasia first found out she was pregnant, she immediately began to pray for a little girl. She had nothing against boys – seeing as though she had a son six years younger than Kolbee – but a baby girl was all she ever dreamed about. Deron, on the other hand, wanted boys to carry on his legacy. It was just his luck to be blessed with two beautiful girls. That was surely some type of payback.

"I'm so sick of these bill collectors; I don't know what to do. I block one, and three more call. How do they keep getting my number?"

Annoyed, Kolbee flopped down on the bed and laid back. "I'm going to change my number."

"And, what will that fix? You'll still be in debt," Tasia shrugged with a chuckle.

"Mama! It's not funny. I'm for real."

"I'm for real, too. I don't know why you just won't call your daddy. You know he'll help you if you ask him."

Kolbee sucked her teeth. "No. That's what he wants me to do. Call and ask him for some money, just so he can ask why. I shouldn't have to ask him for anything. Plus, money can't make up for his absence in my life."

"And, it shouldn't. But... it will help. And, your daddy wasn't completely absent. Give him some credit," Tasia replied.

Though she and Deron hadn't been together in over twenty years, she wasn't going to let her daughter blame his not so present presence, be the cause of her hardships. Kolbee was just learning what adulthood was. Bills had surely shown her how grown she wishes she wasn't.

Sitting up, Kolbee yawned. "I'll pass. I don't need him going back to his little family and telling them our business. I'll figure it out."

"We'll figure it out," Tasia corrected. "I'll pay your phone bill, and car note this month. Next month you're on your own."

Kolbee hopped up from the bed with a quickness. "What! Are you for real, mama?"

Tasia smiled before answering, "Nah. I'm for fake."

"Aaah!" Kolbee screamed, before pulling her mama's short frame into a bear hug. "Thank you! I love you!"

"Mhm. You're welcome, and I love you more. Now, get off me so I can finish getting dressed. What time do you have to be at work?"

"Not until two. I'm closing tonight, so I have a late shift."

"Okay. We'll probably get home around the same time. Ya'll got any sales going on?" Tasia asked, unplugging her charger from the wall and stuffing it into her purse.

That's why my credit card bill is so high now. Not because of her mama alone, but because the duo loved to shop. It was a bad habit Tasia had picked up on when she started fooling around with Deron. He spoiled her to no end, and it got worse when Kolbee was born. He blew a check at the mall without blinking for his girls. Though he had cheated on his main girl, Megan, he'd never in life turn his back on his child or the woman who carried her.

Kolbee had her spending habits a little more under control than her mama, but she did her thing too when she could. Working at Nordstrom as an assistant manager wasn't her ideal job, but it paid the bills that it could. Dealing with customers and employees through retail had taught her to have so much patience. Her spit fire personality didn't waiver, though.

"Nope. You don't need anything else in that closet of yours. I'm surprised things can still fit," Kolbee replied while checking her hair out in the mirror. Her short, reddish-orange curls were longer than she'd like for them to be but she'd been so busy; the hair salon had been the furthest place from her mind.

"Don't worry about what's in my closet," Tasia told her and pinched her ass.

"Stop," Kolbee laughed and swatted her hand away.

"You're built just like me when I was that age. Put some pants on, too. You know Latrell's nappy headed friend be looking at you."

They snickered at Tasia's innocent jab toward her son's friend. With bee stings for breasts, what Kolbee lacked in the chest area she made up for in the ass and hips department. In her younger years, she despised the girls with luscious boobs and an ass to match. But, as she got older, she began to appreciate what the Lord had given her. Her body didn't define who she was as a woman, and that affirmation is one she lived by.

"Have a good day at work. I'll call you on my lunch break," Kolbee told her mama from the front door.

"When you gon' get a man?" Tasia smirked. "You could be calling *him* on your lunch break instead of bothering me."

Kolbee gasped and feigned hurt. "I bother you now? And, I can call you if I want to. Your little boo thang got you feelin' yourself or something."

Giving her a grin, Tasia dropped in her driver's seat. "Sure do. Tell Latrell not to have any fast ass girls in my house either."

"I'm telling your baby daddy!" Kolbee yelled out.

"Which one?" Tasia laughed and shut her door.

Kolbee shook her head at her mother's antics before going back in the house. She had a few hours before she needed to be headed to work as well. Taking a seat back at the dining table, she opened her laptop and pulled up Google Chrome and began typing.

One-bedroom apartments in Kansas City.

Hitting enter, she began to browse the hundreds of living options throughout her city. Though she didn't know when or how she would move out of her mother's place, it didn't hurt to prepare. If the opportunity ever presented itself, Kolbee was hopping on it quicker than an opponent who was down to the last seat in musical chairs.

"Man, quit playing with me Kolbee. Why the fuck you block me?" Bryson questioned coolly.

A few weeks had passed since that talk with her mama,

and Kolbee was two weeks away from the first of the month yet again. On her lunch break, Kolbee decided to go sneak up on her best friend, Alaia, who worked at *Finish Line* so she could vent her frustrations. Before she could make it to the entryway, Bryson and a group of his friends were walking out with multiple bags in their hands.

It was just her luck to run into him after placing him on the block list the week prior. Like those damn bill collectors; Bryson had begun to work her fucking nerves. Not intentionally, but just in general. Everything was annoying Kolbee to no end these days.

Leaning up against the railing he trapped her on, Kolbee tried hard not to suck her teeth. Bryson was a handsome young man. His wicker basket colored skin and grey eyes were what caught Kolbee's attention six months ago at a step show. After a few casual dates, some good sex, and okay conversation; she wasn't too thrilled with the idea of taking things further. Her mind was on how she was going to make a come up to change her lifestyle.

"No reason really. I was just good on you," she replied nonchalantly.

Bryson's head cocked back. "Good on me?" He let out an amused chuckle and licked his lips. "You must be fucking with a new nigga or something for you to just up and cut me off. I thought we were good."

"We were. Still can be if you want to be friends, but I have other things in my life that need my undivided attention. I need to focus on my money right now."

"You can't multitask, damn?" he chuckled, and Kolbee shook her head no with a slight smile.

"Nope. Not unless you trying to pay some of my bills." Her eyebrow lifted waiting to see what his response would be. Bryson just blinked his eyes. "Exactly. We're good, though. No hard feelings. I just need to focus on me. I know you understand that."

"I do, but I don't at the same time. It's all good though, ma. It was fun while it lasted. You take care."

Kolbee leaned into his broad chest and inhaled his musky cologne. "You, too."

As she strutted away in the slides she had replaced for her heels, Bryson shook his head at the way her ass was sitting up in her black suit pants. Though he admired her determination to get focused on her bread, he was pissed that she had cut things off between them so smoothly. Keeping it real, Kolbee had some of the best pussy he had slid up in, and she was cool to kick it with.

"Man. That bitch knows she bad with her fine, red bone ass," one of Bryson's boys chimed.

"Watch yo' mouth, nigga," Bryson scolded him before they walked off. Salty or not about the L he had taken, he'd never let a nigga disrespect Kolbee.

After speaking to a few of the employee's, Kolbee made her way to the counter where Alaia was posted. She had been a store manager at *Finish Line* for the past four years. Thanks to her cool discount, Latrell had every pair of shoes he wanted. Alaia was what most considered the shoe plug.

"You could have given me a heads up," Kolbee groaned as she leaned against the counter.

"I didn't even know you were at work today. What did he say?" Alaia smirked.

She was a brown skin beauty, with long curly hair she kept in a bun, who had just come into her girly ways in the last few years. A tomboy at heart with three older brothers, most of her family thought she'd be into girls. Some of them still did. Her having hardly any figure at all didn't help either. Alaia paid her family no mind, though. If they knew how her skinny ass was taking dick from the highly blessed and favored in the length department, they wouldn't believe it.

"Nothing really. Just asking why I blocked him, and I must have another nigga. Hell, I wish I did. Maybe he'd be willing to let me run up in his pockets. I'm so sick of living paycheck to paycheck; I could pull my hair out."

Alaia's lips tightened so she wouldn't laugh. "Um... you do know you're damn near bald, right?"

"Fuck you," Kolbee hissed and mushed her. "It's a figure of speech."

"You said it, not me. Seriously, though? I know what you mean. We should hit a lick on somebody."

Alaia said it in a whisper, and Kolbee looked at her strangely. "Bitch, what? A lick on who?"

"Does it matter?"

"I mean, not really. I'm down for whatever," Kolbee shrugged. The idea of robbing someone wasn't in her plans, but she would ride with Alaia regardless.

Alaia cracked up laughing and pushed her best friend away from her. "Girl, I'm glad to know you're down for the cause. My ass ain't hitting a lick on no one."

Kolbee rolled her eyes playfully. "I was about to say. Anyway, what time you get off?"

"Six. You close, tonight?"

"Yeah. Unfortunately," she moped before grabbing her vibrating phone out of her pants pocket.

As if she could get anymore annoyed, seeing her father's name flashing across her screen almost caused her to spazz out. Telling Alaia she'd be right back, Kolbee stepped out the store and off to the side before answering his call.

"What's up?"

"What's up?" Deron questioned. "Is that how you answer your phone now?"

The smacking of her lips caused Deron to shake his head. Kolbee was the youngest and damn sure acted like it. She was his baby girl, though.

"I've always answered my phone, the one I pay the bill for, like this."

Deron chuckled. "You and that smart mouth. You get that shit from Tasia, no doubt."

"Nah. I get that sh-stuff from you," Kolbee sassed back. "But, for real. What's up, daddy. You don't ever call me. You must be in a good mood."

"Here you go. I do call; you just don't answer. How you been? You need anything?"

Kolbee swallowed hard. Asking for some money was on the tip of her tongue, but those words went down her throat like a rock before she could voice them.

"I'm okay. And, no. I don't need anything, but you must want something. How's your little family doing in Detroit?" she snickered, and it pissed Deron off.

"Kolbee," he hissed before he began to violently cough. "Quit playing with me. And, you are right. I do need something from you, and it's not all that fucking attitude. Understand?"

Kolbee sighed and rolled her eyes. "I guess."

"Don't guess. You and that sister of yours man," he grumbled with a shake of his head.

"What the hell does she have to do with me or this conversation?" she spat, getting angry. "Look. Tell me what you need so I can get back to my lunch break."

Deron cleared his throat. He hated and loved the relationship he had with his daughters. They meant everything in the world to him, yet his love wasn't enough to bring them closer together. He was putting an end to the shit, today. Regardless if they liked it or not, Kolbee and Logan were going to have to put their differences to the side.

"I need you to come to Atlanta and visit me. It's important, and I don't care what you think you're not going to do because I already bought you a plane ticket. You can be mad at me all you want, but I love you. You and your sister, and I always will. Check your email when I hang up, and I better see your bright face in a few days."

Deron hung up before Kolbee could gather the words in her head to go off. As soon as she pulled the phone from her ear, her email alert went off with a confirmation email from Delta Airlines. She didn't know what her dad had up his sleeve, but Kolbee knew she needed to get prepared for the bullshit.

"I don't even know this damn girl like that," she huffed out. It didn't matter to Deron if she knew Logan well enough or not. She was going to get to know her and her daughter real soon.

3

Deron booked the girls flights for a week after he called them, and Kolbee was still annoyed. Mainly because she had to put her life on hold, but thankfully her vacation week was coming up. Otherwise, she'd be sitting this trip out. More hurt instead of angry like Logan, Kolbee was still coming to terms with the fact that she had an older sister. One she didn't even have a relationship with.

She always knew of Logan, had even stalked her Instagram for a while, but stopped because it made her upset. Deron had cheated on Megan, Logan's mom, but he never lead Tasia on. Tasia didn't know he had an entire family tucked away in Detroit while he was making moves to Kansas City, and she didn't find out until she was pregnant. By then, she had grown to love Deron, and it may sound crazy, but Deron loved her too. It wasn't the same love he had built with

Megan over those six years, but it was love nonetheless. Some shit he couldn't control no matter how hard he tried.

Tasia didn't play not one single game when it came to her child, and she let Deron break the news to her about his other family. All Kolbee knew was that she had a sister. Why she couldn't see her or live under the same roof as she and Tasia were beyond her. Megan's hatred for Deron and his side family was a grudge she held for years. It wasn't until Deron took one of his many visits to Kansas City during his weekend with Logan, did the sisters meet.

Logan was ten at the time and was absolutely in love with her four-year-old sister. She cried the entire way back home to Detroit, and Deron knew she was going to tell Megan. He didn't care, though. Was it foul for him to do that behind her back? Hell, yes. But, Deron was sick of Megan trying to treat Kolbee like she wasn't shit. She could be mad all she wanted to, but she had better take her anger out on him and not his baby girls.

"Mama, why can't you come down there with me?" Kolbee whined as she stood in front of the TV.

Tasia was relaxing on her day off with a glass of chilled wine on a table tray to her right, while her boyfriend Mitch massaged her feet.

"Because you are grown, and I wasn't invited. What are you afraid of?"

"That Megan is going to be there and try to talk slick to me. Then, I'll end up having to punch her ass in the mouth," Kolbee hissed.

Mitch chuckled, and Tasia slapped his arm. "That shit's not funny. I joke around from time to time, but that bitch knows I don't play about my kids. I wish she would say some off the wall shit to you. What Deron say it was for anyway?"

Tasia would be on a redeye had Kolbee called her with some bullshit. Though she was chill during her pregnancy, she and Megan had crossed paths back in the day. Megan was older, but Tasia didn't care. Young or not, she could hang with the best of them when fighting, and Deron knew that. Once she realized that Deron was a dog ass nigga for fooling around on Megan, she didn't take him seriously.

"He didn't say exactly. Just for me to be down there because it was important," Kolbee voiced.

"Hmm. I guess you better toughen up and see what he wants then. Plus, you haven't been to see him in a while. I'm sure he misses you."

"I bet he does," was Kolbee's reply before she walked out of the living room.

Her flight wasn't set to leave out until tomorrow morning, but she wished it were for today. Her nerves were getting the best of her. Something that never happened. Kolbee was usually chill when it came to certain situations, but the idea of being in the same place with Logan was causing her to lose her cool.

Going into her room, she flopped back onto the bed and began to scroll her Instagram feed. She hated how the posts were no longer in chronological order. Seeing posts from two days ago made her roll her eyes. Typing Logan's username into the search bar, she went to her page to see if she had uploaded anything.

It was a habit of Kolbee's no matter how much she hated to admit it. Her big sister was gorgeous, and her niece was even more beautiful. Blessed with the same red hue of hair as Deron's, Logan's was long, luscious, and draping down her back. It was crazy to Kolbee how neither of them had taken after their mother's skin complexion. Their bright skin tone was identical, and their noses looked just like their dad's. The two resembled one another so much, Kolbee often imagined what it would have been like to grow up together.

Having a younger brother was cool, she loved Latrell, but the yearning she felt in the pit of her gut for a relationship with her big sister was one she wanted since she was four years old. In her younger years, she'd question Tasia about Logan's whereabouts, but after a while, she stopped. Even as a youngin' she knew it wasn't a topic that she was going to grasp until she was older. And, even though she was grown and had been for a while, the concept was still slipping through her fingers.

"Maybe this trip I'll get some answers," she said aloud before her phone rang.

Bryson's name flashed across the screen, and Kolbee huffed. She wasn't annoyed that he was calling, but in disbelief somewhat. She had literally unblocked his number hours ago, and she surely thought he must have been sent a bat signal of the removal or something. Shit was weird.

"Yes?" she answered sweetly.

"I miss you, ma. Come pull up on me."

Kolbee rolled over on her side and placed him on speaker. "It's raining."

"What that mean? A little rain ain't ever stopped you from coming over."

"Yeah... when we were fooling around. I'm not pulling up

on no nigga I don't fool with especially in the rain. The dick ain't that good," she laughed, and Bryson sucked his teeth.

"You still on that bullshit. It ain't even raining that hard. I'm trying to eat your pussy from the back and you-"

"Come and get me," Kolbee said cutting him off mid-sentence. Climbing off the bed, she began to prepare her things.

"You playing."

"I'm serious. I'll come over, but you gotta take me to the airport in the morning."

"Man," Bryson dragged with a chuckle. "You about to have me on a flunky mission. Where the hell you going?"

"That's none of your business, sir. You gone take me or not? Let me know now before I be in this bed sleep." Kolbee wasn't about to play with him. Bryson was known to talk a good game, and usually fell through for her, but she wanted to see if he'd switch up now that they were on different terms.

Sliding his hoodie on, Bryson snatched his keys off the dresser. "Yeah. I'll take you. Don't have me waiting outside either."

"Boy, shut up. Your ass about to drive in the rain for this pussy," she rapped, and they both laughed.

"You talking all that shit now. I'll be there in twenty minutes."

"Okay. Drive safe."

"Always."

Tossing her phone on the bed, Kolbee rushed to pack her an overnight bag. Her two suitcases were already packed and ready to go along with her carry on. After sliding into a pair of low-top rain boots and a *From The Bottom* crop hoodie, she hauled her belongings down the hallway, down the steps, and toward the front door.

"You taking your stuff to the car right now?" Tasia asked, and Mitch sat up so he could help her.

"No. I'm staying over Bryson's tonight. He's going to take me to the airport in the morning."

"You just gone tell me, huh?" Tasia joked, making Kolbee groan.

This was the only thing she disliked about living under her mother's roof. Though she was grown, she'd never disrespect her by having Bryson or any of her male friends come through on a consistent basis. Though in her teenage years, she'd snuck a few in. That was then though. Plus, Bryson had his own crib. It made perfect sense to just go to his place. Especially for what was about to go down.

"Mama," Kolbee whined.

"I'm just playing, hush. Be careful, okay? You know I love you, right?" Tasia asked as she stood in her front her daughter.

Kolbee smiled. "I do."

"And, I'll do anything for you, right?"

"Right."

"Good. Remember that when you get down there and need a reminder. I know you're nervous about meeting up with Logan and even spending time with Deron, but it's going to be fine. You are stronger than you think, and they'd be some damn fools not to love and accept you. And, if they don't, fuck em'. Me and Latrell are all the family you need."

"Me too," Mitch said, lightening the intense conversation.

Giving Tasia a hug, Kolbee exhaled deeply. "I'll call you when I'm boarding and when I land."

"And, text me when you get to Bryson's house. He just pulled up."

Mitch slid on his shoes and carried Kolbee's suitcases to the car. He and Bryson slapped hands, and she thanked Mitch before climbing into the passenger seat. Her emotions were now all over the place thanks to her mama.

"You good?" Bryson asked as they pulled off down the street.

"Yeah. Thanks for picking me up."

"It ain't nothing. You want something to eat?"

"You didn't cook today?" Kolbee asked, and he shook his head.

"Nah. I just got home a little before I called you."

"Uhm," Kolbee muffled and looked out her window. She didn't know why his response had her feeling a way. Especially when she was the one who had ended things between them.

"What's all that for?" Bryson asked, peeping her little attitude.

"Nothing. I was just saying."

He chuckled, already knowing what Kolbee was thinking. She could front all she wanted to. "Yeah... alright."

The two didn't talk the entire ride back to his place. Kolbee was on her phone, and Bryson bobbed his head to the slow jams on the radio. He'd usually be playing music from his phone, but he accidentally left it when leaving out.

The rain had slowed up some as soon as he pulled into his designated parking space. He glanced Kolbee's way as she picked her overnight backpack up from the floor.

"You good, now?" he asked.

"I always was. Why you ask that?"

Bryson just shook his head and shut the car off. Kolbee was a horrible liar. Something Bryson didn't take her for, but he wasn't about to press her over the shit. He left her sitting there as he climbed out.

"Come on, fore' somebody snatches your bald-headed ass up."

"Fuck you," she grumbled, but got out and followed him up the steps.

Once inside, Kolbee went right upstairs to his bedroom. The two-bedroom townhouse was decked out in the most elegant décor thanks to Bryson's aunt. She was an interior designer with a vast clientele but always took care of her nephew. Following her upstairs, Bryson couldn't help but shake his head as he removed his shoes. Kolbee was making herself comfortable, and he couldn't understand what this was that they were doing.

"What are you staring like that for?" Kolbee asked as she stripped from her jeans and neatly folded them.

"For somebody who doesn't fool with me, you sure are making yourself at home."

Kolbee stopped removing her hoodie. "Is it a problem? You didn't have to come get me if you had an issue with me being here."

"Did I say I had an issue?"

Kolbee mugged him and rolled her eyes before turning her back to him. She wasn't about to do this with Bryson. Granted, she had placed herself in the predicament but arguing with him was not what she had in mind for the remainder of the night. She had just taken a shower before he called, so she didn't hesitate to slip under his covers once she was down to her panties and tank top.

After removing his hoodie, Bryson hit the lights and climbed in beside her. The TV was on Sports Center, and he was all into until Kolbee began to kiss on his neck. She had sat and played around on her phone for ten minutes waiting for him to say something, but he didn't. Kolbee was spoiled, but he wasn't feeding into her shit tonight.

"Now you wanna be all on me," Bryson said, and she stuck her hand in the band of his boxers.

"I always want to be all on you."

Her voice was sultry and low. So low, he almost missed the words she spoke. Maneuvering herself between his legs, Kolbee removed his long dick from its hiding place, let a trail of saliva drop over it, and stroked him until he was at full length.

"Quit playing and wrap them pretty ass lips around this muthafucka," Bryson voiced, making his dick jump in her hand.

"Nope," she replied and tried to climb back to her side, but Bryson's quick movement caused her to tumble backward. Exactly where he wanted her.

Flipping her over, he smacked Kolbee hard on the ass, yanked the thong from between her ass cheeks and tossed it to the side. "Toot that ass up, then. Pretty ass pussy," he complemented, before slithering his tongue down the crack of her ass to her awaiting hot center.

Kolbee released a deep sigh and arched her back. Her waist to ass ratio was sickening. As Bryson delivered skillful strokes of his slick tongue, sucked on her pearl, and fingered her ass, Kolbee moaned softly. As good as his oral services felt, she was too caught up in her head to relax and really enjoy it. Bryson knew it, also. She'd usually be rotating her hips and twerking his face, but she wasn't.

"What's wrong with you?" he asked, coming up for air.

Kolbee rolled over on her back and shook her head. "Nothing."

She was lying again, but this time Bryson didn't think twice about getting her to fess up. His dick was hard, and Kolbee was lying there looking sexy as hell. He didn't know why she wanted to cut things off with him, even though she claimed it was to focus, but yet here she was in his bed. In his eyes, she was confused... or scared. Whatever the case, Bryson was going to make tonight his last time reaching out to her. He had too much on his plate as well to be playing games.

After sliding on a condom, he placed her legs in the crook of his arms and slowly pushed inside her. He had to close his eyes for a brief second and sit still. Kolbee had the tightest pussy he had ever slid up in, and he had been with his fair share of women in twenty-seven years.

"Shit doesn't make no fucking sense," he hissed.

"I knooow," Kolbee moaned out. "Oh, my gaaawd."

Bryson smirked. She could talk all that shit about not wanting to fool around with him anymore, but as soon as he put that dick up in her, she was singing a different tune. One he thought was music to his ears. Little did he know, Kolbee was planning on making this their last encounter as well. She had caught feelings, and though the sex was good; she wouldn't dare risk the chance of getting hurt. She couldn't. Her ego wouldn't allow her to.

The following morning, it was awkward as ever on the ride to the airport. Bryson was tired as hell from sexing Kolbee in every position imaginable, while she had the energy of a wild toddler who just had a handful of candy. When he dropped her off at the gate, she still didn't reveal where she was headed to, but that was cool. He knew she'd be posting about it on her social media whenever she landed.

After her non-stop flight to *Hartsfield- Jackson Atlanta International* Kolbee yawned as soon as she stepped off the plane. She'd been to Atlanta a few times and each time she was overwhelmed by the number of travelers. Not only that but the fact that she had to take the train to get to baggage claim. That alone gave her fucking anxiety.

As soon as she took her phone off airplane mode, a plethora of texts and calls popped up on her screen. She decided to call Deron back first. He said that someone would be waiting for her at the north terminal, but she had no clue who it would be or who to even look for.

"You made it in?" Deron asked as soon as the call connected.

"Yes. And, I'm already over being here. This airport is a mess. I hope they don't lose my luggage like last time."

"They won't," he reassured but knew it was possible. Kolbee always overpacked. She could be going out of town for a weekend, and she'd pack ten outfits "just in case" something happened.

"Who's picking me up?" she asked, adjusting the phone from one ear to the other.

"You'll know exactly who he is when you see him. Shit, you should," Deron answered.

"If you say so."

"Can't wait to see you baby girl." He was grinning on the other end of the phone, and his excited tone made Kolbee's heart melt. She loved her daddy, but she hated how she had to go without him all her life. He was there, but not physically.

"You too, daddy. I'll call you if whomever this person is picking me up doesn't get recognized."

"Okay. See you in a little bit."

Going to her texts, she replied to Tasia, Bryson, and Alaia, letting them know she made it. It took twenty-five minutes just to get to baggage claim from the train. By the time she arrived, Kolbee was exhausted. Her calves were burning, and she was hungry as hell with an attitude. Thankfully, her luggage was the first set to come around the belt.

"Damn, I'm tired," she huffed out while adjusting her purse so she could pull two heavy ass suitcases.

She headed down to the terminal Deron told her to exit from and took a deep breath. As soon as she stepped outside, the afternoon heat hit her like a shockwave. The heat in Atlanta was of a different breed. The humidity damn near suffocated you. Kolbee glanced around for any sign of the person who was supposed to be picking her up and smiled when she saw who it was.

"Who the hell are you, and what have you done with my little Kolbee bug?"

Grinning, Kolbee let Andre pull her into a hug. The familiarity lifted a weight off Kolbee's being immediately.

There wasn't anyone alive Deron trusted more than his best friend of over thirty years to pick his baby girl up.

"I haven't heard anyone call me that in so long," she replied, and Andre grinned like he was her proud father.

"And, you better not. I gave you that name when Deron first brought you to the crib. How was your flight?"

"Quick. How have you been? You know you could have made him come and pick me up," she fussed while he held her door open to climb into the passenger seat of his truck.

"I wanted to come get you. Plus, he had some shit to take care of."

Kolbee pursed her lips together as if she could smell the lie. Andre hopped in the driver's seat and pulled away from the curb. He and Deron had been boys since before Tasia or Megan ever entered the picture. When Logan was born, he quickly took on the title of her uncle seeing as though Deron's only other brother had passed away years earlier. Andre was usually the mediator between Deron and Megan, and Tasia always found that funny.

A nigga was going to be a nigga. That was a fact. Andre felt bad for Tasia because she was blindsided by everything, so he took Kolbee under his wing and looked out for her and Tasia when he could. Kolbee looked up to him as a father figure in a sense, and Andre had no problem with that. He loved her as if she were one of his own kids.

"So, what you been up to old man?" Kolbee joked.

"Shit. Ain't nothing old about me but my money. I've been good though, can't complain. I'm still married, so I guess that's good," he chuckled.

Andre was the first of the crew to settle down and tie the

knot. He was a certified player back in the day, but his wife Shareese cut all that shit out quick when she got pregnant with their second child.

"Of course, it is!" Kolbee squealed, with a laugh. "I can't wait to see Reese. Does she know I'm in town?"

Andre shook his head no. "Nah. I didn't tell her yet."

"That's not right. Where that daughter of yours at?"

Andre and Shareese's second oldest daughter was seventeen and driving him insane. She was so damn spoiled, and stubborn Andre couldn't understand it. He partially blamed himself, but his oldest son as well.

"At work. At least that's where she told me she was."

"Work! Since when did Shawniece get a job?" Kolbee asked with amusement. That was hard to believe.

"Since we bought her that damn BMW. That's when. Her little ass thinks money just falls out of me and her mama's pockets or something."

"It might," Kolbee snickered.

"Even if it did, she needs to learn some responsibility. What have you been up to, though? How's your mama?"

"You know my mama. Still her funny, crazy self. I told her to come down here with me, but she refused. I think she still got a thang for my daddy."

Andre laughed hard at that one. There was no way in hell Tasia had any type of feelings for Deron. She had buried those long ago.

"Now, that was funny. I couldn't even imagine Tasia still feeling that nigga, Deron."

Kolbee scoffed. "Why you say it like that? What's wrong with him?"

"Shit, nothing. But Tasia used to talk bad to him. That ain't even nothing for you to be worrying about, though," Andre said catching himself before he started rambling. The conversation was innocent, but he'd never want Kolbee to get the wrong impression of her parents from him.

Silence fell over them for a few seconds, and Kolbee's phone started ringing. Looking at the screen, she thought about ignoring Bryson's call but answered it instead.

"What's up?"

"You left your charger," Bryson told her.

"Damn. Okay. I'll just have to buy a new one. I don't know how long I'ma be out here. You can just keep it at your crib until I get back."

"Nah. I'll just drop it off at your crib."

"Um, okay. Whatever's best for you," she said with a shrug. If he wanted to go out of his way, that was on him.

"Yeah. You have fun wherever you at."

Kolbee chuckled, and Andre looked over at her with a smirk. He could hear the disdain in Bryson's voice and shook his head.

"I surely will, honey. You have a good day."

Kolbee hung up the phone and shook her head. "Nigga's man."

"Act just like your damn mama," Andre laughed.

"Better than acting like my daddy, that's for sure," was her reply. Andre didn't have anything to say to that. He knew her response had a hidden innuendo but was staying out of it.

The drive to Deron's large home was long, and Kolbee couldn't recall the last time she had been there. As always, the landscaping was perfect. The flowers blooming out front had been handpicked by Deron's gardeners and his younger sister Deena.

"Logan isn't here yet, is she?" Kolbee looked Andre's way and asked.

"Nah. I volunteered to pick her up, but she declined," he replied with a shrug.

Great, I get to spend some time with him by myself. Kolbee was frowning on the outside, but deep down she was going to cherish this moment. Even if for only a little while until Logan arrived. Andre helped Kolbee with her luggage, and before she could ring the doorbell, Deron was pulling the door open with a grin on his face. Only the grin of a father who loved his child could have.

"Look at you," he beamed with pride.

Playfully, Kolbee mugged him up and down taking in his appearance. "Ugh. I look just like you."

"Shit. That's a good thing. You know I look better than your mama."

"Haha, you wish," Kolbee laughed dryly before falling into his embrace. Deron sighed with content and held her tightly. He was just grateful she had even given him a hug.

"Dre," Deron called out, "Preciate' you for picking her up."

"Next time she gone be taking an Uber like her sister. She done got grown and forget her manners," he chuckled with a shake of his head.

Kolbee grinned. "Thank you, Andre. Don't let this be the only time I see you while I'm in town."

"You got it boss lady," Andre said before climbing back into his truck and pulling off.

"Looks like it's just me and you, baby girl. Come in and get up out this heat."

The duo walked inside, and Kolbee's eyes roamed the walkway with wonderment. So many thoughts were crossing her mind, but she'd hold off at least until tomorrow to start bombarding him.

"So, which room am I sleeping in?" she asked, ready to take her belongings upstairs and shower. Between her plane ride, the drive over and the heat; she was feeling icky.

"Straight to it, huh? You can sit and talk to me for a few minutes before you run off."

"Daddy," Kolbee huffed out while giving him the side eye.

Smirking Deron shook his head. There was no letting up with her. "Upstairs, on the right side of the hallway. Your sister and niece will have the other side."

"Right. Separate us like we've been for years," Kolbee spat with an attitude out of nowhere.

"Don't start that shit, Kolbee. I told you what it was before you came down here, and I don't want to hear anything else about it. You're here now, so you better get rid of that funky ass attitude," Deron scolded.

"Yeah, okay. I'll be down once I'm finished."

With that, Kolbee walked away with a roll of her eyes. The slight mention of she and Logan sleeping in separate areas of the home annoyed her. She was having mixed feelings about a lot of shit, and she was hoping after her shower she'd be relaxed. The tension in her neck was killing her.

After unpacking a few of her things, Kolbee walked across the hall to the bathroom and hopped in the shower.

The first thing she wanted to do once she was dressed was eat. She didn't care what, but her stomach has damn near touching her back she was so hungry. Stepping out the shower, Kolbee wrapped her towel around her and began to wash her face before heading back to the guest room.

The cool air conditioning felt amazing against her hot skin, and she couldn't wait to come back upstairs after she ate to take a nap. That was if Deron didn't have anything planned for them to do. Tossing on a burgundy, spandex one-piece shorts set with the back out, and a pair of vans, Kolbee was good to go. Looking in the mirror, she admired her shapely frame before heading back downstairs.

"Damn, I'm hungry," she said aloud before walking into the kitchen.

"Where you trying to get something to eat from?" Deron asked, walking in behind her.

Kolbee flinched at his intrusion and held her chest. "Damn! I mean, dang you scared me."

"Good. Hopefully enough to make you go change out of that outfit. It ain't that damn hot outside."

Deron was looking at Kolbee with a frown on his handsome face. He knew she was grown, but he didn't appreciate the way Tasia had passed down her genes to their daughter.

"'Change for what? I dress like this all the time, Deron," she joked and pulled the refrigerator door open.

"Well, put on one of them sweater things ya'll women be wearing."

"A cardigan?" Kolbee asked, and he nodded. "It is too hot for that," she laughed.

Deron took a seat at the island while Kolbee munched on

a bowl of grapes. At this point, she just needed something to hold her over until she made a move to get some food.

"How you been? You still working at Nordstrom?" he asked, and she nodded while chewing.

"Yeah, I'm still there. Can't leave no time soon."

"Why's that? You want to work for someone else for the rest of your life?"

"No. But, I have bills to pay and for me to just up and quit my job isn't ideal. At least not for me, it isn't," she shrugged.

Deron licked his full lips, before going into his wallet. Pulling out his debit card, Kolbee eyed him suspiciously when he slid it her way.

"What's this for?"

"Pay whatever bills you need to pay off with this," he replied in an even tone.

Kolbee's jaw clenched, and she slid it back to him. "I don't need your help. You would think after all these years you'd realize that money doesn't move me. That's not what I wanted from you, ever."

"And, you shouldn't let it move you, but I'm just trying to help you out. Your mama told me you still living with her. I don't know why when you could have easily moved out, Kolbee."

"Because what my mama and I have going on in our life doesn't concern you. It never has," she hissed before popping another grape into her mouth.

Deron took a deep breath. He knew they were going to have this conversation some time while she was visiting, but he didn't expect for it to be so soon.

"*You* have always been my number one concern from the day you were born. I don't know what your mama-"

"My mama doesn't have to speak ill of you in any way. She never has. You and I both know, she's much to G for that. *Your* actions are why I feel the way I do, but whatever."

Kolbee shrugged it off because she knew her mouth was about to get real slick, and she'd hate to disrespect her daddy. Regardless of how mad she was with him; her mama hadn't raised her to be disrespectful.

"It's not whatever. I'm not trying to brush your feelings under the rug, so talk to me," Deron pleaded as he followed her out of the kitchen.

"Nope. It looks like we have company, so we'll save this for another time," she replied before going over to look out the window.

Kolbee's stomach dropped to her feet when Logan stepped out of the car and helped a miniature version of herself out as well. Deron looked from her to the window and shook his head. Between Kolbee's attitude and Logan's stand-offish ways, Deron knew he was going to have some major explaining to do.

4

Jordyn's eyes were so wide Logan feared they might pop out of their socket. Logan sucked her teeth as the Uber came to a stop in front of her father's stunning Alpharetta home. A place that she had spent many summers and holidays at. A place that she honestly despised.

Deron had been her superman, and even after meeting her baby sister Kolbee he still could fight the evils of the world in Logan's eyes but him moving and leaving her in Detroit turned her love for him cold. Logan couldn't understand why he'd done that besides trying to be closer to Kolbee and not her. So yes, she was salty as fuck and not looking to mingle with either of them motherfucka's.

"Mommy it's so big!" Jordyn said excitedly.

She'd been before but was too small to remember. Logan opened the car door, and while Jordyn excitedly exited the car, she grabbed the luggage's from the trunk. The Uber driver gave her a gentle smile before pulling off.

"There goes my beautiful granddaughter," Deron said stepping outside.

It was crazy, but it was like he'd shrunken somehow. Logan took in his appearance and swallowed hard. She'd declined seeing him for the last few years out of spite and was now wondering just what the hell was going on with her dad.

"Grandpa!" Jordyn yelled and ran towards him.

She met him on the stairs, and he picked her up. They embraced, and Logan soaked in her father's looks. She was a reflection of him, and so was Kolbee. Logan wasn't as fair skinned as him or Kolbee, but she shared the ginger hair and even had a few freckles on her face that you could see once the makeup came off.

"Damn you so pretty! Just like your mom and auntie," Deron gushed hugging Jordyn.

Jordyn giggled loving the affection because of the lack of male presence she had in her young life. Logan smiled watching them until she realized what he'd said. *Auntie? What the fuck.* She thought as the woman herself stepped outside. Kolbee's narrowed eyes met with Logan's, and they both frowned.

Logan had to admit her baby sister was looking good. Thick, with her red short hair and a naturally pretty face she was very much a Flint woman. It was their eyes. The noses that they possessed and the way they both had adorable dimples that showed they were related. Deron stopped hugging Jordyn and sat her down. He looked at his two daughters and smiled. He was standing in between his heart, and he'd been praying for the moment to be surrounded by them again. He took a deep breath and exhaled taking in the moment.

It had been a long time coming.

"Jordyn, do you know who this is?" He asked.

Jordyn shook her head shyly, and Kolbee stopped staring at Logan to look down at her niece. All the anger she'd felt seconds ago vanished as she locked eyes with the prettiest little girl she'd ever seen. Jordyn looked so much like she did when she was a kid that it was kind of spooky.

Jordyn ran over to Kolbee and hugged her leg.

"You look like me," she whispered, but Kolbee heard her.

Kolbee swallowed hard and leaned down. She hugged Jordyn tenderly and kissed her cheek. Jordyn smelled just like strawberries and looked adorable in her black leggings with her pink top and glittery Converse that sat on her feet. Jordyn could have easily passed for Kolbee's daughter.

"No, I think you look like me," Kolbee told her playfully and touched a piece of Jordyn's red hair that was in two ninja buns.

Jordyn laughed and waved her hand.

"We're both cute, but you stole my look silly," she replied, and everyone laughed but Logan.

Logan looked at Jordyn and narrowed her eyes.

"What I tell you about that silly mess?" She asked her.

Jordyn's light cheeks darkened. She looked up at her grandpa for help, and he chuckled. He'd had three gorgeous women carrying on his name, his legacy. He felt beyond blessed.

"Listen to your mom. You don't talk to adults like that okay?"

Jordyn nodded, and he picked her back up.

"Okay, I'm sorry auntie!" Jordyn replied before Deron took her into the house.

Logan watched Kolbee smile at Jordyn, and their eyes met again. Kolbee looked Logan over and shook her head.

"You don't have as much ass as me. Kind of shaped like SpongeBob," she quipped.

Logan smiled while holding in her laugh. Kolbee was being a bitch, but it was cool she could be one right back.

"And you don't have as much hair as me. Must have fucked with the wrong bitch's man and let her yank your shit out. Instead of drawing on them eyebrows you should have drawn on some fucking edges," she replied and shrugged.

Kolbee rolled her eyes, and they both laughed. Logan could tell Kolbee had natural eyebrows she was just messing with her and Kolbee actually liked her sisters slim thick body. The thing was they didn't know each other anymore, and at the moment all they felt for one another was anger.

"Whatever, you still shaped like a refrigerator," Kolbee retorted and walked away.

"Ya momma," Logan mumbled not wanting Kolbee to hear her. Kolbee was bigger than her and hell she wasn't looking to go toe to toe with her.

Logan followed her pulling her luggage's. She took her bags up to her bedroom and found everyone in the family room watching TV and eating. While Deron was sitting in his lazy boy with Jordyn by his side, Kolbee was on the loveseat alone with her face buried in her phone. Logan chose to settle on the sofa furthest away from Kolbee, and Deron looked her way.

"How is your mom doing?"

Logan watched Kolbee roll her eyes but chose to not comment on it since Jordyn was in the room.

"Good."

Deron nodded.

"How's work?"

"Fine."

Deron sighed. Talking to his daughters and getting a real conversation out of them was like pulling fucking teeth.

"Why don't you and your sister go ride around and have some lunch? I'll watch Jordyn," he suggested and coughed. Logan noticed how her father's fair skin had a yellow hue to it and she frowned.

"Are you okay?"

Kolbee looked up from her phone to look at her father.

"You two should go hang out. I pulled some money out of the bank for you, and you could take one of my cars. It's nice out, and it's still early as hell," he repeated.

"I'm good. I'm going to go take a nap," Kolbee announced standing up.

Logan noticed Kolbee's big ass and rolled her eyes. Kolbee was right she had a natural big ass while Logan had a small but cute round behind.

"Well if you do go out Kolbee wear something to cover that ass of yours up. You shaped just like your damn mama," Deron complained again refusing to let her show off her body in his presence.

Kolbee smirked as she walked out of the room and Logan

stared at her father. She'd been so angry with him for so long that she couldn't think of the last time she'd even told him she loved him. When she was younger, it was her mom that pushed her to separate Kolbee and herself. However, overtime Megan learned to let go of the hurt and anger, but the damage had already been done. Logan had so many questions she just didn't ask them because she wasn't excited about bringing up such painful subjects.

"I missed you beautiful. Your mom sends me pictures on the holidays, but they do you no justice. Did you get the money I sent last month?"

Logan nodded not bothering to say thank you. She used it for Jordyn anyway, so she didn't feel the need to.

"You lost your manners and shit too along with your respect for me?"

Logan dropped her head. She was angry with him and didn't want him to make her feel like the bad guy for feeling that way.

"Please don't. I'm going to take Jordyn to look around," she said standing up.

Deron shook his head not liking that reply. He wasn't perfect no person walking God's green earth was, but he had always been there for his daughters.

"Jordyn go get your auntie and tell her to come down here. We gone go out to eat and do some shopping," he said slightly tired but not wanting to waste any time with his kids.

Jordyn hopped off his lap and eagerly ran out of the living room. Deron sat up, and his eyes fell on Logan. His firstborn, the first person he willingly changed for. He smiled as he admired her beauty. While Kolbee was a walking replica of Tasia, Logan was Megan all over again minus the light skin.

"What's going on with that nigga Rome?"

Logan shrugged. When her father looked at her like she was his everything it made her emotional.

"He's selfish. He rarely sees her, and now that I have completely cut him off from sex he won't even give me any money on the regular. I asked him to pay for dance, and he chose to get tickets to Miami and fix on his car. I'm tired of doing it alone, and now Jordyn is starting to ask questions. Questions that are hard for me to answer daddy," she replied and when the word daddy slipped out Deron's heart smiled.

This was his Logan that he knew was still inside of the angry woman sitting before him. Jordyn and Kolbee joined them in the living room, and Jordyn chose to sit on Kolbee's lap when she sat down.

"A man will only do what you allow for him to do. As a woman, you need to let your demands be known upfront. If you want a ring, let that nigga know. Don't sugar coat shit. Don't walk around going with the flow hoping that will win him over because it won't. Logan, you need to file them papers," Deron suggested referring to child support. Logan nodded knowing that it was something that she should have been done.

"When I even mention it, he makes me feel so bad daddy."

Kolbee sat back quietly pretending to watch the TV. It was weird to be in the same room with her father and sister. Even hearing Logan call him daddy made her feel like an outsider. She didn't know why but it just did.

"Fuck him!" Deron barked furrowing his brows. Jordyn's eyes grew wide, and he quickly shook his head. "I'm sorry about that beautiful. Go use the bathroom before we go. It's right down the hall," he told her needing to speak with his girls alone.

Jordyn slowly exited the room, and Deron looked at Logan and Kolbee.

"I chose you two. Just cause things didn't work out with either of your mothers doesn't mean I let y'all go. Megan and Tasia can feel however the fuck they want to feel about me, but I'm y'all father. It's my blood flowing in your veins, and I was always dedicated to you two. My love for the *both* of my daughters is the reason why I'm alone right now. I could have easily chosen one daughter, but I didn't. I never stopped calling. I came to all the events, and I wasn't present every day, but I was only a phone call away. I know our life wasn't ideal, but damn we had good ass memories. The love has always been there," he said and shook his head to calm himself down.

Deron's guilt was showing on his handsome face. To just heart his daughter, speak of a tired ass nigga angered him. He'd shown her real love and Kolbee too, but still, he felt like he'd failed them.

"Put that nigga on child support and Kolbee what the fuck is going on with your bills?"

Kolbee's jaw fell slack. The way Deron looked at her had her feeling like she was sixteen all over again. She'd remembered a time when she'd got caught drinking by him, but instead of getting mad he ended up finishing the bottle with her. He was that type of father, and while some people would frown on it, it worked for them.

"I owe a few people," she mumbled with her cheeks darkening. She already knew her mama had mentioned something to him behind her back.

Deron sighed. His fucking daughters.

"A few people, huh? Why the fuck haven't you called and asked me for the money? You waiting for them to garnish your shit?"

Kolbee sighed.

"No," she replied with a bite to her words.

Deron nodded.

"You two are so much alike it's crazy. Kolbee go change into something bigger, and Logan go see if your damn daughter done fell into the toilet," he said before walking out of the room.

Logan and Kolbee both rolled their eyes before laughing. They looked at one another and immediately stopped. Logan cleared her throat and stood up. She left out of the room in search of Jordyn while Kolbee went to put on some bigger bottoms.

Three hours later the Flint girls along with their daddy ate inside of Chops Lobster Bar. They'd been shopping and had even taken a small tour around Atlanta. Deron had even taken them by the business he owned; Flint Cleaners. The business had been open for six years and was well known throughout the city. It serviced everyone, but Deron had a lot of celebrity clients that frequented his spot because of the superb service they received. Now they were eating, and Jordyn was attached to Kolbee at the hip sitting in the seat beside her. Logan was lowkey in her feelings. She went to cut her eyes at her traitor daughter and a tall man with hooded eyes the color of roasted pecans approached the table. He leaned down and dapped up Deron while staring at Logan.

His gaze was so intense it made her shift in her seat. Deron coughed as he looked the handsome young man's way.

"How did it go?" Deron asked him.

"Smooth just like you said it would. Your support means a lot man. I can't say that shit enough."

Logan swallowed hard as she watched his lips move. It was clear he was talking to her father. She was so stuck on his looks that she couldn't turn away. He was tall with an athletic build to him. His skin was a mocha complexion that had tattoos going up and down his arms from what she could see, but they weren't completely covering his skin. He rocked a clean ass low fade with a face so handsome Logan found herself openly ogling him. From his hooded eyes to his thick full lips and manicured beard he was sexy as hell.

"You're drooling pick your jaw up," Kolbee mumbled, and Logan rolled her eyes.

"I'm proud of you. Come chop it up with me next week," Deron told the mystery man and coughed again.

The attractive tall man with the cocky smirk and enticing scent nodded. He stole another peek at Logan before walking away. Logan loved how he was wearing something as simple as blue jeans with a white Gucci v-neck and still shutting shit down.

"Daddy are you okay?" Kolbee asked.

Logan looked at Deron and frowned as he coughed again before drinking some water.

"I'm fine my Kolbee," Deron replied.

Kolbee smiled, and Logan felt a twinge of jealousy move

through her. Deron had gone from having their mothers fight for his love to them doing so, and Logan hated it.

"You look good with that hairstyle on you. I know they be in KC on your head. How Tasia doing?" Deron asked Kolbee.

Logan sat back and folded her arms across her chest. Kolbee snickered at how silly her sister was being.

"She's good. Her man is treating her right."

Deron chuckled. He wouldn't even speak on that bullshit Kolbee had said.

"What about you? You making them wrap it up right?" He asked narrowing his eyes at Kolbee.

Kolbee's cheeks darkened as she shook her head.

"Daddy? I'm grown. I've been grown."

Deron smiled and leaned over. He was tall, so it didn't take much for him to reach her side of the table. Gently he kissed her cheek.

"You'll always be my baby girl. Get your life together before you bring a child into this world. Make him walk you down that aisle. Put a title on your name because you deserve it," Deron told her, and Logan blinked away her tears.

Logan knew that Deron wasn't throwing shade, but she took offense to everything he'd said.

"We should go. Jordyn done fell asleep in this motherfucka," Deron said and laughed.

He paid for the bill, leaving a hefty tip like always. The family was soon back in his Mercedes and headed to his place. Deron turned on some Nas, and it took him no time to start playing *Daughters* off Life Is Good album.

With the windows down, the warm Atlanta breeze caressed everyone's skin. Kolbee frowned at why she couldn't ride in the front seat on the way back when Logan had ridden in it on the way there. Logan glowered at how many gems Deron was dropping on Kolbee about kids and life because she couldn't recall hearing that from him before she had her child. She felt like maybe if she had things would have been different for her. While Deron reflected on his daughters with the music guiding his thoughts. The song he was listening to was some real shit.

He'd lived a gratifying life. Traveling all over the world. Been in love, fell out of it and found it again. Been blessed with two gorgeous daughters, money and pretty much anything a man could want still it hadn't been enough. In between all of that he'd failed his daughters in some capacity and that gutted him. To know he'd let them down in any way made him feel like a failure. Deron turned down the song and glanced at the only women he couldn't live without.

"I touched a lot of money girls. I done seen things that would scare most. Made it out of that and still lived to talk about it but nothing I've done has topped making you two. My greatest accomplishments. Y'all family and family sticks together. Life too short to be holding grudges and all that bullshit. You have to live for today because tomorrow is not promised. We'll talk some more while y'all here but know that all this distant shit is dead. I'm putting my fucking foot down," he told them and turned the music back up.

Logan sighed and rolled her eyes while Kolbee rubbed Jordyn's back as she peacefully slept beside her in her booster seat. Logan wanted to say something slick, but like her daughter, she knew when to talk back and when not to. Instead, she gazed out of the window wondering if she would ever be able to have a real bond with her baby sister.

Two weeks seemed to fly by, and Deron had yet to speak with his daughters. He was enjoying the time with them so much that he didn't want to ruin it with his news. While Jordyn was with Deron's only sibling his baby sister Deena at a kiddie spa, Deron was with his girls at the gun range.

While Kolbee was shooting Deron stood beside Logan. He was sipping on his drink while staring down at his daughter. The tension was still there between them despite the things he's said to ease her mind and her angry spirit.

"What exactly is your issue with me baby?" He asked in a low tone.

Logan looked up from her text message with her mom and licked her lips. Deron looked better, but at night she heard him puking out his guts. Every time she or Kolbee asked if he was okay, he waved them off.

"I'm fine," she mumbled and went back to her phone.

Deron snatched Logan's black phone out of her hand and placed it in his back pocket. Logan stood up from the stool she'd been sitting on and glared at him.

"I'm not a kid anymore. I don't have to talk when I don't want to."

Deron sat his drink down and looked at Logan. He knew the owner of the range and was allowed special accommodations that many paying patrons didn't have. He'd walked into the establishment with his daughters, liquor, and wings and the owner smiled at him before he signed them in. As Deron brushed a hand over his hair that was peppered with grey and dark red strands he eyed his oldest child.

"I never set out to hurt anyone. I'm still in love with Megan that hasn't changed we just couldn't make it work, and you know why," he said, and his eyes drifted over to Kolbee who was now shooting a fresh target paper.

Logan could feel her chest tighten. She understood what Deron was saying, but when he'd decided to move to Atlanta, it crushed her. She'd gone from seeing him every day, waking up to him in her home to having time with him on the holidays. Then she couldn't even enjoy that because she had to share that time with Kolbee. Her mom was hurt, she was devastated, and all Deron had left behind in Detroit was broken hearts.

"Forget it. It's the past, and well I don't want to talk about it. Why did you call us here anyway? We're not the Cosby's. We never will be, and you will never be able to right the wrongs you did. You ruined this family with your selfishness," she said in a tone so nasty it made Deron take a step back.

Deron licked his suddenly dry lips as hurt flashed through his eyes. Logan regretted the hateful words the moment they left from her mouth, but she didn't apologize. He'd hurt her, and she didn't mind hurting him.

The saying was true. Hurt people, *hurt people*.

"Damn, I had no idea you were this angry with me. I can take it though. My love for you two isn't conditional Logan. So even when you're telling yourself you don't love me anymore I want you to know that the feelings aren't mutual," Deron said and went back over to Kolbee.

Logan blinked and her eyes watered. She dropped her head and was taken back to a time when her home was in the dumps. A time when her days were lonely and the nights were filled with the sounds of her mother's cries. She looked back up at her father and watched him show Kolbee how to aim correctly. While she missed him, she still felt anger, and the last thing she was going to allow for him to do was make her feel guilty about it.

After finishing up at the range, the sisters along with Deron went back to his place. Logan not wanting to be up under her dad and sister grabbed Jordyn and used her GPS to locate the closest ice cream spot. She decided to go back into the city and knew Jordyn wouldn't mind the car ride. Back home Logan drove a 2012 Cruze, so Deron's $90,000 S-Class sedan was like riding on a cloud. The four-door black car floated up and down the streets while Jordyn sat in the backseat staring out of the window.

Because the weather was beautiful, the windows were down. Logan pulled up to the red light on Peachtree and Williams street and looked to her left briefly making eye contact with a sexy ass guy with mocha colored brown skin.

"It's him," Logan whispered to herself.

The mystery man from the restaurant the other night that she couldn't take her eyes off of was now beside her. Logan swallowed hard, and the light turned green. Horns began to honk as he stared back at her just as drawn to her as she was to him.

It was the way his intriguing eyes pulled her in that had Logan stuck.

"Mommy!" Jordyn yelled scared at the way the cars were honking their horns, and Logan was pulled out of her daze.

Logan slowly drove off and licked her lips.

"Sorry baby," she mumbled.

Logan took Jordyn to the first ice-cream shop she passed and parked in the small parking lot. Jordyn excitedly exited the car with Logan and grabbed her hand.

"Momma I want every flavor! Matter fact just one, auntie Jerricka said eating too much ice-cream goes to your booty," Jordyn said, and Logan laughed.

"I gotta sensor what she says around you little girl and you can have all the ice-cream that you can eat."

Jordyn jumped up and down excitedly as loud music graced their ears. Logan glanced behind her and spotted the red Maserati truck pulling up beside her car. She wouldn't have thought anything of it, but she remembered seeing the fine ass nigga from the restaurant whipping it, and it made her heart beat faster.

She licked her lips and took Jordyn to the small brick ice-cream shop that housed an outdoor seating area and walk up window. The young teenager greeted them with a smile as they walked up.

"Hi! What can I get you?" she asked.

Jordyn's small eyes roamed all over the menu that sat at the top of the window. She spotted a waffle bowl filled with ice-cream and her mouth foamed on the sides.

"I want that one mommy! The bowl with blue and pink ice-cream, candy and chocolate!" she said excitedly.

Logan smiled. She wished eating ice cream could make

her happy like that. She had never been a dairy lover. It fucked her stomach up.

"Um, I guess I'll take the waffle bowl with the blue and pink ice-cream with some M&M's on it, and I'll also get a strawberry smoothie...um..." Logan stammered over her words as the most alluring cologne she'd ever smelled invaded her senses.

Logan's eyes lowered as she slowly inhaled it and she could hear someone clear their throat.

"Hey, Bezo!" The young cashier said in a chipper, voice.

"Aye Shay, you good?"

Logan stood by nervously trying to play it cool. His voice was deep and carried that southern drawl to it. As he took a step closer to her and Jordyn, she could feel his body heat.

"We good! I was at the Fox Theater too. You killed it like always!"

Logan groaned growing tired of whatever the fuck was happening, and Bezo gently touched her waist.

"I'm sorry beautiful. I wasn't trying to interrupt your moment and whatever they want put it on my bill Shay," he said, and his hand fell.

Jordyn glanced back and up at the tall, handsome man and smiled.

"My granny said I can't take anything from strangers," she told him.

Bezo chuckled. He looked down at the pretty little girl and shook his head. When he smiled at her, the diamonds on his bottom row of teeth sparkled, and they fought over attention with the diamonds in his chain and watch. Jordyn watched him carefully while grabbing onto Logan's leg.

"I'm just trying to be a gentleman. Maybe if your mom wouldn't have pulled off on me we could be friends already," he replied, and his eyes went down to Logan's plump little ass.

Bezo was used to being with thick women. Natural or the unnatural way so Logan was on the smaller scale to him, but she was so sexy with her's that he really didn't mind.

Logan wore black leggings with black and pink Huaraches and a fitted matching top. Her mid-back length dark red hair was in loose waves and hanging down her back.

Bezo was so intrigued by her beauty and anxious to see her face up close. At the restaurant, he'd noticed how pretty she was, but out of respect for Deron, he didn't say anything.

"What about you, what can I get you red?" He asked, and his eyes went to her hair. It was so pretty and from what he could tell it was real. He'd never come across a black girl with naturally red hair.

That was sexy as fuck to him.

Logan licked her lips and nervously turned to Bezo. Their eyes connected, and her pc muscles involuntarily started to clench together. *Damn!* He was fine, and Logan could tell by the cocky grin on his face that he knew it. His teeth were white which was always a plus. Even his bottom grill had a sexiness to it that she liked. Then there was his fade. It was lined up just right and the line in it made it sexier. It was similar to the haircut Mitch had in "Paid in Full" and also the fade Deron used to rock back in the day.

My daddy's haircut. Logan thought.

The way his hooded eyes peered down at her made her swallow hard. In blue Balmain jeans with wheat high top

Nike's and a white V-neck, he looked attractive, to say the least. His jewelry and style wasn't over the top but it still demanded your attention.

"Your beautiful as hell," Bezo admitted with a slip of the tongue and Jordyn smiled.

"She's the prettiest mommy in the whole wide world," she told him.

Bezo chuckled. *Already* he liked Jordyn. He looked at Logan and admired her beauty.

"Yeah, she is. Let's get some ice cream and grab a table," he suggested and stepped around them.

Logan stood back frowning while Bezo paid for their dessert and waited at the stand for it to be made. He'd been so caught up in Logan's beauty that he forgot to order himself anything. Once everything was done, they all sat at a nearby table that had a bright red umbrella over it, and Bezo watched Jordyn tear into her ice cream.

"This is so good, thank you!" Jordyn said and stuffed her face some more.

Bezo nodded, and his eyes landed on Logan who was looking at anything but him.

"You like your shake? Is it sweet enough?" He asked, and his business phone started to ring.

Logan turned to him and nodded. She watched him pull out two cell phones, and she frowned again.

"Thank you. It's good, and if we're keeping you, then you can go."

Bezo shook his head, frowning at the words she'd said.

"Why would I do that? Maybe next time we can hit up

the aquarium," he said, and Jordyn stopped eating to smile at him.

"Oooh mommy yes! My daddy said he would take me, but he didn't. He never showed up," she said and started back eating her ice cream.

Jordyn's innocent words angered Logan. Never did she think she would have a child with a dead-beat ass nigga. She balled up her fist, and Bezo leaned over to massage her thigh. He was confident that with or without her pops Jordyn would be good.

"It's clearly his loss. Why not let me take you two out?" He asked in a low tone.

Logan took a sip of the milkshake as Jordyn stared at Bezo.

"What's your favorite color?" she asked him.

Bezo smiled at her.

"Green, what's yours?"

"Pink and purple and sparkle," she replied.

Bezo chuckled. He had no idea that sparkle was a color. He drug a hand over his fade as his eyes briefly scanned the road before turning his attention back to Jordyn.

"Who's your favorite princess?"

Jordyn's thin brows bunched together.

"Ummm...Elsa," she replied.

Bezo nodded trying to think of who the fuck she was talking about. He didn't have any small children in his family, so he was lucky enough to miss the Frozen wave.

"What about princess Jordyn?" He asked grinning.

Jordyn laughed like he'd told her the funniest joke.

"Silly I'm not a real princess," Jordyn said and went back to her food.

Logan smiled until she realized what Jordyn had said.

"Silly?" She questioned, and Bezo looked at Logan.

"It's cool," he said not bothered by what Jordyn called him. Hell, he'd been around kids that cursed more than adults so to him something like silly wasn't a bad word.

"Still she doesn't need to say that to people older than her," Logan replied and frowned at him.

Bezo leaned towards Logan as she glared at him and his hand went to her soft thigh.

"Relax, you too pretty to be frowning so much," he whispered as his business cellphone rung again. Bezo dismissed the call, and soon two new Chargers were pulling up to the ice cream shop blaring loud rap music. A group of men emerged from the vehicles and headed their way. Bezo sighed as he stood up.

"Nigga you should have seen that shit, it was crazy. We were laying motherfucka's out!" One man said animatedly with his shirt tore at the collar.

Logan shook her head and started to clean up Jordyn. She didn't want her baby caught up in no mess.

"Oh yeah? Y'all nigga's need to fall back for a sec," Bezo said, and red Benz truck pulled into the lot beside his car. He watched the scantily clad women emerge from the truck, and he shook his head.

"Who the fuck invited them?" He asked looking the women way.

His right-hand nigga Trey smiled showing nothing but gold teeth.

"I did we bout to hit the club. What the fuck you doing over here?" He asked until he spotted Logan standing up. He grinned as he checked her out.

Bezo went back over to Logan as music started to play from one of his people's cars. The women began dancing, and liquor was passed around as weed got lit up. Logan moved quickly to her father's car with Bezo on her heels.

"You still taking us out?" Jordyn asked glancing back at Bezo.

Bezo nodded with his hands in his pockets. He knew he hadn't done anything wrong, but he could tell that Logan was now angry about something.

"We gotta convince your mommy to let me do that."

Logan rolled her eyes and helped Jordyn get into the car. Bezo grabbed her hand and pulled her closer to him before she could walk to the driver's door.

"I just need a second of your time. I don't remember ever having to work so hard just to get someone's attention," he told her not being cocky but just being honest.

Logan smiled.

"Maybe that's the problem but look I have to go and this ghetto ass move your people just pulled was not cute. Thank you for the ice cream."

Bezo shook his head. He felt like once she looked at him, she would know who he was. She still hadn't, and honestly, his ego was slightly bruised by it.

"That's nothing. Let me take you and your daughter out. What's your number?" he asked staring down into Logan's eyes.

Logan stared back at him breathing hard. She was here

visiting. Not looking for men to court her but Bezo was cute and tempting.

"I don't know," she mumbled, and Bezo nodded.

He didn't know either what was going on. He could see by the look in Logan's eyes that she was attracted to him too, but she was holding back for reasons unknown to him.

"Six," he said, and her eyes wandered up to his.

"Huh?" Logan asked.

Bezo stepped closer to her and touched her soft hand. Their energy together was perfect. Logan could feel the sparks invade her body from his hand.

"I'm saying six is how many times you frowned since I pulled up on you. Let me change that. I got a lot of women in my family. I know how this shit go. Some nigga didn't know what he had, and it hurt you. I'm saying though," Bezo stopped talking to lick his lips. "Let me make what he tampered with right. I'll do all of that plus more," he promised her.

Logan dropped her head thinking about what Bezo said as Morgan walked up. Morgan was a beauty queen. You could easily turn on the TV and see her gracing music videos or cut on her Snap Chat and see her living the life as she called it. However out of all the things that she did including attend Clark Atlanta to become a nurse her favorite thing to do was ride Bezo's dick, and that was in the literal sense. Since she'd met him a year ago, she'd been crazy over him.

"Bezo lets be out! I'm hungry as hell!" She whined walking up and pulling on his arm.

Logan noticed the brown-skinned thick beauty and

smiled. Morgan was attractive, but Logan didn't lack self-confidence, so she wasn't stressing her thirsty ass.

"If you see me again I just might take you up on that offer," Logan told him knowing she would soon be leaving Atlanta. She smiled at Bezo and walked away.

Bezo watched her intensely as she slipped into the Mercedes and drove off. Morgan couldn't hide her jealousy as she watched Logan pull away.

"Probably a rental," she mumbled, and Bezo chuckled.

"Look better than that Uber you be using as a limo and shit," he said and walked away.

Logan and Jordyn rode around Atlanta checking out the sights until the sun fell and night washed over the lively city. Logan headed back to her father's home, and on her way, she called her mom.

"Hey, baby! How is my angel doing?" Megan asked answering on the first ring.

Logan smiled at the sound of her mother's voice. Her mom was a strong black woman. She'd shown her how to become one, and there was nothing she felt like she couldn't do in life as long as she had Megan by her side.

"She's asleep now. Today was interesting. Dad got mad at me because I said the family wasn't perfect. Was I wrong for that?"

Megan sighed.

"No and yes. The family will never be perfect. No family is but you can have your own form of normal. You don't have to hate your father baby. I hate I even talked shit about him around you," Megan replied.

In her younger years, she'd spewed hate towards Tasia,

Deron, and even Kolbee. The fact of the matter was she was hurt, and they were part of the reason why. Megan had passed that down to her daughter, and now she regretted it.

"Kolbee is your sister and Deron is your father. I don't want you to waste any more time hating them. I wish I could go back and do things differently, but it's not too late for you. Kolbee didn't ask to be placed in that situation, and neither did you. Hell, none of us did. It's all on your lying ass father, and I've even forgiven him. It's time for you to do that as well sweetie," Megan told her.

Logan nodded listening closely to the things her mother was saying to her. As she pulled up to her father's home, she spotted the ambulance parked near the front steps. Her heart started to pump faster as she pulled near the garage.

"Ma, I have to call you back, the ambulance is here!"

"The what!" Megan yelled.

Logan ended the call and quickly exited the car. She ran up to a crying Kolbee as Deron was rushed into the back of the ambulance on a stretcher. Logan looked at her little sister worriedly.

"What happened?"

Kolbee shook her head. Her light skin was flushed from her crying. Her eyes were swollen, and she was very shaken up.

"I found him downstairs coughing. It's like he started, and he just wouldn't stop. He started to vomit so I called 911. I don't know what's wrong with him," Kolbee replied.

Logan shook her head. She wanted to console her sister, but they were too disconnected for her to feel comfortable doing so. Instead, she rubbed her arm and went over to the emergency medical technician.

"That's my daddy," she said making Kolbee roll her eyes.

"We're taking him to Well Star North Fulton hospital mam," the technician said before getting into the back of the truck.

"I'll ride with them," Kolbee said following after him.

Logan quickly went back to the Mercedes and got in. Jordyn started to wake up from her sleep as Logan followed the ambulance to the hospital.

"Where we going?" Jordyn asked looking out of the window.

Logan was too lost in her thoughts to speak. Silently she followed the truck to the hospital. Deron was immediately taken to the back and Logan, Kolbee and Jordyn sat in the waiting room. Deron's baby sister Deena rushed into the hospital half an hour later. Deena was forty and looked better than most women half her age. Her youthful brown-skinned face was etched with worry as she ran towards the girls. Sadly because of the situation, she knew Logan better than she knew Kolbee, but she loved them both the same.

"The neighbor called and said the ambulance was over at the house. What happened?"

She sat in-between the girls and Logan shook her head. She was trying to hold it in for Jordyn and was starting to lose her strength.

"Kolbee said he was throwing up and she got worried. Is something wrong with him auntie Deena?"

Deena sighed. She couldn't believe that her brother still hadn't told them of his secret. She grabbed Jordyn that was starting to fall asleep again and held her tightly. Deena's sad eyes looked at both of her nieces, and she shook her head.

"Your father has pancreatic cancer. He's known for about six months now. It seemed to happen out of nowhere. One day he was fine then he was having abdominal pain. His urine was different, and I forced him to go get it checked. He didn't want to do chemotherapy, so he tried radiation therapy. I thought it was going good," she replied, and a few tears fell down her face.

Kolbee stood up and walked away while Logan stared straight ahead. She was hurt, and a part of her was angry with him. Why hadn't he told them?

"Will he die?" she asked quietly, her pain bubbling to the surface and making her voice sound shaky.

Deena shrugged. She'd prayed, talked with God and now it was up to him.

"If he's meant to be here he will," she replied.

Logan stood up before she fell apart and rushed out of the hospital. She found Kolbee sitting down near a bed of flowers with her legs pulled up to her chest. Logan sat beside her and started to really bawl. There had been so many times when she wanted to reach out to her dad. Call him and just say hello but she hadn't. She ignored him, talked down to him every chance she could and now possibly she was about to lose him.

She was so hurt that her chest began to ache.

"Girls please come in!" Deena yelled walking outside with Jordyn by her side.

The sisters stood up and went with her back into the hospital.

"He's stopped breathing, and he has on his will do not resuscitate. We have to honor his wishes. Do you all want to go see him?" Deena asked.

She was a mess, but for her nieces, she would hold it together.

"What are you saying?" Kolbee asked wiping her face.

Logan glanced down at her daughter and saw her staring at them curiously. Logan grabbed Kolbee and pulled her over to the side.

"He's gone. She's saying that he's dead and he doesn't want to be brought back," she said slowly.

Kolbee shook her head. She never really had him and like that he was completely gone. More tears fell from her eyes as Logan grabbed her hand. Logan took Kolbee over to the chairs and helped her sit down. Deena and Jordyn went to Kolbee's side as the nurse took Logan back to Deron's room.

Logan slowly stepped in and saw that the lights had been dimmed low. She closed her eyes as her heart pumped wildly in her chest.

"My beautiful red-haired girl. Daddy loves you." She could hear Deron say. Logan opened her eyes and with blurred vision went over to her resting father. He looked like he was asleep as he laid on the bed. She kissed his cheek and inhaled his scent before sitting down in a nearby chair. Logan tried to stop crying but she couldn't. The pain she felt was almost unbearable.

"Why do you keep hurting me, daddy? Why did you do this?" she asked balling her hands up into fists. "I hate you for this...do you hear me? I fucking hate you for doing this!"

Logan wiped her face and took deep breaths to calm

herself down. She looked at Deron and her eyes crinkled as she blinked back tears.

"I never stopped loving you, daddy. You hurt me, you hurt mommy, but I always loved you and now...I'm just so hurt," Logan mumbled and started to cry harder.

She couldn't find the right words to say. She couldn't have one last talk with the man that helped create her. Her pain was too great, and the only thing that felt right was to cry.

5

NOTHING IN THIS WORLD COULD PREPARE KOLBEE OR Logan for their father's untimely death. Nor did arranging a funeral within the same week. A funeral they didn't want to plan, nor discuss. Logan was taking Deron's departure the hardest. She felt herself slipping into a depressive state just thinking about all the times she had been rude to him. Not just rude but mean spirited for his actions of over twenty-five years ago.

Puzzled by his silence to let them in on his illness, Logan sat paralyzed with grief. Kolbee was hurting as well. The small amount of time she got to share with Deron was short-lived, and she wished she had come down or reached out sooner. But, there wasn't anything either sister could do now.

As the family gathered at the alter around his casket, Logan let more tears fall as her frame began to quake with sadness. She was a complete mess even though she told herself she'd hold it together for Jordyn. Seeing Logan so emotionally hurt, Kolbee stepped her way and wrapped an arm around her shoulder. The two hadn't hugged since they'd been in town, but Kolbee didn't care about that. They needed each other now.

"I can't believe this," Kolbee whispered, and Logan sniffled.

"Me either," was Logan's choked reply.

Wiping her face, she turned and headed back to her seat on the front pew leaving Kolbee to have a moment of her own. Disheartened and at a loss for words, Kolbee stood over Deron's body with tears in her eyes. She didn't know what to think, what to say, or even how to feel. *Who knew this would be the last time I ever got to see you*, she thought before wiping the lone tear that rolled down her cheek.

Deciding against kissing his cheek, an action she felt would haunt her, Kolbee sauntered back to her seat. Jordyn's tiny arms wrapped around her aunt's waist before she nestled her head underneath her.

"Don't cry, auntie. He's in a better place," Jordyn whispered.

Kolbee didn't know how accurate her statement was, but the fact that she was trying to cheer her up made Kolbee hug her back. She needed all the love she could get at this moment in time. Once the pastor gave the eulogy, the immediate family filed out of the sanctuary behind the pallbearers. A few stuck around to speak and thank them for showing up, while others went to their cars. They were headed to the burial site in thirty minutes.

As friends of Deron's gave their condolences to Kolbee

and Logan, the sisters were zoned out in a space of their own. Light smiles covered their faces, but that was only to be polite.

"Who the hell are all these people anyway?" Kolbee asked in a whisper to Logan.

"I have not a clue," she replied.

The church was filled to capacity with every seat taken. Logan knew her daddy was loved, but damn. She had no clue he was loved like this. Most of the people in attendance were paying their respect to him and his family. For years Flint Cleaners had taken care of many in the Atlanta and Detroit communities, and Deron's business was one of the most successful black owned. His clientele stretched from the older widowed gentleman who lived around the corner from the cleaners, to high paid celebrities who refused to take their clothing to anyone else. Deron was an OG in his hometown of Detroit, and it amazed the sisters how many people had traveled to see him be put to rest.

"Mommy, I have to use the restroom," Jordyn squeaked on bouncy legs.

Grabbing her hand, Logan faced Kolbee. "Are you going to be good until I get back?"

"Yeah. I should be fine. I see Andre and his family, so I'll go talk to them."

"Okay. Let's go J,'" Logan told her daughter.

Watching the duo walked away, she felt a twinge of jealousy. Logan had Jordyn by her side while grieving and she had no one. Not even a little human who would cheer her up on her sad days. Tasia was supportive like only a mother could be, but Kolbee was already yearning for a different type of affection. A particular fondness only a man, a lover, a homie, or friend could provide.

Bryson had reached out to give his condolences, and Kolbee appreciated his efforts, but he was in Kansas City. She hated to sound selfish, but she needed him there in the flesh. As much as she hated to admit it, she had caught some sort of feelings for him. The loneliness she felt that entire week was starting to creep up on her again.

"Kolbee Bug, you good?" Andre asked as he and his family walked up.

Her face lit up when she saw them. Shawniece, his daughter, was her daddy's twin. Her round face, thick eyebrows, dainty nose and thin lips all came from Andre. Every other feature she possessed was passed down from her mother. Shareese was a Jamaican beauty who easily stood out in any crowd. She and her daughter's gorgeous dark skin and long, course hair had Kolbee wondering what she'd look like with long hair. It had been so long since she went for the short cut.

"Hey Kolbee," Shawniece spoke before the two hugged.

"Hi, ya'll. I appreciate ya'll so much for today."

Andre waved her off. "We're family. Ain't no need to thank us. Where your sister and niece at?"

Jordyn skipped up to them and announced their presence. "Here we are. Hi, Sha-Sha," she grinned and hugged the teenager.

Jordyn had only met the young girl a few times, but she took a liking to her immediately. So much so, that she had given her a nickname. Logan smiled before taking a deep inhale. She was exhausted, and before she let it be written all over her face, she would just smile.

"Hey," she spoke softly. "Is everyone almost ready to head to the gravesite?"

"Should be. Let me go and make sure everyone knows where we're going. Still a private location for the repast, right?" Andre asked for clarification.

"Yes, unless anything has changed since last night. That was up to you, Deena, and our grandparents."

Though Deron was well loved, his parents wanted their son's day not to be made a mockery of. Many people had questions regarding his illness, and today most certainly wouldn't be the day they got answered. Nor would any other day. Deron had kept his business to himself for a reason, and he parents wanted to respect his wishes even in death. It didn't matter how anyone else felt; Deron was their child.

"Nah. No changes," Andre replied.

"Can you see where Den- oh!" Shareese chirped. "There he is. Girls, ya'll remember my son, right?"

Kolbee and Logan both blinked their eyes at the dangerously fine man who had just somehow snatched their breaths away simultaneously. There were tons of good-looking men in attendance, and though it was the wrong time and place to be lusting over any of them, the sisters couldn't help but steal glances every so often. The men had peeped Deron's offspring's as well but would never disrespect him by trying to push up on them at his funeral. He'd haunt their asses from his grave.

"Damn," Kolbee let out, and Logan chuckled. Her baby sister was a mess.

Damn was absolutely correct, and the only word she could muster up in her vocabulary to describe what her eyes had fallen upon. She remembered Shareese's son and hated him at one point, but she didn't remember him being that fine, nor that built. The white button-down shirt was fitting his muscular upper body like a glove. Kolbee didn't think a man in a suit could look so damn good, but she was wrong. Her eyes wandered down his torso to admire the black slacks he was wearing, and the slight bulge didn't go unnoticed either.

He's definitely packing some big shit, or those pants are too tight, she said to herself.

"Hey. I'm Logan. We met a few times when I lived here. How old are you now?"

"How you doing, Logan? I'm Denali. It's kind of rude to ask a man his age, ain't it?" he joked, and that got a smirk out of Logan while Kolbee damn near stared a hole into the side of her head. *She needs to fall back;* she thought already staking claims.

"I assume so. You can't be too old. Shareese still looks young as ever," Logan complimented.

"Thank you, honey. And, he acts old but still in his twenties. Around the same age as Kolbee if I'm not mistaken," Shareese answered and glanced Kolbee's way.

Denali looked her way as well. *Got damn*, he thought to himself. It was bad enough they were still in church having these dirty thoughts, and they both had the nerve to be cursing. It had been years since Denali laid eyes on Kolbee, and he was mad about it. She had grown from the snaggle tooth, red-head who used to chase him through his parent's home, to a fucking stallion that needed to be tamed.

While he was gawking over her maturity, Kolbee was impressed as well. Denali's skin was coco powder brown and looked coated in a layer of coconut oil. He had the type of skin that glowed because it was well taken care of. His hair was in a fade, with a crisp line-up to match.

Decorating his face was a full beard that was perfectly trimmed, connecting to a thin mustache. Kolbee didn't know how tall he was, but he was towering over all the women even with heels on by at least a foot or two. And, she was 5'9 with heels, so that had to make him well over six feet. Denali was grown man fine. The type that had Kolbee wondering where his ass had been all this time. At this point, she was ready to settle down and raise a family. Fuck the small talk. As enthralled as she was with him, Denali was highly intrigued himself.

The classy dress pants Kolbee chose to wear did nothing to hide her voluptuous curves. While buying an outfit for today, all she could hear was her father's voice about covering up more. She had granted the majority of his wishes, but there was only so much she could do. Denali was envious of those pants at the moment. Even more so envious of every man he watched walk behind Kolbee and sneak a glance at her ass. It was so big; he could see it from the front.

Kolbee grinned. "I know this isn't young Denali who cut my hair when we were younger," she sassed and crossed her arms.

Chuckling, Denali shook his head. "You still mad about that?"

"Clearly. I had to be bald for the rest of my life because my hair wouldn't grow back."

Denali's eyes went wide. "You lyin'."

"She's lying. She told me she cuts her hair all the time," Jordyn spoke up, and Logan said her name in a hiss. She knew better than to be in grown folk's conversation.

"Good lookin' out J," he said and held his hand out to give her a five on the low. "I apologized so much for that; I ran out of breath."

"And, tears," Shareese added.

Logan was looking puzzled, so Kolbee decided to fill her in. On one of his many visits to KC, Andre had to take nine-year-old Denali with him. Shareese was nine months pregnant, and on bed rest, so she couldn't do too much around the house. Back then, Kolbee had long hair similar to Logan's length now, but Denali didn't believe it was hers. In his attempt to find out the truth even after Kolbee promised all the hair on her head belonged to her, Denali snipped young Kolbee's luscious ponytail from her head.

She cried for days after the incident, and Denali got the worst beating of his life from Shareese and was placed on strict punishment by Andre. Though Denali wasn't biologically his son, Andre had been the only father figure in his life since he was five months old. In Shareese's eyes, Andre was his daddy. She was so pissed off when the duo returned home, that she cancelled Denali's tenth birthday party that had been scheduled for months.

"I was so sad about my hair," Kolbee pouted with a smile.

"I'm sorry about that. I hope I didn't make you have low self-esteem or anything like that," Denali said.

"Does it look like I have low self-esteem?"

Kolbee asked the question, and instead of answering Denali just gazed at her with a handsome grin on his face. Whatever tension he had caused when they were younger had morphed into something else.

"Not in the slightest, Busy Bee."

Kolbee's face flushed with embarrassment and astonishment. She couldn't believe he remembered. Like Andre, Denali had made up his own nickname after hearing his dad call her Kolbee Bug a few times. He wanted his own nickname, and by the looks of it, the effects it had on her back then were totally different now. She was seeing him in an entirely different light.

"Wow. Okay, Denali River," she joked back, and Logan chuckled.

"Well, I'm glad you two are getting along, but we need to get moving. Aunt Deena just called and said the family cars were pulling off in five minutes," Logan announced.

"So, who's riding where, or does it matter?" Kolbee asked.

"We're in the second limo behind our grandparents. Unless you wanted to ride with someone else."

Kolbee shook her head no. "No. I was just wondering. Andre, where are you going to be?"

"I drove, but if you want me to ride in there with ya'll, I can."

"I'll ride with them," Denali spoke up and said. "If it's cool with ya'll?"

"Um, yeah. Sure. That's fine," Logan answered once Kolbee hadn't replied.

"Aight. Let me grab my phone off the charger, and I'll meet ya'll outside."

As the crowd dispersed, Logan couldn't help but ask Kolbee what was up between she and Denali. Their attraction to one another was evident, but she didn't want to make assumptions.

"So, did you two fool around back in the day or something?"

Kolbee's eyes tightened in confusion. "Who? Denali and I?" she laughed.

"Yeah. Why you say it like that?"

"Because. I've never looked at him like that. It's kind of weird, you know. With him being Andre's son and all."

Logan shrugged. She didn't see what was weird about it. "I don't see how you *didn't* look at him like that. Did we not see the same person back there?"

Kolbee laughed as she climbed into the back of the family car. "We most certainly did. It would feel out of place and distasteful to even think about him in that way."

"So, you're telling me you didn't gawk over that bulge in his slacks?" Logan whispered closely to her ear.

Kolbee's eyes lowered, and she grinned. "I have no idea what you're talking about."

"Mhm. I'm sure you don't. You know Kolbee; I think we're going to get along just fine. I know we haven't been the closest in years, but you're still my sister, and I love you. Daddy passing away makes me not want to take anyone for granted. Any moment we share, I want to cherish."

The heartfelt words made Kolbee's eyes water. She wasn't a very emotional person, but today she was. Over the years, she had come untuned with her feelings. Once a person barely moved her in a negative way, she was good on them. In her eyes, if the vibe was off between them, they were off. There was no use in prolonging something only to end up hurt or worse.

"Me too. I don't care how old we are now; I'll always need my big sister." Leaning her way, the two hugged. "Love you, sis."

"Love you, sis," Jordyn mocked with a grin on her face. She was all into a learning game on her iPad but didn't miss the opportunity to repeat her aunt's words.

Shaking her head, Logan kissed her daughters head. "You're too much, baby."

After leaving the burial site, immediate family and friends who received the location of the repast congregated together. Deron's aunts had the venue decked out only the way they knew their nephew would had he been alive. Though they too were mourning his death, today was a celebration of the life he lived.

Sipping on a mixed drink that tasted more like alcohol than anything, Tasia took in her surroundings. For so long before she found out about Megan and Logan, she had been secluded from this part of Deron's life. She never pressed him about meeting his family, and he never fed her lies about meeting them. Their affair was understood. That was until Deron caught feelings and knocked her up.

True, it takes two to tango, but Deron had somewhere along the line stepped out of place. After finding out she was pregnant, Deron flew her to Detroit so she could meet his parents. They couldn't believe he had stepped out on Megan, but there wasn't anything they could do about it. Deron had made his bed, two of them actually, and he had to lay in them.

Tasia was treated no differently than Megan. Mrs. Flint was highly upset with her son, but she would never take her frustrations out on the young girl. If anything, she wanted to give Tasia a heads up that Deron was already a family man if he hadn't done so. Thankfully, he had. Of course, she was pissed off at first, but she wouldn't dare blame herself for his inconsideration.

Watching her oldest child sing to Jordyn as they danced on the floor, Tasia smiled. Kolbee was her everything no matter how old she turned. She was so thankful for the brief moment of love – or what they thought it was – between her and Deron. They had created something beautiful together.

"They look just like him," Megan observed, interrupting her thoughts.

Glancing up at her, Tasia didn't bother to mumble a reply. Picking up her cup, she took a sip and continued to mind her business. Letting out a sigh, Megan pulled the chair out across from her and sat down. The two stared at one another for a few moments. All the hate Megan had for Tasia for ruining her happy family had dissolved throughout the week.

It made no sense to hold onto a grudge with a woman who had been left in the blind just as much as she had. The cattiness and petty banter would probably still continue between them through their daughter's, but they could at least be cordial. Something Deron always wanted them to be. Megan was willing to do that for him now. Now, after years of coming at his neck for his deceitfulness.

"I'm sorry," Megan voiced.

"No need to be."

"Can you let me just say what I have to say? I know you don't too much care for me and trust me the feelings used to be mutual on this end, but not today. Not on his day."

Tears pooled in Megan's eyes, and Tasia reached over to grab her hand. This was tough for them both. Now as an adult, and under the circumstances, Tasia figured she'd lighten up some.

"Deron would shit a brick if he saw this right now," Tasia laughed, and Megan joined in wiping under her eyes.

"Girl. He'd think the world was ending seeing us be this friendly. Really, though Tasia. I want to apologize. Over the years, I've said some fucked up things to you and that was only because Deron had pushed me to go there. It wasn't right, and though our girls are grown now, I felt the need to squash whatever tension there is between us."

"I thought we squashed it the last time I whooped your ass."

Megan clenched her jaw but sucked her teeth when she saw Tasia smirk.

"Girl, don't play with me. I almost reach across this table on your ass."

"And, I would have had to embarrass you in front of your child."

The two shook their heads and chuckled. It had only been a few occasions when the two had come to blows, and they were tied with equal wins and losses. Arguing over the phone didn't cut it for Tasia one time, and she booked a flight straight to the D to handle hers. Deron knew he had two feisty women on his hands, but he didn't know the extent until they were tested.

"So, we're good?" Megan asked.

Tasia slid her the bottle of Crown, Deron's favorite, and gave her a soft smile. "Take this shot, and we're great."

Logan couldn't believe her eyes as she tapped Kolbee on the arm. "Well, I'll be damned. Look at them."

"Girl, they're drunk that's why. My mama is not friendly."

"And, you think mine is? We should go take some shots with them," Logan suggested.

Kolbee had already had a few cups of something her aunt Deena had concocted, but she'd still take a few. The positive energy in the air was electrifying and had Kolbee feeling a way. It felt good to be in the presence of family under the circumstances. She just hoped after today; they didn't forget about her like they had in the past.

The dumbfounded look on Logan and Kolbee's faces would take days to wipe off. Two weeks after the funeral, Deron's attorney reached out to them regarding his will. Instead of mailing a letter out, Deron wanted him to meet with them face to face. Some news could only be shared in person. Sitting between the two, Deena held her breath waiting for either of them to say something.

"Why would he do that?" Logan was first to voice her concern. "He left us the house? For what? Neither of us lives here."

"But, you could," Deena said.

"What other surprises do you have for us? I have to get back to work." That was Kolbee. She was in a funky mood thanks to Bryson, who she swore she wouldn't let get to her, but she had.

"A few more. Mr. Flint not only left you his home, but you two are now owners of *Flint Cleaners*. The property in Detroit was closed down when he moved but has been overshawdowed by a Megan Thompson for the last two months."

"What!" Logan screeched. She couldn't believe her mama had kept that secret from her. "Auntie Deena, you knew about this?"

"I knew about a lot of things, sweetie. But, you know how your dad is."

"Do I? He's still secretive from his fucking grave," she hissed, and Deena gasped with shock written across her face.

"Logan. Come on now. Don't act like that," Kolbee said softly. This was all too much for her as well.

"Don't tell me how to fucking act, okay, Kolbee? Everyone in my life is clearly too sneaky for me. Paul, what else?"

He cleared his throat before continuing. "There's a shop in Detroit and one here in Atlanta. He preferred that you leave the one in Detroit to Megan, while you two ran the location here."

"Oh, give me a fucking break."

"Logan Flint," Denna spat. "You better chill your ass out, and I mean it. Deron has done nothing but take care of you your entire life, and the one time he asks you to do something it's a problem? You're thirty fucking years old. Whatever hurt he caused you back then, you need to let go. Your mother has."

"I'm not my mother," she replied dryly with a mug on her face. She was so tempted to hop the hell up and leave this meeting, but she rode with Kolbee.

"Paul, please go ahead," Deena insisted once she broke her icy gaze from her niece.

"Besides the home and his two businesses, he also left each of you a trust fund. Logan, yours comes along with one for your daughter Jordyn," Paul explained before sliding them each a piece of paper.

Kolbee always told Deron she didn't want him to coddle her with funds, but she'd be lying if she said she wasn't anxious to see what he had left her. She still had bills to pay, and they were only collecting interests by the months. Reading over the contents, Kolbee's eyes ballooned damn near out of their sockets. The six-figure number had her seeing stars.

"This is a joke," she whispered to herself.

"It's not," Paul replied. "I have been Deron's attorney for the past ten years, and there wasn't anything he loved more than you two girls. He was a friend of mine, more than a client. I know money won't bring him back, but know he always had you guys in mind when he went to work every day."

Logan was stuck. She wasn't new to money but never had this amount just been given to her. Overwhelmed with everything happening at once, she broke down crying. Kolbee looked her way and shook her head.

"I'm not sure if those are sad or happy tears, but you better wipe them away. Remember what you told me?"

Logan sniffled and wiped her face. The day of Deron's funeral she told Kolbee that she wanted to grow a closer bond with her and make her daddy proud. This was her chance.

"I do."

"Okay, then. No need for all that. We're sisters Lo. Blood. We go through shit, grow through it, and get on with our lives. Daddy loved us both, regardless of how we felt back then. His decision may have been selfish at the time, but he knew what he was doing. Building a legacy. We have to continue his. It's only right."

Grabbing the tissue from her aunt, Logan blew her nose. Kolbee had a point. Though she felt every bit of betrayed, Deron had done his absolute best to be the best father to them both. He'd be crushed to know his baby girl; his first born was acting out the way she was. Actually, he wouldn't. Logan had always craved his attention, and surely that wouldn't stop with him being gone. A parent's job was never done.

"You're right. How much time do we have to make a decision on the move?" she asked Paul.

"As much time as you need. He has workers in place until either of you get there."

"Either of us?" Kolbee questioned. "Which one of us did he think wouldn't show?"

Deena pursed her lips together and glanced Logan's way. "Who do you think? Ms. Spoiled behind over here. I tell you, Deron did a number on you two. Meet me at the house when you're done, okay girls," she said standing to leave. Her presence was no longer needed now that the more substantial topics were out of the way. Her part of the will was addressed first.

"We'll be there," Kolbee told her. Deena kissed the girls on the cheek and made her exit.

Glancing down at the letter again as Logan and Paul conversed, Kolbee shook her head. She couldn't believe two months ago she was stressing and about ready to climb a damn pole to get some funds in her bank account, and now she had enough to get her out of debt plus more. Placing a kiss on the D initial tattoo with a crown positioned over it on her wrist, Kolbee looked up at the ceiling.

"Thank you, Daddy," she whispered.

Deron had always been a king in her eyes, no matter how much she tried to front on him.

6

"I see Deena is doing good. I'm happy she dropped that weight that she picked up when that man left her," Megan said making Logan shake her head.

"I thought you two got along."

Megan looked at her daughter.

"We did until she called herself checking me about my issues with your dad. I had to let her know real quick I'm not the one and after that, I stopped taking her calls. She felt like Deron could do no wrong. But how are you? You okay?"

Logan nodded. If Megan asked her one more time if she was okay, she was positive she would scream at the top of her lungs. While she loved and appreciated her mother at times Megan did work on her nerves.

"I'm fine mom," she murmured looking at the face gracing her cellphone screen. On her explorer page was none other than the man Bezo himself performing at the Barclay Center.

Logan was speechless and couldn't stop the corners of her mouth from lifting up.

"So, he is somebody," she mumbled.

Jordyn leaned over and looked at the photo. Always curious and eager to be up under her mom she smiled.

"That's the ice-cream man mommy!"

"Who is the ice cream man?" Megan asked and glanced over at Logan.

"Nobody!"

Logan glanced into the backseat giving Jordyn a look that made her keep her mouth shut and Megan smiled. She knew sooner or later her grandbaby would spill the beans. Everyone knew that Jordyn couldn't keep a secret.

"Tasia was cordial," Logan said changing the subject.

Megan nodded. She'd spoken her peace for all the wrong things she's spoken about Kolbee. It only felt right, but she wouldn't ever consider Tasia her friend. Too much bad blood had happened between them however they could get along for their girls. Deron was no longer alive, so it would have been childish to still be at each other's necks.

"Tasia was Tasia. Like I said before. I just wish things could have been handled better in the past, but we still have time," Megan said and stopped the car. She was pulled over at the gate that she would be entering. She sighed as she threw the car into park. She was trying to be strong for her daughter and herself. While she'd been apart from Deron for years, she still loved him and hadn't given her heart to another man. She was truly heartbroken to have to say goodbye to him.

"The moment you need her back just let me know, but I will say she's going to be a good distraction for granny. It will also give you time to deal with the cleaners and your relationship with your sister. I was happy to see you two smiling and getting along. Do it for him and yourself. Okay?"

Logan looked at her beautiful mom and smiled.

"Okay."

Megan leaned over and pulled her only child into a tight embrace. Her eyes watered as she rubbed Logan's back.

"I'm so sorry your daddy left us but he's in our hearts, and we will make sure his memory lives on. You can call me at any time, and if you need me to fly back down just to give you a hug, I will be there. I love you," Megan said and let Logan go.

Logan stared into her mother's eyes as she could feel herself become emotional.

"I love you too and let's not talk about dad right now."

Megan nodded. She understood that her daughter needed time. Hell, they all did. Nothing would get accomplished in a few days or even weeks.

"I understand. Jordyn give your mommy a hug and a kiss."

Jordyn quickly unbuckled her seat, and everyone exited the car. Logan hugged her daughter tightly as she inhaled her sweet-smelling scent. Like always Jordyn smelled of strawberries.

"Mommy it's okay. Pop-pop will be fine, and he's in a better place. Auntie will take care of you. Don't cry," Jordyn told her.

Logan nodded, and tears fell from her eyes. She pulled back and stared at her beautiful creation.

"I love you, and I'm going to miss you so much. I will call

you every day, so I can see that pretty face. Be good with granny."

Jordyn grinned at her.

"Will my daddy come see me?"

Jordyn's question made Megan roll her eyes and Logan take a deep breath. Logan put on her biggest smile for Jordyn.

"I'll make sure of it. Kisses."

Jordyn kissed both of Logan's cheeks and smiled at her.

"Kisses! Bye, mommy!"

Logan stood up and helped her mother retrieve the luggage out of the trunk. She waved them goodbye before getting back into the car. Logan called up Rome as she pulled away from the airport.

"I'm sorry to hear about your pops. I could have flown down to see about you," Rome said taking the call.

Logan rolled her eyes even hating the sound of his voice.

"I just need you to be there for your daughter. She's flying back with my mom now, and she wants to see you. I need you to go see our child Rome. She misses you plus like I told you last night. I've decided to move so you need to spend as much time as you can with her."

Rome sucked his teeth as the music in his background went down.

"I got work and shit like that. I can't bring her back with me Logan. You the one that decided to up and move not me. Don't put that on me," he said angrily.

Logan's skin grew hot at his words. Her arched brows furrowed as she pulled onto the highway.

"Put what on you? Nigga you need to go see your daughter. She misses you! Got damn your so fucking sorry. All she needs is her daddy," Logan started to cry and decided to end the call.

She tossed her phone angrily into the passenger's seat and shook her head. She couldn't stop her angry, tears from falling. She'd lost her father. Missed out on time with him because of grudges and yet Jordyn had a father that was of good health, and he wouldn't see her. She didn't want her daughter growing up and resenting her father, but as of now, it looked like it was a good chance that she would.

Logan decided to stop by Boogalou Lounge to have a few drinks. Kolbee wasn't answering her phone, and while Logan knew a few people that stayed in the "A," it wasn't anyone she wanted to chill with like that.

Logan brushed her straight hair out and added some clear gloss to her lips before getting out of the car. It was six in the evening on a Monday still the lounge was filled with chilled adults vibing out and having a good time. Logan wore an off the shoulder green romper with green YSL slides. The weather in Atlanta was getting hotter by the day making it hard for her to rock her jeans during the daytime. Logan's hair was flat ironed bone straight, and she had a bare face.

Without Jordyn, she felt odd. She was used to her baby girl being her shadow and with her gone Logan missed her already. She quickly found a swing to sit on that was by the bar and sat her small clutch in her lap. The music was loud while Plies rapped over a sweet ass beat.

"What can I get you beautiful?" A bartender asked looking at her.

Logan thought of Deron and smiled.

"I can do a Crown Vanilla on the rocks," she replied.

The bartender nodded, and her chinky eyes softened as she looked Logan's way.

"I knew your father, and I'm very sorry for your loss. Any kid of Deron's is good with us. The drinks are on the house," she said before walking away.

Logan's eyes widened shocked that she was spotted by a stranger before an all too familiar scent hit her.

"She is my rock, bust at the op, hold down the spot, beast with the box, shawty be wet, dope in the pot," Bezo rapped walking up beside Logan. Bezo turned his Mitchell & Ness cap backwards and looked down at Logan. His warm minty breath brushed against her skin as he leaned closer to her. "I didn't get to see you at the funeral, but I did stop by. I'm sure people been telling you this shit since it happened, but I am sorry for your loss. Your pops was a stand-up dude and was loved by this city. He looked out for me and invested in me when my own people wouldn't. If you need anything just let me know and I got you," he told her.

Logan was brought her drink. She thanked the bartender and took a large sip to calm her nerves. She wasn't ready to discuss Deron and definitely didn't want to do it with a stranger.

"Thank you," she said in a tone for only their ears.

Bezo nodded. His eyes slowly trailed up and down Logan's body, and he licked his lips.

"It's the third time. Now you belong to me," he semi-joked.

Logan smiled. She tossed the drink back and asked for another one. Bezo ordered her some food not wanting her to get sick, and he grabbed her hand. The way the niggas stared at Logan in the lounge made him uneasy. He was used to the women he ran with getting attention, but Logan was in a lane of her own. The look that she wore confidently pulled men into a trance much like it had with Bezo.

"Come chill with me," he suggested and gently tugged on her hand.

Logan stood up, and more men glanced her way. While she wasn't thick as her sister, she had a body. One that many men adored including Bezo. He grabbed her drink as the bartender was sitting it down and allowed for Logan to walk in front of him. The lil fatty she had on her swung as she walked slowly.

"Where do I go?"

Bezo looked up at Logan's face briefly taking his eyes off her ass, and he smiled. It was then that Logan got to see he was kind of matching her. He wore blue jeans with a dark green Saint Laurent T-shirt and Maison Margiela sneakers. His beloved Jesus piece hung from his neck while a diamond-encrusted watch sat on his wrist.

Bezo's hand sat at the small of Logan's back as he directed her to his section that was being preoccupied with a few of his people. His boys grinned when they saw him coming, however, the look Morgan gave him was deadly. Morgan's full lips pulled into a thin line as she sat her drink down.

"Aye, this Logan and this my people," Bezo said showing Logan where to sit which was on the opposite side of Morgan.

Logan gave his friends a quick wave as they both sat down. A few girls walked over to Bezo wanting his autograph and Morgan took that time to strike. She wore a black racer back dress with Fenty sandals and her shoulder length hair in a bun. She looked pretty, and as Logan stared back at her she wondered if she would have to re-arrange her pretty face? For Morgan's sake she hoped not.

"Your dad was that fine ass man that owned the cleaners, right?" Morgan asked.

Bezo's cousin shook his head. He tapped Morgan's leg as Logan frowned at her.

"Aye chill out," he told her, and Morgan smirked at him.

"What? He was fine as hell. I see why he was screwing all them young ass girls, hell if he was still alive I would have taken a ride on it," she replied and before she could laugh all of Logan's liquor was being tossed her way. "Oh my God!"

Logan jumped up ready to beat her ass but was stopped by Bezo who caught the tail end of Morgan's comment.

"Calm down sexy," he whispered bear hugging her.

Logan said nothing as she stared at Morgan so hard it made Morgan nervous. Crown Royal covered Morgan's hair and clothes. Her eyes even stung from the amber colored alcohol. She stood up and wiped her face as she glared Logan's way.

"I was just joking. I know you're from Detroit and up their life is rough. People probably get killed every damn day, but down here we don't carry ourselves like that. At least act like you have some class about yourself. And to think you came from money. Shit I can't tell," she said before walking away.

Once Morgan was out of the lounge Bezo let Logan go. A few of his boys chuckled at how nicely she'd handled Morgan. However, Logan didn't find it funny, and she knew the minute she saw Morgan again it was going down.

"Relax, drink this," Bezo said passing Logan a cup of D'ussé.

Logan shook her head and crossed her arms over her voluptuous chest. Bezo looked at her sexy ass pout, and he chuckled.

"Don't be like that. You wearing my favorite color, you walked into my favorite lounge and you blessing a nigga with your presence. I thought I was supposed to be making you smile," he told her.

Logan rolled her eyes. She hated that he was so charming with his sexy ass.

"Yeah, you're really doing a good job at that," she quipped.

Bezo passed her the drink again and leaned towards her. He didn't wanna come off too strong, but Logan's presence just kept drawing him near.

"You smell good as fuck too. You should chill with me tonight," he said sitting back.

Bezo was now stretched out with his leg brushing against Logan's. His head was turned her way, and those intense hooded eyes of his were trained on her. Bezo would admire her face for a few seconds before checking out her body. He hoped her little spat with Morgan didn't turn her off of him.

"I don't think that's a good idea. I only came in here for drink nothing more."

Bezo shook his head. Once again, those eyes of his were on Logan's body.

"That's a shame baby. I was hoping to put a real smile on that pretty face of yours," he confessed and the lustful gaze he gave Logan made her push her thighs together.

"I should be going. My daughter is gone, and I could be using this time to catch up on some rest."

Talks of Logan's daughter momentarily shifted Bezo's thoughts.

"I could help you do that too but where your daughter go?"

Logan ignored his comment about helping her rest and looked at him. She knew that if they were to be alone rest would be the last thing on either of their mines.

"Back to Detroit with my mom," Logan replied wondering if her baby had fallen asleep on the plane.

Bezo nodded.

"How she dealing with all of this?"

Logan sipped some of the D'usse. She glanced over at Bezo and frowned.

"Why do you wanna know? Why would you be interested in how my daughter is doing?"

Logan's tone was nasty, and Bezo along with his boy next to him looked at her as if she was crazy. Bezo grabbed Logan's food from the waitress and thanked her. He ate a few wings before passing Logan one.

"You and that mouth. I'm sure you get away with shit ugly bitches wouldn't dream of trying still you need to calm the fuck down. If I ask a question it's because I'm genuinely concerned," he told her as two more of his fans walked up only it was men this time. Bezo leaned up and looked at them.

"That new mixtape on it nigga. You stay putting on for us," the tallest man said and dapped up Bezo.

"I appreciate it. All I ask is that you listen to what I'm saying in these songs. That street life not about shit. Get your education and don't fall victim to that life," Bezo told them before the young boys walked away. He sat back and when he glanced over at Logan he noticed she was already staring at him. "What?" He asked showing off his pretty white teeth. His grill was missing in action still his smile was perfect.

Logan shook her head. He'd shown her a glimpse of what he was about, and she hated to admit it, but she was impressed.

"Nothing. I saw you on my explorer page. Jordyn called you the ice-cream man."

Bezo chuckled. *Finally,* Logan knew who he was.

"I do a lot of shit, but rapping is my passion. I was born to do that shit. It saved my fucking life baby," he said and shook his head.

The way he talked about his profession impressed Logan.

"A million followers, six mixtapes and you still indie. What's up with that?" Logan asked making Bezo smile.

He dropped his head and licked his lips. Logan made him nervous. Usually, he was confident and relaxed around women.

"For now, I don't need to sign with anyone. If that changes, you'll be the first to know beautiful. Let me take you out."

Logan made herself another drink, and Bezo sat up to run his large hands through her silky straight strands.

"Is it real?" His cousin asked, and they all laughed because they knew it was.

Bezo looked at him and frowned.

"Nigga stop it. My baby don't rock no fake shit," he said making Logan smile.

"What do you plan on doing to your pops business?" He asked.

Logan looked away from him and pursed her lips. She wanted to have a break from her real life, and Bezo's questions weren't making that easy for her to do.

"I don't wanna talk about that."

Bezo's eyes peered at her curiously before he slowly nodded.

"I met him years back when I was a teenager. I was banging and doing all kinds of wreck less stuff. He helped me out and gave me a lot of advice that I needed. He looked out for a nigga, even helped my mom save her house from being foreclosed. That was the kind of man your pops was. A real stand up dude," he said, and Logan sat her glass down.

Logan stood up angrily, and Bezo stood up with her. Because he was so popular in Atlanta most of the people in the lounge glanced his way being nosey.

"What the fuck is the problem? I just want you to know that your pops was loved," he said staring down into her eyes.

Logan's eyes were narrowed into slits as she glared up at Bezo. She just wanted to chill and have a few drinks. She didn't need a trip down memory lane.

"Look I came here to chill. I don't want to talk about my father, yet you keep talking about him. Are you hard of fucking hearing or something? You can't just look good you got to know how to take direction nigga," she said angrily.

Bezo chuckled to calm himself down. He grabbed Logan's clutch off the seat she was sitting on and passed it to her. Sexy or not he wasn't kissing no bitch's ass. He didn't give a damn how good she looked. It was clear Logan had some issues that she desperately needed to work through.

"It's all good shawty. I know you dealing with some things, but that mouth and attitude is reckless. I'm not trying to go down for popping your ass in it, so I think it's best you leave. Hitting women ain't never been a niggas style, but you seem like the type that like to try a nigga. You be good, and I'll keep you in my prayers," he told her before sitting back down.

Logan tucked her lip in as his boys eyed her with blank looks on their handsome faces. Logan felt anger and embarrassment sweep over her. However, because she was so stubborn, like her daddy, she had to say something to save face.

"Nigga please don't think I was pressed to sit up under you. You're a fucking fake ass rapper with some whack ass mixtape covers. Look like you did that shit on your cellphone and don't even get me started on your music. It was trash too. Damn near made my ears bleed with them cheap ass beats. You aint shit but a black Vanilla Ice. Fuck you," she said angrily before walking away.

Bezo was shocked by her words before he started to laugh. Logan angrily stormed out of the lounge so angry with him that she could have beaten his ass.

7

"Mama," Kolbee groaned. "I hate the humidity here."

"What do you want me to do about it Kolbee?" Tasia asked, chuckling into the camera.

The two were on FaceTime, and Kolbee was going through her dramatics for the day. After she and Logan discussed Deron's will with Paul, went over the pros and the cons with their mother's and with themselves; they made the decision to move to Atlanta. More thrilled than Logan, Kolbee was excited about the new transition in her life. At the moment, Kansas City wasn't offering her anything but depression, so she welcomed the fresh scenery with open arms.

Logan, on the other hand, had herself and Jordyn to pack up and move. Though she saw no need to, she gave Rome a heads up about their relocation. And, of course, he didn't have much of anything to say like always. It was as if Logan was talking to a brick wall with his deadbeat ass. Either way, that wasn't stopping her from making the move.

Flopping back onto the bed, Kolbee sighed. "I don't know. It's boring here."

"Where's Logan and Jordyn?"

"Jordyn is visiting Megan, and I don't know where Logan is. Probably out. She's always out finding something fun to do without me."

"That's because you isolate yourself. Go out and roam the city. There's plenty of stuff to do; you're just being lazy."

"No. I'm just having one of those days," she sighed heavily.

Kolbee most definitely had her lazy days, but today wasn't one of them. She had been up since seven that morning, roamed the house, FaceTimed Jordyn on her iPad, showered, ate, scrolled social media and all. She still felt like blah. Deron's house was big enough and with him missing from it, Kolbee felt small. The four walls she was tucked behind kept her from facing the reality of her situation. The reality of her life now.

"You know Deron wouldn't want you sulking around like this," Tasia advised.

"That's the thing; I don't know what he would have wanted. How could he not want to prepare us for this?"

"Death is never something someone is prepared for. No matter how much they think they are. You just have to take it one day at a time. Has Andre been by to see you?"

Kolbee nodded. "Yeah. The other day. Maybe I should,"

Kolbee's sentence was cut of by the sound of the doorbell. She stood from the bed and yawned.

Tasia smiled. "Well, looks like you have a visitor. Call me later, okay?"

"Okay. Love you."

"Love you too."

Sliding the phone in the pocket of her cotton lounge shorts, Kolbee trekked down the long hallway, down the steps, and toward the front door. Live video monitors were to the left in the study, but she didn't bother to go look at them. Whoever had stopped by had intentions of being let in. A pleasant surprise crossed her face when she pulled the door open. In all of his milk chocolate glory, Denali stood at the top of the steps with a chill expression on his face. One Kolbee couldn't read quite yet, but she was determined to overtime.

He was dressed down in a pair of basketball shorts, a plain v-neck, with a pair of Air Maxes on his feet. Before he headed to work for the day, he decided to stop by and check up on the girls. In a sense, he felt obligated but didn't want to seem overbearing.

"Well, hello hair cutter," Kolbee greeted and crossed her arms over her chest.

"Let the past remain in the past, girl," he said with a shake of his head. "What's up? What you in here doing?"

"Absolutely nothing. You want to come in? I can feel myself starting to sweat already," she said, moving to the side.

Denali took her invite and moseyed inside. He had walked through the front door of Deron's home on plenty of occasions, but the energy had never felt like this. He didn't see how they were staying in here, but he wouldn't speak on that. Everyone had their own way of handling grief. Feeling like an intruder though welcomed in, Denali waited for Kolbee to walk ahead of him before taking a seat on the sofa.

"I know you in here bored than a mufucka," he chuckled after hearing no sound of a TV playing.

"And, I hope you didn't come by to be bored with me and discuss how bored I was," she smirked.

"Nah. I was actually headed to work early and decided to slide through. Where the other two at?"

Kolbee shrugged. "Jordyn is with her grandma, and I don't know where Logan is. I must have dozed off or something before she left out. Where you work at?" she asked, crossing her legs at the ankle.

The motion caused Denali's eyes to drift from her pretty face to her thick peanut colored thighs. Kolbee's hips were spread wide over the navy blue cushioned couch. He was trying his hardest not to let his gaze turn lustful. Denali was a man. A man that damn sure appreciated a woman's natural curves. In the era of plastic surgery to enhance said features, Kolbee's genetic makeup by God and her mother's genes were welcoming. In his field, he saw way too much fake, pumped bodies. Bodies that were only glorified on a social media platform by mufuckas who didn't even know your real name.

"I own a gym," he answered, and Kolbee grinned. That made him grin as well.

"For real? Damn, that's what's up. So, are you a trainer of some sort or do you just manage the building?"

"I'm a trainer. Been in business going on three years."

"Wow. That's impressive. Congratulations. No wonder you look like that," she said with a lifted brow.

Denali chuckled. "Like what?"

Like you can lift me up and eat me out with one hand, she thought but didn't say it aloud. Compared to her slim hand and bony fingers, Denali's were wide, thick and looked exactly like he lifted weights for hours on end. There wasn't anything Kolbee loved more than a manly man.

"Like you're in excellent shape is all. You used to be skinny when we were kids."

"Yeah, well I haven't been a kid for a very long time," he replied smoothly.

His answer made chills coat Kolbee's thighs. Grabbing the pillow, she placed it over them and licked her lips.

"Clearly. Anyway, what brings you by? If I knew I was having a guest, I would have been a little more presentable," she said bashfully.

"Nah, you look good. I mean, you straight. Don't let my intrusion take you out of yo' comfort zone."

Kolbee didn't know if that was a compliment, or not but she'd take it. "Thanks."

"I was just sliding through to see how ya'll were doing with the move and all. See if ya'll needed anything."

"We're doing as best as we can. Haven't completed adjusted but I'm sure we will with time."

"Ya'll will. Deron was loved out here, so anything ya'll need is already taken care of," Denali replied and went to stand, but Kolbee's outburst question made him halt his movements.

"Did you know?" she asked meekly.

Denali knew exactly what she was referring to. On the one hand, he could have lied to her, but he didn't want to ever be considered a liar in her eyes. Andre had told him of Deron's failing health two weeks before he passed away. As his best friend, he had confided in his wife, but his son as well. Denali was old enough to understand, but even still he was crushed by the news.

He nodded his head, and Kolbee swallowed hard. "I did."

Looking away from him, Kolbee focused her attention on the backyard. She could vaguely remember visiting him and running around on the playset he bought just for his girls. An accessory Logan had cried over until he gave in and purchased the thousand-dollar set. *Deron loved you girls*, that all she had been hearing since stepping foot in Atlanta, but did he really?

Did he think hiding his illness from them was going to make the pain hurt less? Was he expecting for them to forget about him because they hadn't gone through any treatments with him? Kolbee didn't understand it at all.

"Why would he do this?" she mumbled, as tears clouded her vision.

Denali took a deep breath, walked toward where she was and sat down. "To protect ya'll. If you knew how much he talked about you and Logan-"

Kolbee's head snapped around with fire in her eyes. "Ya'll!? I'm so sick of hearing about *you and Logan this, you and Logan that*. What about me! When have I ever been a priority to him!? A priority to anyone on this side of the family?!"

Tears streamed down her cheeks. She couldn't hold it in any longer. She had nothing against Logan, not anymore at least, but she was still so sick of hearing every single person refer to them together. This was the first time in either of their lives that they had been around each other for more than a few days. They didn't have the same experience growing up, going to school, learning how to drive, talking about the birds and the bees or even the littlest things like how to light a grill. Kolbee loved barbeque, and though Tasia could cook, the outdoor task was something she envisioned doing with Deron.

As selfish as it may sound, she wanted her daddy's love all to herself for at least once. All her life she had come in second to Logan, and she was so fucking tired of it. Even in death, Deron was putting them against one another, and he didn't have a clue.

Denali wasn't versed in being affectionate with many women, but he wanted to learn with her. Unbeknownst to Kolbee, he had felt the same way sometimes. Other times, he simply didn't give a fuck that the man who helped create him, left his mama to fiend for herself and raise him alone while he started another family. Many of nights he wanted to reach out to him because he was a man now, and he could never see himself leaving his child behind. It was a pussy move.

But, that was the difference between his dad and Deron. No matter how Deron had explained his absence to Kolbee and Logan, nothing made up for it. In their eyes, mainly Kolbee's, his death was just a way for him to get out of being a father anymore. Though harsh to think that way, Kolbee couldn't control her angry thoughts. She was heartbroken, and anger was the stage she was relishing in at the time.

Grabbing her elbow, Denali pulled Kolbee closer to him. She let him, and he wrapped his arm around her shoulder.

Resting her head on his chest, he rubbed up and down her arm soothingly.

"I know you don't think Deron made you a priority, but he did on plenty of occasions. What I'm saying may not convince you, but at some point, you have to remember the good times. I know you two shared some."

Kolbee sniffled. "We did, but I also remember the times he didn't show up and Andre did instead. He was sending his best friend to do a job he signed up for but couldn't clock into work. That was selfish. All my life I've come second in receiving his love. Always. Fuck if I was born last. That shouldn't matter."

"I know you're grieving and still hurt, but I honestly think you just want something to be mad about, Kolbee. You know Deron as well as I do. The man did his best."

Kolbee lifted up slowly, and Denali removed his arm from around her. He wasn't trying to piss her off, but she was pissing him off with trying to discredit a man he saw bust his ass for everyone in his life; including him. He didn't have to do shit for Denali and wasn't obligated to, but like Andre, Deron too was a stand-up nigga. If there was a responsibility to be handled and they could, they would be on it.

Two seconds away from slapping his ass, Kolbee had to take a deep breath. She didn't know what gave him the impression to get so loose at the lips with her, but she wasn't feeling it.

"I don't know who you are, and you clearly don't know me, to try and tell me what the fuck I should be upset over. Deron may have treated you like the son he always wanted, but you're not. Until you've been in my shoes and walked the soles out of the mufuckas, don't ever fix your lips to compare your relationship with him to mine. It'll never be the same."

The grit in her tone made Denali feel bad for a second, but he shook the feeling off. Kolbee didn't know shit about him either, and maybe it should stay that way. Though he was pissed at her for talking to him like she was crazy, he'd let her slide just off GP for being in her crib. There'd be no next time though.

"You got it, Busy Bee. A nigga crossed his boundaries a little bit, but I know where they're at now. I'ma gon' head and head to work," he said, standing up from the couch. Kolbee did the same.

"And, I wish you'd stop with this damn name," she said with a roll of her eyes. She tried playing it off like it annoyed her, but it honestly made her jittery on the inside.

"I could, but I'm not. It's our thing."

Our thing, she said to herself. In a way, she liked the sound of that. "I guess, Denali."

"On the real though, my fault for coming at you like that. That was mad disrespectful, ma."

Kolbee giggled. "Why you sound like a nigga from New York?"

"I was living out there for a little bit. Their lingo catchy than a mufucka," he said with a shake of his head. "So, we good?"

Stubbornly, Kolbee shrugged her shoulders. "We could be great if you told me all the good food spots around town. I didn't even cook this much back home."

"Damn shame girl. What you gone do when you get a man."

"Who said I didn't already have a man?" she questioned with a serious expression on her face.

"Word?" Denali chuckled. "Nah. I know you don't have one cause that nigga would've helped you move your shit up here."

"Maybe he had to work, smart ass. Everyone isn't a business owner like you."

"Ain't that much work in the world to have my woman move across the world and not help. That nigga better find another occupation."

Kolbee smiled at his caring manners. She wasn't surprised by them though. Andre was his father and had raised him to be a hell of a man.

"I'll let him know that when I call."

"See. Why you calling him? He should be blowing your line down making sure you good. Or what? You the type that like space?"

"A little of both actually."

Denali nodded and opened the door. "Bet. I'll remember that."

"For what?"

"For myself. What's today, Wednesday? I'll see how you doing in a week. I'll text you some food spots."

Kolbee didn't like that. She was hoping he could actually take her to some of the food places himself, but she wouldn't let him know that. Not now at least.

"You would need my number for that."

Pulling her phone from her pocket, Kolbee unlocked it and handed it to him. After saving the number, he gave the phone back.

"I'm locked in now, so don't go missing on a nigga. I know where you live," he joked, and she smiled.

"Trust me; I won't. I'll be texting you for a list of places every day."

"You can text me about other stuff too. I know you need somebody to listen to your big-headed ass." What he really wanted to say was he could take her out to eat, but didn't.

Kolbee gasped. "My head is not big! Fuck you," she laughed just as her phone began to vibrate in her hand.

"Yeah, yeah. Get in the house for you sweat up out them little ass shorts."

The look in his eyes made Kolbee lick her lips and step back inside the door. "Have a good day at work, ugly."

"Your pretend boyfriend," he shouted before hopping in his charcoal gray, Dodge SRT.

Shaking her head at his petty jab, Kolbee glanced at her screen prepared to take the call and sucked her teeth at the name on the screen.

"Yes, Bryson?"

"Damn, I can't call now? Why you answering the phone like I get on your nerves or something."

You do, sometimes, she thought but played nice. "You don't. I was just in the middle of something. What's up?"

"I'ma be in Atlanta tomorrow. Little bro got a tournament or some shit that way. Can I see you? I miss you, bae."

Truth be told, Kolbee missed him too. She only saw him once when she went home, and that was her decision. Being home with her mama and little brother were the only people she wanted to be around. Her best friend Alaia had to break into her room and go off for ignoring her texts and calls.

Seeing Bryson would make her feel not so lonely in this big city. He was something familiar. A feeling she sometimes craved.

"You can. And, I miss you too," she replied before laying back on the couch.

Denali could joke about her having a pretend boyfriend all he wanted to, but little did he know she was about to be taking him to all the food spots he'd suggest.

UNTITLED

Kolbee was drunk, and the only thing she wanted to do was lay down. Bryson had been in town for three days, and she was so glad he had come in town. His presence was very much missed, and so was his spectacular head game. After his brother's basketball game Saturday evening, one of Kolbee's older female cousins on Deron's side invited her to kick it at the park with her and some friends. That was four hours and five drinks ago.

    The setting at Washington Park reminded Kolbee of back in the day at Swope Park in Kansas City. Old school cars lined the sidewalks, people were everywhere socializing, shooting dice, playing basketball on a court nearby, and the woman responsible for Kolbee's drunkenness was selling liquor from under a tent. Posted up on the back of a pickup truck with her arms around Bryson's waist and head on his shoulder, Kolbee yawned.

"Un, un! Ain't none of that. It's still early, cuz," Yazmeen, her older cousin said.

"I'm so sleepy. It's all that liquor and the heat," Kolbee replied sleepily.

"You ready to go, bae?" Bryson asked.

"I want some dick," she whispered in his ear while tracing her hand down his chest and kissing his neck.

"Aye! Don't make me beat this nigga ass out here Kolbee," one of her male cousins shouted from across the park. He was only a few years older than she was, but he didn't care.

"Girl," Yazmeen snickered. "Don't get this man beat up and sent home out here. You know everyone knows whose daughter you are."

"Says the bitch who got me pissy drunk," Kolbee sassed and gently pushed Bryson so he could scoot up some.

Hopping down from the back of the truck, she made sure the dress she was wearing was in place. It was another hot day, but thankfully some of the shade from the trees had helped alleviate her from getting sunburn. The stretchy material was sticking to her damp skin, and beads of sweat trickled down her back. Men were used to seeing round asses and pretty faces, but Kolbee's was a new one. They gawked at her with vulture eyes, and Bryson clenched his jaw.

"You straight? I'll pull the car over here, so you won't have to walk." He didn't want every nigga at the park to have their eyes transfixed on her ass when she did mosey by. Thankfully, she agreed.

"That's fine."

When he walked away, Yazmeen couldn't resist laughing. "That man knew what was up."

"What?" Kolbee asked cluelessly.

"Your body is sickening, hoe. He ain't ever about to let you walk by all these hounding ass niggas again," Yazmeen and her friends laughed. Though they were frequent visitors to the park, every week there was a group of new niggas trying to holler. It never failed.

She knew her cousin was right but took up for her boo. "Nah. He knows I'm drunk is all. What you doing when you leave here? I know you aren't driving."

Yazmeen waved her off. "Girl, please. I do this every weekend. I'm good. We might head over to a little after-hours spot if these hoes are down. I gotta check in with my man."

"You always checking in with that bum ass nigga," her friend scolded.

"The same bum ass nigga that got you smoking on that blunt like a fucking junky, bitch. Don't do my nigga."

"Trust me, baby. The only person that wants to do him is you."

The friends fell out laughing at that. They were used to their bickering about Yazmeen's boyfriend. He may not have been shit, but that nigga had some of the best weed in town. As Kolbee said her goodbyes, Bryson pulled up, and she hopped right in. The coolness of his leather seats felt so good against her warm skin.

"You hungry?" he asked, turning out of the parking lot.

"Not right now. I just want to sleep this liquor off. Damn. I can't believe I got this drunk."

"Me either. You were going to be mad as hell had I not

shown up. You would've been out there all night fooling with your cousin."

Kolbee shook her head and shrugged. "I would've called my other nigga to come swoop me up."

Bryson looked over at her and had the right mind to slap her in her damn forehead but told himself to chill. Kolbee had said it so nonchalantly, and with her damn eyes closed he thought she was playing. She hadn't even cracked a smile.

"You already got you a nigga down here, huh?" he pressed minutes later.

Kolbee was dozing off not paying him any mind. "What are you talking about?"

"I'm saying, you talkin' 'bout calling another nigga coming to pick you up on some disrespectful shit. I ain't with that."

"Okay."

"Okay?" he asked slightly raising his voice. Kolbee's eyes slowly peeled open and Bryson chuckled. "You a muthafucking trip, man."

"You over there upset on some shit that didn't happen. You need to chill, for real. I'm not trying to hear all that on this drive home."

Kolbee had always been bold with the words coming out of her mouth, but Bryson was taken aback just then. The liquor in her system wasn't helping any either. While he was tripping off her slick comment, Kolbee was wondering what Denali was doing. She wished it was the passenger seat of his car that she was reclined in right now.

Instead of texting her like he said he would, Denali had called her that night when she was in bed. They stayed on FaceTime catching up on old times and talking about his training business amongst other topics. It was refreshing for them both, especially for Kolbee. Their conversation was authentic and not forced. Those were the type she enjoyed. Not ones where she stayed arguing all the time.

An hour later, Bryson was pulling up to Kolbee's new home. She had given him the address before dozing off. Shutting the engine off, he gently shook her so she could wake up.

"Kolbee, wake up. We here. Shit, I think this is it."

Adjusting in her seat and to the night's dark skies now, Kolbee stretched and unfastened her seatbelt. "Dang. I slept the entire ride."

"I know not to go on a road trip with you," Bryson joked and climbed out.

He had every intention of spending the night with Kolbee, but he didn't know they'd end up at her place. Bryson came prepared, though. Grabbing his overnight bag out the backseat, he closed the door, hit the locks on the rental, and followed Kolbee up the front steps. The house was surprisingly quiet when they walked inside, and Kolbee was glad. Introductions of who Bryson was and why he was there was something she was not in the mood to explain to her auntie Deena and her kids who were staying the night.

Making it to her bedroom, Kolbee couldn't get through the door before she was pulling the dress from her body. Had she known she'd be standing outside in the heat all day, she would have brought a change of clothes. She hated being sweaty. Bryson closed the door and found him a spot on the opposite side of the room to place his belongings. Kolbee was just about to grab her towel from the back of the door and head to the shower, but he stopped her.

"Come here right quick, Kolbee," he called out.

"What?" she whined, wrapping the towel around her panty and bra-clad frame. "I need to get in the shower."

"This will only take five seconds, woman. Bring your ass here."

Releasing a heavy sigh, she stomped over to him. "Wh-"

Bryson grabbed her by the chin and kissed her hard. Pulling her body closer to his, he gripped her juicy ass cheeks in each hand and tongued her down so good, Kolbee felt lightheaded. Pulling away, she blinked up at him with a questioning gaze.

"The only nigga you need on your mind is me. When I'm gone, you can do whatever you want to cause' I know you will anyway," he told her.

Bryson just had to come to grips with what they were doing; casually dating. Kolbee was no longer interested in taking things further, and Bryson had to respect that. With her up and abruptly moving to Atlanta, he had no choice but to. She wasn't offering anything else, especially not a long-distance relationship.

All Kolbee could do was nod her head, before heading to the shower. She liked Bryson and their time spent together had created some dope memories, but Kolbee knew that was as far as it was going to go. She had her eyes on someone else. That someone else being deemed off limits in her mind. Denali was basically family, but she couldn't control the feelings that had somehow produced since Wednesday night when they were on the phone.

After the two showered, Kolbee snuggled deeply under the covers with Bryson laying between her legs. He was skillfully sucking on her clit as her legs began to shake. She was so tired she could have fallen asleep straight after her shower, but Bryson had other plans. Gripping the curly afro he had let grow out some; her back arched away from the sheets as her orgasm coursed through her body.

"Ssss," she hissed out.

Her heart was beating wildly, and her eyelids were heavy as hell. Licking her lips, Kolbee exhaled a deep breath, and Bryson kissed her plumps lips.

"You always taste so fucking good," he growled in her ear.

After securing the condom he didn't want to wear but knew Kolbee wasn't going to let him hit raw, Bryson slid inside her tight walls with a little push back, but he knew just how to handle that. Gripping her thighs, he pressed them back against the sheets and went deep.

"Ughhh! Fuck!" Kolbee gritted out.

She could have honestly gone right to sleep after that vicious tongue lashing she received, but she wasn't an unfair lover. As much as Bryson loved to please her, she didn't mind him getting any. Fifteen minutes, and a different position later, Bryson was releasing his seeds into the latex and breathing hard as hell.

"Damn," he huffed, falling onto his elbow on the bed.

Kolbee felt like she needed another shower, but for now, she'd just wash up. Stepping onto the plush carpet, her steps halted when little knocks were heard at the door. The smaller voice following behind it had her praying the door was locked.

"Kolbee, you awake?" her little cousin Deanna called out.

"Yes. What's wrong, boo?"

"I want some ice cream."

Kolbee's face frowned in confusion. "Where the hell her mama at?" she said to herself. "Okay. Give me ten minutes, and I'll make you some. Did you ask your mama if you could have ice cream?"

"She's sleep," Deanna replied, and Kolbee shook her head with a grin.

She and her cousin were more alike than she thought. Kolbee was super sneaky as a kid and stayed getting in trouble for stuff just like this. After telling Deanna to wait for her in the living room, Kolbee went to handle her business in the bathroom. Looking at herself in the mirror, she smiled thinking of Jordyn's funny self and the new accolade added to her name. Being an auntie to Jordyn was an honor and getting to know her little cousins brought out the caregiver in her immediately. She was so grateful for the little people in her life.

8

♪*Do I find it so hard*
   When I know in my heart
   I'm letting you down every day
   Letting you down every day
   Why do I keep on running away?♪

While Jay-z rapped about almost losing his family, the sisters thought of Deron. Quietly they sat in the car as their future stared back at them. **Flint Cleaners**. The sign was big. The establishment was of course bigger. It sat on Monroe Dr in a large white building that took up a chunk of the space on the busy street. It stared at the sisters as they both peered back at it.

"Wow, so this is real. We own this," Kolbee said, and Logan glanced over at her.

Slowly Logan nodded.

"Yeah."

They watched people travel in and out of the business, *their* business for several minutes before finally finding the courage to exit the car. Logan and Kolbee went into the cleaners and was greeted with big smiles. Flint Cleaners had been in business for over four years and had mostly the same employees. Deron loved his company and had chosen to run it himself, so he was the boss and had no one up under him however in his absence his sister Deena had been helping run the place.

She walked from behind the counter smiling. She wore a Flint Cleaners black collared standard work shirt with black slacks. Her almond-shaped eyes were somewhat sad as she walked up to her beautiful nieces.

"Today is one of those days girls. I can feel your father up and through this place. I'm so glad to see you all. Everything is easy, and in time you all will be running it without a problem. Let me show you around," she said and began to give them a tour of the building.

In the front entrance was a large white desk that housed a register along with a long black sleek counter to place your bags on. Behind the counter were racks and racks of clothes. The building smelled of fresh linen. In the front were four chairs perched on each side of the front door along with two pop machines. A coffee machine also sat to the side against the wall.

In the back of the building away from the customer's eyes were the pressing machines, the supply closet and the laundry room with the heavy-duty washers. Deena showed the sisters how to work the register and where to store the money. She also gave them all access codes to the building and the computers in the back. While Kolbee was shown how to payout the employees and call up payroll Logan was given the rundown on the upcoming events.

Flint Cleaners donated a lot of money and were invited to two luncheons to receive awards for their efforts to support Atlanta's youth. Logan felt a surge of pride for her father move through her as she looked at all the receipts he had for giving away money.

"Wow I had no idea he did all of this," she said putting the receipts away.

Deena nodded eyeing her oldest niece. The spoiled one of the bunch.

"You didn't care to know sweetie. Your father always wanted you girls here with him. I'm going to show Kolbee this stuff, Mr. Brown could use some help at the front," she said and walked away.

Logan sighed. She loved her auntie, but she was growing tired of her coming down so hard on her on behalf of Deron. He was her father, and she didn't feel it was Deena's place to continually talk about it.

"I'ma have to sick my momma on her," she said and laughed.

Logan went to the front of the cleaners and stood beside Mr. Brown. He was one of the oldest employees that Flint Cleaners had. He loved the small break from the home that the job provided him with and was hurt to see Deron go. Deron was like family to him.

"Hey, pretty girl. I wanted to go take a bathroom break. You think you can manage to register?"

Logan nodded as a tall man with creamy brown skin walked through the door. He talked animatedly about something on his phone as he walked to the register totting two Nordstrom bags filled with his jeans. He placed them on the counter, and his eyes landed on Logan.

Yung Cho licked his lips as his eyes gave her a deliberate once-over.

"Aye let me hit you back," he said before ending his call.

Logan shifted from one foot to the other as she stared back at him. She'd seen him online rapping. He'd been featured in a few popular songs, but that was the extent of her knowledge of him. What she could admit was that he was sexier in person.

Yung Cho stood tall at six feet three with a lean build. He had long inky black hair that was usually in two braids to the back or hanging wildly on his head. He had a short beard that was always lined up along with a mustache that he kept groomed. Yung Cho had a small gash at the bottom of his face, but it roughened up his pretty boy looks and didn't take anything away from how handsome he was.

"I heard Mr. Flint had some bad ass daughters, but I just had to see for myself. You are gorgeous shawty."

Logan nodded. She'd been enthralled in how good he looked until he brought up her father. That had brought her back to reality.

"I'm fine. How can I help you?"

Yung Cho stared at her. His light brown eyes bounced all over the cleaners before they landed back on Logan. He put his phone in his pocket and passed her the bags. He was trying to be respectful to the man that had kicked knowledge to him daily but was finding that hard to do. Logan was by far the sexiest woman he'd come across in quite some time. She was definitely to fine to let her get away.

"Shit I um...shit I needed this cleaned. Can you do that for me?"

Logan looked through the two bags then at Cho. She nodded, and he smirked at her. He licked his lips, and she saw that he had an abnormally long tongue. It was so long her mind immediately went to nasty thoughts.

"Sure, let me take down your info."

Yung Cho shook his head.

"It's already in their sexy. Look up, Chauncey Wright. You don't know who I am?" He asked.

Logan smiled.

"I had no idea what your real name was. Sorry I'm not one of your fans sweetie," she replied, and Mr. Brown walked up.

"Chauncey, how is your mom?" He asked, and Yung Cho looked at him.

"She's good Mr. Brown. Can you make sure this beautiful ass girl don't mess up my clothes?"

Mr. Brown nodded, and Yung Cho chuckled. While Mr. Brown took Yung Cho's things to the back Yung Cho stared unashamedly at Logan while she pretended to dust off the counter.

"I got a show tonight. You should come through," he suggested looking at her.

Logan stopped dusting to peer his way. He was yet

another rapper trying to get on. She glanced back to see if her sister or auntie was walking up before replying.

"I shouldn't. I have a lot going on, and I just don't have the time."

Yung Cho nodded as he walked up on Logan. He smelled like weed and cologne. His attire was relaxed as he wore grey sweats with a black tee. Logan didn't want to glance down at his imprint, but she couldn't help it. She immediately spotted it and Yung Cho chuckled.

Yung Cho placed a flyer for his intimate show on the desk in front of Logan and touched a piece of her long red hair. He'd been eyeing it since he'd walked into the building and damn that turned him on. He leaned towards her as she stared hard at the words on the colorful flyer.

"Let me introduce you to the "A" sexy. Come out and when you get to the door tell them your name," he whispered, and as Logan looked up, he was heading for the door.

Deena and Kolbee joined Logan shortly after in the front of the cleaners, and Kolbee picked up the flyer. She looked it over and smiled.

"I like some of his songs. He was just here?"

Logan nodded, and for some reason, she thought of Bezo. She then thought of how persistent he was with being all up in her damn business and she rolled her eyes.

"Yes, he was, and my best friend is flying in tonight. I think we're going to hit this up. You should come."

Deena smiled as she watched her nieces naturally fall into their sisterhood. Many nights she'd prayed for her brother and his girls. She hated that it had taken something tragic for it to happen, but still she was thankful.

"Nah I'm going to chill tonight, but if I change my mind, I'll let you know. Do let me know how them niggas is looking though," Kolbee said, and Deena playfully swatted her on the butt.

"Watch your language. Right now, you two need to adjust to your new life. These boys not going nowhere. They can wait," Deena said and walked away.

Kolbee glanced over at Logan as Deena disappeared into the back.

"But what about my coochie? Can she wait? Hell, I'm horny as hell," she said, and Logan laughed. She had been thinking the same thing.

"Maybe we more alike than we thought we were," Logan said and smiled at Kolbee.

"I miss you so much! Do you miss me?"

Jordyn nodded with her big red curls all over her head. She was in her pajamas and eating ice cream. One of her most favorite things to do.

"I do but mommy...my....my daddy didn't come. He didn't pick up when granny called," she said and her slanted eyes watered.

"That hoe ass nigga," Jerricka mumbled from the bed.

Logan swallowed hard and looked at her baby. This was her life, her heart, the reason she was still forging ahead, and it angered her that she was in pain.

"Mommy will fix all of it. You know how we pray every night?" She asked, and Jordyn nodded. Logan smiled at her.

"Well, mommy wants you to pray for your daddy. Ask God to move him towards you. Okay?"

Jordyn's sad face brightened up.

"Will he? Will God give me my daddy back?" Jordyn asked excitedly.

Logan nodded.

"Even if it's a new one he will sweetie. I love you," Logan told her before Jordyn ended the call.

"Suck that shit up and drink this. No tears tonight boo! I promise you the minute I get back to Detroit I'm tossing three Snicker bars into his tank. Remember we did that shit to Ross when he cheated on me in high school? Well it still works. Rome's old dumb ass gone wake up to a non-driving car I promise you. If he can't go, see my baby then his ass doesn't need a car. Fuck him he can catch the bus or better yet walk," Jerricka said, and Logan laughed.

Logan tossed back the shot of Patron and shook her head. That tequila wasn't nothing to play with.

"Hey is my niece okay?" Kolbee asked stepping into the room.

Jerricka had met her hours ago and was in love with Kolbee. Jerricka felt like Logan and Kolbee were just alike and was happy to see them trying to move past all that they'd been through.

"It's her bitch ass daddy. He is such a punk. I hate him," Jerricka vented.

Kolbee shook her head. It angered her to think of someone hurting Jordyn. That girl was everything to Kolbee.

"But damn how could anyone not love her? She's so perfect. What's the problem?"

Logan sat up and looked at her baby sister.

"He's mad that I don't want him. He's trying to hurt me but, in the end, it only hurts her. I honestly don't know what to do, but I will take dad's advice and file for child support. Maybe If I do that he'll see that I'm not playing with him."

Jerricka and Kolbee nodded. Jerricka looked at Kolbee and smiled.

"So, you sure you don't wanna come?" She asked, and Kolbee shook her head.

"Not this time but you two ladies have fun and like auntie said leave them, boys, alone. They can wait!" Kolbee said and wagged her finger at them before they all laughed.

"Yes, they can wait until I see a young, rich, nigga then I'm popping it for a real one," Jerricka joked mimicking Rick Ross. She loved the boss and was always saying things like she needed a young, rich, nigga in her life. However, jokes were all it was. Jerricka was a full-time nurse in school for her masters. She was fully capable of taking care of herself.

"We need to go before we get too drunk to leave," Jerricka said as she got off Logan's bed.

Logan nodded, and Kolbee told them goodbye before going back to her room. Logan put on some perfume before she grabbed her purse. She was buzzing, but her tolerance for liquor was high, so she wasn't drunk. While her best friend wore a grey t-shirt dress showing off her curves Logan wore a black mini dress with thigh high open toed boots. Logan's long red hair was pulled back into a sleek bun, and she wore black matte lipstick. She looked sexy, and so did her best friend that was rocking her blunt cut bob in sexy beach waves.

Logan and Jerricka made drinks to go and climbed into the Mercedes. Logan tried to not think of her problems, but it was hard to do. She was living in her father's home, helping run his business and driving his cars. He was everywhere yet he still wasn't there. She missed him. Regretted the things she'd spoken to him when he was alive then there was Rome. Logan was feeling overwhelmed with all the issues in her life and was glad her best friend that she'd known since third grade had flown down to spend some time with her.

"When are you coming back to pack up your place?"

Logan shrugged. She honestly didn't know when she would have the time to. The cleaners was a full-time job, and even after it was closed, they seemed to always have something to do. Learning the ins and outs of the business wasn't as easy as her aunt had promised them it would be.

"I'm not sure. I'm still trying to figure all of this out," Logan admitted.

Jerricka rubbed her arm soothingly.

"Well I'm going to miss you, but I feel like this is what you and your sister should be doing. You did lashes in the "D," but this is your own business. You and your sister could really make a living down here, and I know Jordyn would love the weather. I just hate you had to lose your dad to gain it you know?"

Logan nodded. Her eyes watered, and she swallowed down her emotions.

"Not tonight Jerricka," she said quietly, and Jerricka nodded.

Jerricka turned on the radio as Logan downed her cup of Patron and juice. Migos cut on, and both women got hype from the music. They were in Atlanta. The city had an aura to it that made you feel so alive. The weather was nice, and they were looking beautiful. They felt invincible. For the moment Logan's mind was free from worry, and she was loving it.

As she pulled up to the address that had been on the flyer, they spotted all types of rides. From foreigners to old school's cars lined the block. Jerricka looked at the sign outside of the building and laughed so hard tears came to her eyes.

"Why didn't you tell me this was the strip club?" She questioned.

Logan's shoulders shook as she joined in with her. She felt dumb because she'd looked at the name and thought nothing of it. Although she was thirty she'd only been to Atlanta to visit Deron, so she had no clue about the various strip clubs that it had in the area.

"You know I'm boring as hell at home so why would that change down here? I thought it was the club," she replied.

Jerricka smiled while wiping her wet eyes.

"I mean it's still the club just one that chicks get naked at. I just would have worn something simple had I known. We all done up for this shit. These niggas are really gone be on us. You know they can smell an out of town chick," she said, and Logan nodded agreeing with her.

Since she'd been there men had been on her left and right.

"Well if it's whack we leaving," Logan said and found an available space to park.

Once the ladies were admitted into the club, they bought a booth one of the last three available and ordered food and bottles. Jerricka liked to tip dancers like it was going out of style so while she grabbed singles a familiar face joined Logan in her booth.

Bezo was looking like money in his black Givenchy outfit. On his feet were black Buscemi's while vintage Bugatti 508 frames sat on his handsome face. He soaked in Logan's beauty as he took a seat next to her. Four of his boys blocked the opening of the section making it impossible for someone to pass through without their permission.

"Look at you miss lady. Still mad at my black Vanilla Ice ass?" He asked and chuckled.

Logan inhaled the weed and cologne that floated off his body, and she nodded. She was kind of happy to see him, but she wouldn't dare let it show. Bezo's hand went to her thigh, and gently he squeezed it. His head heavy from all the liquor in his system fell back, and he relaxed in his seat.

"I been thinking about you baby. Never thought I'd see your mean ass up in here though. Where your phone?"

Logan with her heart doing an irregular beat passed him her phone. Bezo put all three of his numbers in and called each one so he could lock her number in. He gave the phone back to her as Jerricka entered back into their section. Jerricka had dancers with her and bottles. Bezo smiled at Jerricka as he pulled money from his pocket. It wasn't singles, but he decided he'd still toss a few. In his mind stripping was like hustling for bitches. He respected them and would help in any way that he could. Bezo would never look down on the next man at how he got his money up.

"Jerricka this is Bezo," Logan said as he tossed the twenties at a brown skinned beauty.

Jerricka grinned tossing singles.

"I know who he is. The question is how do you know him? And why the fuck didn't you tell me best friend?"

Bezo chuckled. He liked Jerricka already. He leaned towards Logan and placed a kiss on her cheek. He was happy as fuck to see her and trying to play it cool.

"Yeah, baby why you ain't tell her? You wanted her to wait until you was pregnant to drop the news and shit?" He joked.

Bezo went back to tossing money, and Jerricka's eyes grew wide as she looked at Logan.

"What's going on?" She mouthed to Logan.

Logan shrugged, and they both laughed. Logan made a drink while Jerricka and Bezo went crazy making it rain. They brought so much attention to their section that the DJ was moved to give them a shout out.

"We got the A-town's own Bezo in this bitch. His latest hit is lighting up the fucking charts and he looking to do a tour in a few months. We see you nigga!" He yelled, and the crowd went wild.

Logan and Jerricka watched as women broke their necks to get into the section. Bezo's people politely turned their thirsty asses around. Bezo sparked up a blunt and looked at Logan. She'd been invading his thoughts since he'd met her. She was pretty, but truthfully her attitude needed help, so he wasn't sure why he felt such a pull to her.

"You been good?" He asked blowing smoke out of his mouth.

"Yes, I have," Logan replied frowning.

Bezo leaned towards her and gently blew smoke into her

mouth to give her a charge. Praying the weed mellowed her mean ass out some.

Logan coughed as she blew the smoke out of her mouth and Bezo and Jerricka laughed. Bezo stroked her cheek as he stared at her.

"Relax and let's try that again," he said and gave Logan another charge. Only this time his lips brushed against her's. Logan closed her eyes and slowly inhaled the weed. As she held her breath, Bezo massaged her thigh. Her skin was soft, she was looking sexy as ever and smelling even better. She had his dick hard as fuck.

"You sexy as fuck," he told her and buried his face into her neck. His beard tickled her as he kissed her soft skin.

Logan glanced over at Jerricka and saw she was talking with one of Bezo's boys. She blew the smoke out of her mouth as Bezo raised his hand up her leg.

"You keep running from me, and I keep finding you. What's that telling you? Maybe I'm what you need in your life Logan," he said and bit her neck.

Logan moaned. The music cut off and the lights dimmed low.

"Aye, we got Yung Cho in the building putting on for them eastside niggas. If you fuck with him like we do, then y'all need to stand y'all asses up!" The DJ yelled, and most of the women went crazy.

"It's almost time!" Bezo's boy yelled reminding him of why he was there.

Bezo sat up and looked at Logan. He pulled some money out of his pocket and passed it to her.

"This for your food and drinks. You need to go, baby. I'll hit you up later to explain shit," he said and stood up.

Jerricka not needing to be told twice jumped up. Logan looked at the hundreds before knocking them off her lap. She stood up as the music began to play. Bezo's cousin glanced back at him and shook his head. He was the biggest one resembling Shaquille O'Neal in height and weight. He also worked as Bezo's bodyguard when he went on tour.

"They deep as fuck. We gone let that nigga slide tonight," he said knowing when to pick his battles.

Bezo nodded knowing they would catch Yung Cho slipping and he sat back down. Jerricka looked from him to his boys and shook her head.

"Is it safe for us to be here? I mean don't have us up in some drama where we could catch a bullet."

Bezo shook his head. If only Jerricka knew. He'd been shot at more times than he could count. As long as he had his cousin watching his back, he was okay. That nigga was the reason why he was alive.

"You good relax. Logan come here," he said pouring himself a drink.

Logan sat down and looked at Bezo.

"He invited me here," she said as Bezo stared at her.

Bezo frowned as he took off his glasses.

"Who?"

"Cho! The nigga on stage," Jerricka said then stood on the couch in the booth to get a better view of his performance.

Bezo smiled before lightly chuckling. He took a bottle of Moet to the face and drunk some of it down before sitting it on the table.

"How the fuck did you manage to pull two of the biggest rappers in Atlanta, and you just got here? Must be that hair and that pretty ass face. Word of advice though tell that nigga to kick rocks." Bezo went to grab the bottle again and quickly turned to Logan. "Did you have that hoe ass nigga around your daughter?" He asked thinking of how drama seemed to follow Yung Cho.

Logan shook her head, and his tense jaw relaxed.

"Good that nigga still banging. Remember when I told you, your pops saved me and shit? He helped me leave all that alone. He knows a lot of the bloods and they respect him, so they was cool with me falling back so I could do my rap shit. Plus, I was never jumped into that shit I just claimed it because it was what all my niggas was doing at the time. Chauncey bitch ass still is on that tip. Don't have that nigga round your daughter Logan. He dangerous," Bezo warned her.

Logan nodded.

"So, you're telling me the gang just let you walk away from them?"

Bezo shook his head.

"I'm telling you that I do what the fuck I want. I don't answer to no niggas but that nigga do. Too many people funding his career. Then he uses them niggas for protection cause he talk a lot of shit and now he got enemies," Bezo replied.

Logan nodded halfway listening to him. The weed was giving her a buzz and the longer she stared at Bezo, the more she wondered about how big his dick was?

"Okay but you still on that too. You came here tonight to fight him," she said calling Bezo out.

Bezo pinched her cheek and kissed her forehead.

"Baby we grown ass men. We don't fight no more. Come here," he said and pulled Logan firmly to his side. Bezo leaned down and gently kissed her on the lips. Logan moaned as she grabbed his shirt. Bezo's soft tongue slid into Logan's mouth as Jerricka started coughing loudly to get their attention.

"Nigga you must wanna catch a hot one tonight," Yung Cho said walking up to Logan's section in search of Bezo. Yung Cho looked at Bezo's cousin and pulled his gun out. People started to leave out of the section, and Cho's boys ran over with their own weapons drawn.

"Aye Bezo!" His cousin yelled not bothered by the niggas before him.

Bezo stopped kissing Logan and stood up. Jerricka rushed to Logan's side and shook her head. Seeing men with guns had sobered her ass up really quick.

"Listen this is crazy," Jerricka whispered to Logan.

Logan nodded. She had been around weapons all her life. She knew how to shoot well because of Deron. She was more concerned about catching a stray bullet. They had no names on them and took innocent lives every day.

"Bezo and Cho," she said walking up to the madness.

Bezo and Yung Cho looked Logan's way along with the other men. Briefly, the beef was forgotten. The men admired her beauty until Yung Cho realized that she was chilling with the enemy.

"You came but you on the wrong fucking side. What the

fuck you doing with this nigga?" Yung Cho asked angrily. His pride was wounded, but he refused to let it show.

Logan feeling closer to Bezo grabbed his hand, and he looked at her. She had no interest in watching anyone lose their life in front of her.

"Let's go. Okay?"

Bezo pulled his bottom lip into his mouth, and Logan tugged on his arm. Yung Cho stared at her as his heart pumped wildly in his chest.

"Damn okay. I guess you'll be attending another funeral in a minute," he retorted and before the words were completely out of his mouth, Bezo hit him in the face with his gun.

Chaos broke out in the club as men began to fight. It was Bezo's people against Yung Cho's. Logan and Jerricka ran like their life depended on it as gunshots started to go off.

Pop!

Pop!

Pop!

"Oh my God! This can't be happening!" Jerricka yelled accidentally peeing on herself. She'd talked mad shit about being from Detroit, but she was actually raised in the suburbs and had never heard a real gun go off a day in her life.

"Come on!" Logan hissed and pulled her out of the club.

They ran to the Mercedes and quickly got in. Logan drove like she was on the Fast and The Furious as she pulled out of the lot. The gunshots made it out into the parking lot, and they spotted people running as they drove away from the building.

Once they were free from harm Jerricka sighed. Logan's

cell phone started to ring, and Jerricka with shaky hands picked it up.

"It's Bezo. You should see if he's okay," she said and answered the call.

Logan cleared her throat as she took the phone from her.

"Are you okay?"

Bezo coughed, and she could hear loud music playing in his background. Logan had never been into street men, so the whole scene had her out of her element.

"I'm good. Them niggas started shooting on some hoe shit. You know I would never put you in harm's way. Where you at?" Bezo asked her.

"You're telling me to keep my child away from him when clearly you are more than just a rapper. Me and my friend could have been killed tonight. I think it's best for us to lose each other's number," Logan replied and ended the call.

Bezo called her back repeatedly, and she ignored his calls. Jerricka glanced over at her and gave her a sly smile.

"It's good you hung up on his ass anyway. I pissed on myself when them niggas started shooting. We can't go around nobody until I change my clothes. I will not be known as your pissy ass best friend," she said, and they laughed.

Thank you, daddy, for watching over us, Logan thought as she rode back to his home. Once they finally made it back to Deron's place. Logan parked, and Jerricka quickly exited the car. As Logan got out of her seat, a red Jaguar truck pulled up behind her's, and she shook her head.

Bezo's shirt was loose at the collar, and his glasses was now gone from his face. He hit the locks on his truck, and

Logan walked away. Silently he followed them into Deron's home.

"I'm sorry about all that," he apologized before Jerricka bolted up the stairs nodding. Logan locked up behind them and went upstairs with Bezo on her heels. His eyes took in the immaculate home and admired how the late Deron had laid it out. Logan took him to the guest room since Jerricka was sharing a room with her and she closed the door. Bezo took off his shoes as she took off her dress. "I would have never let you stay had I known that shit was going to go down," he said looking at Logan.

Logan ignored him and went to the bathroom. She turned on the shower and Bezo being the man that he was followed her. He leaned against the large porcelain sink as Logan stood before him in a black thong and black lace bra. His eyes wanted to admire her beauty, but he was more concerned with where her head was at.

"I like you," he said quietly, and Logan's angry eyes snapped to his.

"You don't even know me. You want me, that's the better way to put it," she said, and he nodded.

Bezo did want her, but he was also interested in getting to know her as well.

"You right. I do want you. The minute I saw you at the resturant I thought of different ways I could make you cum. But I'm also feeling you past that sex shit. I see you dealing with a lot and I wanna be there for you. I'm not about to front like I know how you feel. I never knew my pops. Couldn't tell you what that nigga looked like, so I don't know your pain. What I do know is that with anything life can get better if you work at that shit. You so fucking angry that you probably making shit worse than what it is. Let somebody be there for you, damn!"

Logan turned her back to Bezo and shook her head. Even with Deron being her father she couldn't think of the last time she felt like a man had her back. Her issues with her father had kept her away from him, and Rome showed her soon enough what he was about which wasn't shit. Logan got used to having her mom as her everything and had found comfort in that.

"Why do you even wanna be there for me?" She asked sounding more like a child instead of a grown woman.

Bezo walked up behind her and hugged her from the back. His presence, his touch calmed Logan down in ways that she wasn't expecting it to.

"Because something is pulling me to your pretty ass. On some real shit, I don't do that fate bullshit, but we just keep bumping heads. Everybody deserves to have somebody holding them down. I thought women liked when a man wanted to get to know them. You act like you turned off by it," he said, and she sighed.

"It's not that...I'm just wondering why you're doing it? What's your motive? I mean if sex is what you want then we can get that over with now. I can't take another man giving me empty promises Bezo."

Bezo nodded. He'd listened to his mom and sister cry over broken hearts and could see where Logan was coming from with her statement.

"It's Bellamy, and I rarely make promises, but when I do, I always keep them. I'm not trying to hurt you, and I don't have no motives. I wanna see how many times I can make you smile. I wanna give you a reason to never wanna leave the "A." Can I do that? Can I show how it is to fuck with a real one?" He asked allowing for his hands to slip between her legs.

Logan's eyes closed as Bezo massaged her through her thongs. He kissed her neck, and she slowly nodded. She wasn't sure if it was the liquor from earlier. The adrenaline that was still pumping through her veins or the man himself that was driving her wild with his presence but at the moment Logan was willing to give him a chance.

Bezo helped Logan take off her underwear, and he quickly discarded his clothes. Logan glanced down at his pretty dick that hung heavy between his legs, and she cleared her throat. She stepped into the shower, and he followed her. Logan tried to grab his member, and Bezo shook his head.

"Nah shawty. You want this dick you gotta give me some dates first. I don't know what the fuck you think this is," he told her, and Logan frowned at him. He smirked at her pout as she started to wash herself up.

Bezo grabbed some shampoo and poured it gently on Logan's hair. It immediately curled up into tight coils, and Bezo's dick got harder. He quickly spun Logan around and dropped down to his knees. When the light colored pubic hair stared back at him, he smiled. He leaned in and placed a gentle kiss to her vaginal lips.

"You are too sexy," Bezo said and pulled Logan into his arms. He tried to lean down to kiss her, and she shook her head while smiling.

"Nope no dick for me, no kisses for you," she replied.

Bezo nodded. He started to tickle her sides, and Logan pushed him back. He grabbed her again and slapped her ass. His hooded eyes peered down at her adoringly, and Logan felt herself getting lost in his gaze.

"I know you hurting. I can see it in your pretty eyes. All I wanna do is make it better. You just have to let me," Bezo said before pulling her into a passionate kiss.

Two days later Logan sat with Jerricka in the backyard as they fired up Deron's grill. They made a few drinks and were discussing life. Jerricka was leaving in two days and trying to catch up with her best friend on everything that she could.

"So, spill the beans. How did you meet him?"

Logan put on her sunglasses and peered up at the bright sky. Bezo just wouldn't go away. She kept running into him for some reason and now he'd found a way to invade her thoughts. She thought of how good it felt to lay next to him the night of the shooting and rubbed the goosebumps that had raised up on her arms.

"I first seen him right before my dad died. Bellamy says that my father was there for him and his family. I didn't get into the story behind it, but he said my dad helped save his home and things like that. I then saw him with Jordyn and after I took her and my mom to the airport. Its like we keep running into each other. I don't know what to do."

Jerricka sipped some of her mixed drink that had watermelons and kiwi's floating around her large glass.

"Interesting. Did y'all have sex?"

Logan's brows pulled together.

"No, I wish we did. I'm horny as hell. I'm tempted to call up Uriah," she replied and they both laughed.

Jerricka smiled at her.

"But do you like him? I don't think I've ever seen you smitten over anyone. Not even with Rome bitch ass."

Logan snickered.

"He's cool but I just don't know. I have a lot going on and I don't need any distractions right now. What about you?"

Jerricka chewed into her bottom lip before grinning at her best friend. Her smile was telling Logan all that she needed to know.

"Who is he?"

"A doctor. I met him at this luncheon a few weeks ago. He's different than what I'm used to but its in a good way. We fucked on the first night and Logan it was the best sex I ever had. I cried," Jerricka replied saying the last part in a whisper.

Logan laughed and playfully hit Jerricka's arm.

"I bet you did. Just be careful. You know your track record with men in the medical field isn't good. Protect your heart or we will be sweetening up his gas tank too."

Jerricka nodded while smiling. She was so happy to be around her friend again.

"I will, and you do the same. That shooting mess was crazy. Make sure he's a good guy before you have him around Jordyn."

"He promised me that he was and.... I believe him."

Jerricka stood up and glanced Logan's way.

"Okay just be certain that he is because if anything happens to my baby he gone need all his fans and gang members to keep my ass off of him," she said before going over to the grill to check it.

9

SOME EXCITEMENT IS WHAT KOLBEE NEEDED IN HER LIFE at the moment. Since she couldn't confront Bryson face to face about the empty threats she was receiving from some female back home about leaving her "man" alone, she decided to take a trip to see Denali. Hardly did she ever receive Instagram messages, and while she was scrolling her newsfeed earlier in the day, the icon caught her attention. Thinking it was spam, Kolbee had rolled her eyes before opening it but laughed obnoxiously loud when she read its contents.

The girl, because Kolbee wouldn't dare call her a woman, had her mistaken for some kind of punk. Though she'd served several hoes with words that could cut through their skin, she saved her fingers a break and simply typed an okay. She'd never argue over a man. Never had, and after Tasia told her how she used to act out over Deron, Kolbee knew that was not her thing. A nigga was going to do him and move however he saw fit.

In Bryson's case, he knew just how cold Kolbee could turn once she felt played. If he thought she had cut him off before, he was about to learn the real meaning behind her cut off game being strong. The fact that he was all up under her no more than two weeks ago when he came to town annoyed her.

"Niggas are disgusting," she groaned right when her phone rang. Pressing the phone icon button on her steering wheel, Logan's call came crooning through her speakers. She was happy to see her sister calling because they hadn't talked in a few days since Jerricka was in town.

'What's up, Lo?"

Logan sighed. She'd just said goodbye to Bezo and was upset that he could lay beside her all night and not try to have sex.

"I'm horny as hell and sleepy with a slight hangover. Where are you at?"

"I needed some fresh air. I'm headed up to Denali's gym. How was your night out?" Kolbee asked, switching lanes.

"Interesting to say the least, girl. So, you know I originally went out to see Cho, but when we got there, I ran into Bezo again. It's like he has eyes and ears on me or some shit. Things got crazy, and Cho's people ended up shooting at Bezo and his people," Logan said, still shocked by the events of her night out.

Kolbee gasped. She wasn't expecting to hear all of that.

"Damn. You should have woken me up for that shit. That's crazy."

"I know. We don't live them type of lifestyles, so I was shaken up, but I was more focused on making it home. I have a daughter to live for you know? Jerricka was so scared she pissed on herself girl," Logan said, and both sisters laughed.

"Her scary ass. That's funny as hell. You need to be careful with them. They're on some east coast versus west coast type shit. Rapping is not that fucking serious," Kolbee said, and Logan smiled.

"You're right! Bezo promised me it was all Cho. He even followed me home girl. We didn't fuck although I tried to. He said that I had to take him out first girl. I'm like did the roles reverse or what? These men are way too sensitive for me," Logan cracked.

Kolbee nodded her head agreeing with her.

"I be saying the same thing. But for real you need to watch yourself. We already lost daddy. Jordyn and I don't wanna lose you to some bullshit that has nothing to do with you," Kolbee reiterated to her.

Logan smiled at the sweet words her sister spoke to her. What a difference time made to some people.

"I'll be okay, I promise. The guns didn't freak me out. You know daddy always had us around them, but I don't like being in shoot outs. So, yes. I'm going to steer clear of Cho. Bezo is different, but he's also a rapper. I don't know If I'm built for that lifestyle," Logan admitted.

"I know girl. Tell that nigga Bezo to let us come to the studio one time. Now I bet that's an experience," Kolbee said pulling into the parking lot businesses. Squinting her eyes, she searched for the building with *Westin Gym* and pulled into an empty parking spot a few doors down from it. Westin was Denali's last name, and he thought it was kind of catchy for a brand name as well.

"The studio? Hell no. You're tripping," she was laughing but was somewhat serious.

"It'll be fun, Lo. Just ask him and see. I'm about to go in here, and bug Denali so send me a text and let me know what he says."

"Ya'll would be kind of cute together you know," Logan grinned from the other end of the phone.

"I bet. Bye girl."

Hopping out her ride, Kolbee adjusted the Adidas fanny pack she had around her waist. Knowing she was coming to a gym, she dressed accordingly – so she thought – in a pair of gray leggings, dri-fit pink Adidas tee, and the pink EQT Adidas. They were super comfortable. She was dressed girly, but ready to put in work had Denali wanted to test her agility.

Walking in, she was greeted by a teenaged girl at the front desk. She had a love for working out but also needed a summer job, so Denali hired her on. As long as she got her work done first, her membership was free.

"Hi. Welcome to Westin. Are you a member here?"

"I'm not. I'm actually here to see the owner. Is he available?"

The young girl looked stunned for a second before shaking her head. "He's in the middle of training until ummm..." she squinted her eyes at the schedule on her desktop screen, "Oh! He should be free in just a few minutes. Would you like to wait?"

Kolbee grinned. "May I take a tour?"

"No, you cannot," Denali's husky voice called out from behind her.

And, damn was she a sight to see. Women ranted and raved about men in gray joggers, but their appreciation was equivalent to a mans when he saw a woman in gray leggings. A woman with some ass that is. And ass Kolbee had lots of. The strap of the fanny pack reveiled how tiny her waist really was, and Denali had to refrain from smacking the young boxer he trained in the back of his head. He was staring entirely too hard for his liking.

Spinning around, Kolbee faced him with a smile. Her eyes were filled to the brim with lust, as nasty, disgusting thoughts filled her mind. She was concocting a plan on how to remove the sweat from every inch of his body... with her tongue. It was the only way she wanted to remove it. The towel could wait its turn.

"I would hope that's no way to greet a potential client."

"Of course not, gorgeous." Denali charmed her easily. Complimenting her was an easy task. She was gorgeous, and the fact that she showed up at his place of business unannounced meant she had been thinking of him. So, he hoped.

"Aight, Denali. Same time tomorrow?" the young trainer asked ready to head home.

"Same time. And tell your chef I said to cut back on the carbs just a little bit, aight. You have to make weight in a few weeks."

He nodded, they dapped hands, and he was on his way out the door. Pulling the towel from the band of his shorts, Denali used the opposite end to wipe behind his neck. It was still early in the day, and he had a few more people to work out, but he needed to put some food on his stomach first. His first mission was to see why Kolbee was standing in front of him like he owed her an explanation for something.

"What brings you by Busy Bee?"

Kolbee looked down at her outfit and frowned up at him. "Do you see my outfit? What do you think I'm here for?"

"A midday quickie?" Denali joked, and Kolbee sucked her teeth before walking pass him.

"You wish that were the reason I came up here."

Drawing the towel back, he swatted her ass. "Nah. That's what you wish."

"Ouch! Damn. These leggings are too thin for you to be playing," she griped, then gasped when Denali openly caressed her ass cheek.

"My fault. You shouldn't have all this out anyway. Thick ass."

Kolbee was left standing there as he sauntered by her to his office. "I know this nigga didn't just massage my ass," she asked herself. It was shit like that that she couldn't handle. He may have done it playfully with not much thought to it, but Kolbee knew better than that.

Following him into his office, Denali decided to multi-task. Pulling his prepped lunch that consisted of brown rice, baked salmon and steamed broccoli out the fridge, he popped it in the microwave and waited for Kolbee to close his door. She did, slowly. Taking in the large office, she was highly impressed at his accomplishments. It was refreshing to see a black man chasing after his dreams and placing his failures on the back burner.

"This is amazing, Denali. You've accomplished all this, and you're only how old?" Kolbee asked, marveling over his awards from the city of Atlanta and other states.

"Twenty-seven. And, thank you. Shit wasn't easy at all."

"I can only imagine. You're doing great, though. Making me feel like I haven't done a damn thing in my life," she chuckled but was slightly serious. Kolbee had never been intimidated by a man, but now she was having second thoughts. Denali was striving successfully in his business, had been for years, and Kolbee was no where near her goals. In fact, since moving to Atlanta, she didn't even know what they were anymore.

Denali pulled his food from the microwave and sat down. "Don't think like that. Aren't you running the cleaners?"

"Yeah, but that was passed down to me. Not something I had to work hard for. Had my daddy not passed away, I'd still be in KC struggling. Working a job that only paid certain bills, with certain benefits. I don't know; I guess I'm still in that stage of 'what the hell am I doing with my life'." Kolbee huffed, feeling dejected.

After taking a few bites of his food, Denali cleared his throat. "Ain't nothing wrong with that. At least you know what you need to do from here on out. Did you go to college?"

"Yeah but had to drop out because of tuition."

Denali frowned. "Deron knew you-"

Kolbee put her hand up to stop him. She already knew what he was going to say. "He didn't find out until a month later, and by that time I didn't care anymore. I know he would have given me the money, but I didn't want him too."

The truth was she already felt like a failure and asking

Deron for that amount of money made her cringe. Thanks to him every debt she owed was now paid off in full. It hardly put a dent in the money he had given her.

Denali shook his head. "Stubborn. I get it, though. You wanted to prove to him that you didn't need him... is that it?"

"Sure. I'll let you make whatever assumption you'd like."

He stared her in the eyes and smirked with a chuckle. "Aight. You ever get around to going to any of those restaurants I sent you?"

"A few, but that was a few weeks ago."

"With your man?"

"I don't have a man, thank you," she smirked.

He polished off the remainder of his food and drank from his bottle of water before responding, "That's not what Deanna told me."

Kolbee couldn't do anything but shake her head. The night she got up to fix her cousin some ice cream, Bryson made his presence known as well. Being the inquisitive seven-year-old that she was, Deanna couldn't help but ask if he were her Kolbee's boyfriend. Of course, Bryson said he was which annoyed her. That next day while they grabbed a bite to eat, Denali stopped by andn Deanna made it known that Kolbee and her boyfriend went to get food.

"Well, he's not," Kolbee answered.

Denali's eyebrow lifted in surprise. "Whatever you say Busy Bee. As long as he knows that."

"Mhm. So, do you train those plastic surgery Instagram models, too?"

He choked on his water and shook his head. "Maaan. Here you go."

"What?" Kolbee shrieked with humor laced in her tone. "I'm just asking a simple question. Your gym is in the heart of Atlanta, where I know woman get work done just to make it seem like they've been in the gym for months. When, they've really been at home chilling, on bed rest."

"What you got against plastic surgery? Shit, it could benefit you, too."

Kolbee cocked her head to the side. "Fuck you, okay. I'm happy with my a-cup boobs."

Denali smiled. Shit, he was happy with them if she was. "As you should be. I see you got on your workout gear. What you came to do today?" he laughed.

"I came prepared just in case you wanted to work me out."

Denali's eyes lowered, as a smirk crossed his face. Her choice of words was meant to come off as innocent, but there was nothing about Kolbee Flint that gave off innocence. She was bold when needed to be, quiet when in deep thought, and observant to the littlest of things. Like how Denali had removed one of his hands from his desk to adjust his growing erection in his shorts.

Kolbee kept the smile on her face before standing up. "So, what's up? Can I get a quick work out session or do I have to pay first?"

He stood from his seat and placed his food container in the plastic bag it was previously in. No matter how many lunch bags Shareese bought him, Denali was still a hood nigga at heart. He wasn't wasting a plastic bag if he didn't have to.

"If you serious, yeah. Don't expect me to take it easy on you either."

Stepping up to him, Kolbee replied, "Good. I don't like anything easy, anyway."

She was stunned when Denali grabbed her by the front of her neck and brought his lips close to her ear. So close, she felt them move when he began to speak.

"Neither do I."

Pushing him away, Denali had a serious expression on his face and a hungry look in his eyes. He had just eaten, but he wouldn't mind something sweet on his tongue. And, he just knew Kolbee was sweet. Her sexual pheromones were invaded his office space and making his nose tingle in a good way. Kolbee's chest was heaving up and down, and her panties had long ago been soaked.

"I-I um. I'll just meet you in the gym," she stammered.

"Yeah... you do that."

Kolbee couldn't get out of his office quick enough. As soon as the door closed, she placed her hand where his hand had been around her neck and smiled. She liked that aggressive, freaky shit, and stars danced in her eyes at the thought of him doing it again.

"Damn you, Denali River," she hissed before strutting toward the gym area. A good workout to burn off her sexual frustrations was surely needed now. Just as she unclipped her fanny pack, a text from Logan came through on her cell.

Bezo said we could come through the studio on Thursday. Is that good with you?

Yeah. I'll be at the cleaners all day, so I'll need the excitement.

Okay. I'll let him know.

Kolbee liked the flirting she and Denali were doing, but still felt a way about him being Andre's son. She was sure this trip to the studio would present nothing but potential candidates. Kolbee wasn't necessarily looking for love, though it'd be nice, she just wanted a nigga to kick it with around the city. Casual dating, if you would. The thing was, Denali wasn't feeling the same way. He knew whose daughter she was and what she meant to Andre, but that wasn't his problem. Kolbee's bubbly personality in his life was something he had been missing and wanted to keep around for as long as she would let him.

The bass from the music thumped obnoxiously loud through the walls and shook the contents inside of Kolbee's cup. The only reason she had taken the drink was because Bezo opened the new bottle of Dussé in front of her. She knew to not ever drink from a bottle that was already open. Especially around a group of cocky niggas she didn't know.

He was inside the booth putting the finishing touches on a track, while his entourage bobbed their heads and rapped along. Logan or Kolbee had a clue what the song was, but the beat was hitting, and his lyrics made it sound even better. In Logan's hand was a bottle of water. She drove them to the studio and wanted to be able to drive home as well. Plus, she felt like she was still recovering from when Jerricka was in town.

"He can really rap," Kolbee whispered in her ear.

"Can't everyone from Atlanta?"

They laughed, and Kolbee shook her head no. "Hell, no. Some of these niggas friends need to tell them to give it the fuck up. This isn't what they were called to do. God is not pleased with their asses."

Logan placed a hand over her mouth and laughed. She had long ago realized that her little sister always came with the jokes. The funny thing was, they were facts as well. Logan lifted her head up right when another group of men walked through the door. She and Kolbee weren't the only two women there, but they were the best looking for sure.

While the scantily clad women were dressed in mini dresses with high heels like they were at a club, the sisters were casually dressed. They each rocked ripped denim jeans, Logan had on a white loose-fitting v-neck tee, while Kolbee had on a cream onesie with her back out. Comfortable shoes were on their feet. Focusing her gaze on the incomers, Kolbee sipped from her cup and eyed the light skinned male, with long dreads pulled away from his face into a ponytail.

While everyone greeted and showed loved to him, Kolbee nor Logan mumbled a word. They were both raised to speak when entering a room; not the other way around. Mr. Light Skin had a mug on his face when he stepped in front of them. Kolbee looked over at Logan before looking up at him. He didn't say anything for a few seconds. Just let the awkwardness build up.

"Can you back the hell up," Kolbee hissed.

He smirked. "She does speak."

"When I need to."

"I hear that. Who are you? I never saw you before."

"Nigga, who are you? Why you all in my damn face," Kolbee spat.

He looked shocked at her reply but introduced himself anyway. "I'm Sir."

Kolbee shrugged. "Okay."

The volume had been cut low, so everyone heard their interaction and started laughing. Sir had to even laugh himself. That wasn't the standard reaction he was used to getting when he told people his name. He was what he considered well known, but Kolbee just proved that he wasn't. At least not to her knowledge anyway.

"Aye. Who these girls belong to?" Sir called out as Bezo stepped out the booth.

"Not you, nigga. Ya'll good?" he asked, and Logan nodded her head with a smile. He was so sexy when he was in his zone. "Come here," he called out to her.

Logan walked over to him and stood in between his legs while he sat on a nearby table. Between him and Yung Cho, she didn't know what she had gotten herself into. Leaving the seat open next to Kolbee, Sir took it upon himself to fill the space. Kolbee immediately got a whiff of his musky cologne. The weed smoke was so potent in the air; she already planned to strip from her clothing at the door when they made it home.

"What's up? Why you acting like that?" Sir asked, trying to spark conversation.

"I'm not *acting* any kind of way. What's up, Sir?" she

asked with a grin. He was fine, and just trying to make sure she was having a good time. That was it.

"You enjoying yourself? I see that cup running a little low."

Kolbee looked onside her cupped before downing the little she had left. "My first and last. Thanks though."

"Can I get your name, shit. You one of the baddest bitches we done had come through here."

"First of all, learn some fucking manners. I'm not a bitch, so watch what you refer to me and her as," she said nodding toward Logan. Bezo peeped the motion and gave her a questioning gaze without saying anything. She shook her head and mouthed that she was good.

Sir sat up some on the couch. "My fault. If I had a name on you, we'd be good in the future."

"High hopes of seeing me again, huh? That's cute," she chuckled. "The names Kolbee, with a K."

He nodded. "Dope name, ma. You new to the A? You gotta be. Your accent is proper as fuck, shawty."

Kolbee laughed. This wasn't the first time she had heard that. "Been here for a few months."

"That's what's up. If you like partying and shit, you should definitely fuck with me," Sir offered. "I can get you into all the clubs, concerts, whatever."

"And, why would I want to fuck with you?"

He grinned. "Shit. Why wouldn't you is the better question."

They laughed, and Kolbee thought it wouldn't hurt to have another male friend to kick it with. It was just the distraction she needed from Denali's fine ass. Total opposite in looks, Sir was caramel skinned, not nearly as buff, had the prettiest full pink lips on a guy, and his dreads were neatly twisted. If his eyes weren't so red from blowing backwoods, she'd see his natural brown eye color.

"You're funny," Kolbee said and looked her sister's way when she heard her laugh out loud, before covering her mouth. Bezo was over there saying some nasty, goofy shit in her ear and Kolbee was sure she caught contact from the blunt he was puffing on.

"And you're fine as fuck. You rocking the hell out of this short cut, for real," Sir complimented only the best way he knew how.

He had come across tons of pretty women in his life, but Kolbee was natural with it. Unlike the other bitches he had already fucked and smashed to his partners across the room, Kolbee had him intrigued.

It may have been from her being a fresh face, or the diamonds that were sparkling on her K initial necklace, and diamond tennis bracelet. With the money she inherited, Kolbee tried not to go overboard with her spending after paying off her debts, placing some in her savings account and giving Tasia a hefty amount, but it was tough. She never had so much money to her name at once.

Had Tasia not cursed her out for trying to trade in her car that was only two years old, she would have been pushing something foreign with a different year on it. She couldn't bring herself to drive any of Deron's just yet. That was still a milestone she needed to cross. But, until then she was plotting on her next purchase. She still shopped at the non-name brand stores, but the expensive ones had seen her face as well.

She could make any brand look good; didn't matter whose name was embroidered on it.

"Thank you. Do you rap, too?"

"Hell nah," Sir laughed but stopped when he saw her eyebrow lift. "It ain't shit wrong with rapping, but that ain't my thing baby. I'm more of a behind the scenes type of nigga, honestly."

Kolbee didn't know what job that was the definition of, but she honestly didn't care either. She was just trying to make small talk until Logan was ready to go. Pulling her phone from her purse, she saw a text from Denali saying he wanted to see her, but she left the message unopened. Seeing him this late at night only meant one thing; for her at least. And she had been drinking brown? Kolbee shook her head. Nope. She was not about to set herself up.

"What's your number. Maybe we can link up one of these weekends," she told Sir.

She typed his number in and saved it. "You better hit me up too," Sir grinned.

"Of course. My phone would have never been pulled out if I had no intentions to."

"Yeah, okay. I'ma get out your way though. Enjoy the rest of your night. Don't be afraid to drink these bottles, either. We good around here."

Kolbee smiled. She heard him loud and clear, but she'd have to pass. Instead, she grabbed one of the water bottles she knew no one had tampered with and twisted the cap. After taking a generous sip, she felt someone staring at her. Locating the culprit, Kolbee looked the brown chick girl and her posse over. They were mugging, and she assumed it was because Sir had just been all in her face. Kolbee chuckled and turned her head. There wasn't a nigga alive that had yet to bring her out of character. Especially one that wasn't hers.

Across the room, Logan leaned on Bezo as he listened to the producer play his latest song back for him. Some days in the studio he was chill, and some days he didn't mind the turn-up. He would tell his boys to bring up a few people through to get shit popping and they would.

As Logan replied to a text from Uriah questioning where she was at, Bezo was peeking at her screen. It wasn't any shame in his game, and after learning that she had also attracted Cho, he was playing her close. Bezo wasn't sure what it was, but he preferred her near him.

"Who the fuck is this nigga?" he questioned grabbing her phone.

Logan rolled her eyes.

"No one and with all of these groupies you got up in here you the last one that needs to be questioning me."

Bezo chuckled. He licked his full lips and placed Logan's phone in his back pocket. Hugging her tightly from behind, he placed his face in the crook of her neck. The women in the room took notice of the intimate act and sent even more jealous glares Logan's way.

"Chill out. They here with my boys. I don't even know half of these motherfucka's," he replied.

Logan sighed. His voice was raspy cause he'd been rapping all day, and the tone of it sent chills down her spine. She closed her eyes briefly and wondered just what was she doing with him.

"It's fine anyway. We're just friends," Logan said, and Bezo frowned at her words.

"Friends huh? How is my princess doing? And when is she coming back? You on that bullshit Logan trying to keep me away from her."

Logan shook her head while smiling. Bezo smelled her hair before kissing her neck. Since Logan had stepped into the studio with her sister all eyes had been on them. Word was spreading that Deron's daughters were bad. The type of fine that you immediately wanted to wife up and Bezo was staking his claim. He wasn't about to let Logan get away from him.

"Bellamy, that's my daughter," Logan said, and Bezo bit her neck gently as his hooded eyes quickly scanned the room making sure everyone was behaving.

"I'ma tell her how you were hating on her and shit when she comes home. Now when is she coming back? I wanna take ya'll out plus my mom is eager to meet you. You know she was close to your pops."

The mention of Deron and Bezo's mother had Logan ready to go. Slowly, she peeled herself away from his arms and glanced back at him. Bezo noticed her change in mood but chose to not speak on it. He was seeing firsthand that Logan had some serious issues with her father.

"I'm going to head out. Where's my phone?"

Bezo passed Logan her phone and grabbed her arm. Logan looked up at him, and her eyes slid over his relaxed fit. He wore black jeans with a white beater, and a pair of black, gold and white retro Jordan's. An icy Bezo chain hung from his neck while his black Mitchell & Ness cap sat on his head.

He smelled of Bond. 9 cologne and looked so damn sexy it made it hard for her to be angry with him.

"What?" Logan asked, and Bezo shook his head.

"You and these mood swings," he replied with a shake of his head.

Logan groaned, and Bezo had the right mind to yank her ass up. Her attitude was off the fucking chain.

"Look. You know how I feel about my dad and my daughter. You are doing too much. We don't even know each other," she told him angrily.

Bezo smirked. He bit down hard into his bottom lip, and before Logan could walk away, he pulled her into his booth. Bezo pushed her up against the door and grabbed her face. Logan glared up at him as her heart raced.

"We don't know each other, huh? If that's the case why the fuck was you trying to have a nigga pound on that pussy? I've never met somebody that didn't want you to be fucking nice to them. Damn, what the fuck is the issue and I'ma need for you to talk like a fucking adult about the shit. Ain't you thirty?"

Logan was so mad the veins in her neck were popping out. She pushed Bezo's hands away from her face and smoothed down her hair. He was continually probing, poking at some shit that wasn't any of his concern.

"Sex doesn't have to equate to love; so calm down," Logan said commenting on the most natural topic she could discuss.

Bezo took a step back and chuckled. Logan was something else.

"Aye, you really act like a nigga and shit. It might not mean that for you but don't speak for everyone else. I'm not out here sticking my dick in random bitches. I'm beyond that, and I thought that you would be too. I'm not your enemy so you can let your guard down. I just wanna get to know you and you making the shit impossible."

Logan looked to her left, and he grabbed her face tenderly. Her sad eyes traveled up to Bezo's handsome face, and she exhaled.

"Why?" She asked quietly.

"Why what?"

Logan swallowed hard.

"Why are you so interested in me like that?" She asked him, and Bezo pulled her close to him.

"Because you're special and even with all that mouth I can see that," he said and kissed her lips. For now, that was the only answer he was providing her. She could take or leave it.

Logan exited out of the booth followed by Bezo. With talks of hooking up with him once Jordyn came home she was in a much better mood. As he hugged her from the back once again Logan's eyes connected with a girl that reminded her of the bitch she had to toss the drink on at the lounge and she tried to pull away from Bezo.

"That's her sister calm down. After that disrespectful ass shit she pulled she's not allowed up in here," he told Logan.

"Aye Bezo, that shit is hitting nigga!" One man yelled excitedly about the beat that Bezo's producer was playing.

Logan liked the beat but *damn*. It felt like the producer had honestly played the shit a million different ways.

"Yeah, this the one I was telling you about. Where the weed at?" Bezo asked, and Logan looked back at him. Bezo and Logan watched his boys start to make lean, and Bezo chuckled.

"What you pouring Boon?" Bezo asked his cousin although he already knew.

Boon was a biracial tall cutie with light brown eyes and nice full lips. He glanced over at Bezo and chuckled.

"*East Atlanta niggas drink lean not liquor,*" Boon rapped reciting a line by Gucci Mane, and both men chuckled.

"These niggas about to start wilding baby," he commented.

Logan shook her head wanting no parts of that.

"I'm gone. You be good since you so concerned with me and my life."

Bezo grinned down at her. He knew her words had more to do with her not wanting him to be on some fuck boy shit and he liked that. Finally, she was coming around.

"You be good. You the one I gotta watch. Go straight home," he joked and kissed her on the forehead.

"You okay?" Logan asked when she walked back over to Kolbee.

"Couldn't be better. You ready to go?"

"Yeah. Bezo said it's about to get wild in here so... yeah," she laughed, and Kolbee cocked her head to the side.

"His ass better be leaving out too, then. What he think this is?" she said standing to her feet.

"Got damn red!" some nigga yelled out.

"You know a bitch is thick when she got ass in jeans," another one added, and they slapped hands.

Kolbee was disgusted. "Yeah, lets shake before I end up slapping one of these ugly ass niggas and these hoes."

The groups of girls were bickering in low whispers in the corner, but Kolbee paid them no mind as she made her way to the glass door. The wild shit that was about to go down had everything to do with them, and that was enough embarrassment to last them a while. Kolbee didn't want to add to it. Bezo walked them outside to Logan's ride, and Kolbee climbed in while they talked. She was happy her sister was getting close to Bezo. He was chill and came off very respectful to them both.

Pulling her phone out, Kolbee decided to reply to Denali's text but stopped when she saw he had texted her again. Twice actually.

Don't forget I know where you stay, big head ass girl. She laughed at the one. Her head was indeed big, but it fit her body.

Aight, bet. Just for not replying, I'm adding time to your workout routine tomorrow. And you better show up.

Kolbee groaned in agony. She knew fifteen minutes added to her hour-long workout was going to kill her. "I should just go over there." Sucking her teeth, she looked at the clock, then the time he sent the text. "Damn. That was over an hour ago. I'm fucked."

"Why are you pouting?" Logan asked climbing into the driver's seat.

"Denali," was Kolbee's only reply. She didn't even want to utter what was going to happen to her in the morning.

In return, Logan just smirked. Her baby sis was going through the motions, and she found it to be so cute. She knew when either of them gave in to temptation; it was going to be a situation neither of them could control.

10

"I'm telling you, Kolbee. Mr. Roberts entire face lit up when his wife brought him lunch the other day. It was the sweetest thing ever," Brittany gushed from behind the counter.

Kolbee smiled softly. She loved Mr. Roberts. He was an older gentleman who had been working for Flint's Cleaners since it first opened six years ago. He had been by Deron's side through the thick of the business, helped him remodel, and most importantly laced him with knowledge. Mr. Roberts didn't have to work at all. His kids were in their thirties, and he was retired. It was just something he enjoyed doing. Something to get him out of the house a few days out of the week.

"I want that one day."

"What? Brittany asked. "Your man bringing you lunch?"

"Yeah, but the love aspect of it. She didn't have to do that, and I'm sure it wasn't planned either. It's always the thought that counts."

"Yeah... well, my thoughts are not so clean right now," Brittany whispered as she stared out the front window.

Walking up with a plastic bag in his hand, Denali pulled the door to the cleaners open, and Kolbee swallowed the lump in her throat. For some reason, she seemed to get nervous around him now. Like she couldn't contain the stirring in her belly whenever he was in her presence. It happened even while they worked out. But, she welcomed it. She had no choice but to because it wasn't leaving anytime soon.

Clad in a white wife-beater tank, and some jogger shorts on Denali still looked good. He seldom wore anything besides workout gear. But, he'd get clean and on his grown man attire in a heartbeat if need be. Behind the counter, Kolbee was wringing her fingers. She was not expecting him to pop up on her today. Any day for that matter.

"What a pleasant surprise," she greeted with a smile.

"I know right. I brought you something to eat," he said placing the bag on the counter. Brittany's eyes shot over to Kolbee, and she smirked. The two had spoken way too soon about the act of love. Denali was pulling out all the stops with Kolbee, and she couldn't understand why. Sure they were friends, but did he feel the chemistry and connection between them as well? He had to.

"Awww," Brittany gushed. "She was just getting ready to take her lunch break."

"Perfect timing," Denali replied.

"Right. Let's go to my office."

Denali grabbed the bag and followed Kolbee to her office. Once inside, she closed the door after him and just stood there. Denali was explaining what all the containers had, but she honestly hadn't heard a word. She was still stuck on the fact that he had brought her lunch. The simply gesture had her tripping out. He stopped when she hadn't responded to a word he said.

"Why you just standing there like that?" he asked.

"Why'd you bring me lunch?"

Denali's face masked confusion, and he tossed his hands out. "Because I thought you might have been hungry? Am I in trouble or something?" he asked with a chuckle.

Kolbee sighed and closed her eyes. *Maybe I'm overthinking this,* she thought. Denali was standing right in her face when she opened her eyes, and she jumped back some hitting the door.

"What's wrong?"

She shook her head. "Nothing."

Denali ever so gently, caressed her neck with his large hand. It was so soothing, Kolbee almost released a soft groan. "Don't lie to me, Busy Bee."

He knew what calling her that did. "I just... nothing. It's just strange how you bring me lunch."

"Use your words. What's strange about it? Can I not bring you lunch or something? What's up?" He removed his hand, and Kolbee's stomach dropped.

"Are we friends?"

"Yeah. I mean, shit. I thought we were. To some people we may seem like family because of how close our fathers were, but nah. We don't share the same blood."

"So, we're just friends?" She just wanted to make sure she was tripping, and not both of them.

Denali nodded his head. He didn't know if she was asking him a trick question or not, but he was going to give her the same answer. "Yeah. We're friends Kolbee. Now, what the hell is wrong with you?"

Kolbee slid out of his bubble and stepped around to sit at her desk. She had her answer. Though it wasn't the answer she wanted, she would live with it for now to save face. She'd be damned if she embarrassed herself for looking too deep into a friendship and making it more than what it was.

"So you wouldn't mind me hooking you up with one of the workers here?" she asked just for shits and giggles on her end.

Denali sucked his teeth and flopped down in the vacant seat by the wall. "Who? Ole girl out front. Hell nah. Ain't nothing wrong with her, but I'm good."

Kolbee laughed. "Why not? Brittany's a pretty girl."

"Exactly. She's a young ass girl that I can't do shit with but look at. I need my woman about her business, about her bread and all about me."

She pursed her lips together in a smirk. "Is that right?"

"One hundred percent. Someone like you."

Kolbee's eyes shot open in surprise. "Me?"

"Yeah. You chill as fuck, running this cleaners like it's been yours for years, and you got the best conversations when you're not in your feelings."

Rolling her eyes, Kolbee bushed on the low. "Whatever. I am not always in my feelings."

"Shiiit," Denali dragged. "It's all good though. That just

means your in tune with how you feel. How you feeling today, anyway?"

His question didn't alarm her. Denali always checked on her well-being. Not because he was obligated to do so, but because he genuinely cared about her.

"Today is one of my better days, actually. I was talking to Brittany earlier about college, and I think I want to go back and finish. I only had two years left. I can knock that out in no time."

Denali smiled wide. "For real?"

Her heart beat wildly at the interest he always showed. "Yes. I mean, why not. I'm not doing much of anything else," she shrugged.

"That's true. I'm proud of you, ma. Let me know when you start looking into colleges. There's a lot to choose from down here."

"I know. I can't wait to tell Logan. I know she'll be happy for me."

The bond the sisters shared was crazy to Kolbee. After years of not talking, their connection once reunited was stronger than ever. It was exactly what Deron wanted. Kolbee smiled softly thinking of him and his bossy ways. She hoped she was making him proud.

"She will. Jordyn, too. How's that chicken? I used a different kind of seasoning this time," Denali asked.

Slicing a tender piece of the chicken breast, Kolbee chewed slowly with her eyes closed. She could complain all day about Denali working her out till her limbs were on fire, but he always replenished her with nutrients. She was used to Bryson's quick and easy meals when she stayed with him, but

Denali's cooking was on another level. It was healthier but wasn't bland at all.

"Mmm. It's so good," she moaned out, and Denali froze.

"Kolbee," he hissed, and her eyes shot open. She had never heard him say her name like that. "Don't... don't moan like that with your eyes closed and shit, aight? At the end of the day, I'm a man. I can't have that vision of you in my head when I leave here."

Licking her lips, Kolbee nodded her head. "Sorry," she said lowly.

She didn't know how to respond to that. He asked for her opinion, and she was giving her honest truth. Cutting another piece, she picked it up and held the fork out for him to sample.

"Here. Try it yourself."

Denali obliged and ate from her fork. Some shit he would never do with anyone. Not even his little sister Shawniece. Chewing, he had to nod his head in approval. He wanted Kolbee to be the first person to taste test his new blend of seasonings.

"Yeah, it is hitting," he said.

"I swear. You'll have to send me the recipe, so I can make some on my own."

"I'll be selling it soon," he announced and Kolbee placed her fork down.

"Selling it at the grocery stores?"

"That's the plan, but I'm starting small first. I just had to see if it passed inspection," he grinned, and her eyes went wide in admiration.

"Wow. I'm so lucky to know you. Like, for real Denali.

What can you not do? This is amazing. When you get famous, don't go acting all fresh on me."

Denali chuckled and ran a hand over his head. "Never that. You the one been acting funny style now that you got some abs coming in."

Standing from the desk, Kolbee lifted her shirt with *Flint's Cleaners* embroided in the corner and ran a hand over her stomach. Though she had just eaten, you could still see the definition of her abs peeking through. Grinning, she did a little jig in Denali's face before flexing.

"Yes. Just wait until I get to show them off," she beamed.

"You still got some work to do," he said pinching her side that wasn't as toned yet.

She slapped his hand away, and Denali snatched her up by her waist bringing her closer to him. Sitting in the low chair brought him eye level with her belly button. A stirring in his groin moved with lightening speed as his hand crept from around her waist. He teased the hem of her skinny jeans at the thigh. Kolbee was trying her best to control her breathing. They had to stop meeting up in offices this way.

Feeling the heat from her center, Denali pulled his hand back and stood to his feet. Kolbee leaned against the desk. His touch had her stumbling, and he had barely touched her. His possessiveness and need to feel her every time she touched him had her yearning for more of him. More of whatever it was he was trying to give her without words. She needed it; desperately.

"Denali," she called out, and he closed his eyes.

"I know. I'ma keep my hands to myself. It's just you... never mind," he breathed in frustration.

She moved from the desk to behind him, facing his back. She didn't touch him though. Afraid of what may happen had she even placed a finger on his defined back.

"It's just what? Tell me," she pleaded lowly.

The innocence in her voice when she wanted to know something made Denali grit his teeth. He felt obligated to bare his soul to her. Whatever questions she needed answers for, he wanted to be the one to answer them all. And if he didn't have the answers, he'd retrieve them.

"You know what it is."

Her head dropped in defeat and annoyance. She knew what it was, but she wanted him to say it. Denali wasn't trying to take things with her further because of Deron. His respect for him wouldn't let him. The thoughts that coursed through his mind about his baby girl were foul enough, but Kolbee didn't care. Fuck that line of respect right now. She wanted him to violate it, disrespect it, and straight obliterate it until there was no sign of it.

"Whatever," she huffed with an attitude. "You always do this bullshit."

Though he didn't want to, Denali smirked. Her feisty attitude was so sexy. He knew he kept starting shit with her, but when the time was right, he was going to finish what he started. Put out the fire he kept igniting in her body and most definitely between her thick ass thighs. Only when Kolbee walked away from him did Denali turn around. She was roughly putting her lunch away and mumbling obscenities under her breath.

"You mad?" he asked.

"Leave me alone. Matter fact, get out."

Kolbee was so damn frustrated with his hot and cold ways; she could slap him and that sexy smirk from his face. Denali stepped over to her desk, and Kolbee's head shot up.

"I'm not playing with you. Gon' over there with your indecisive ass."

"Nah. Tell me you're not mad first."

Her face went serious. "I'm not mad," she enunciated through clenched teeth, and he laughed.

"Give me a hug, and I'll believe you." He stepped closer, and Kolbee scurried to the opposite side of the desk.

"Quit playing! I'm not hugging you Denali. Grow up."

"You grow up. The least you can do is give me a hug for bringing you lunch."

"What!" Kolbee screeched. "Nigga, I didn't ask for you to bring me lunch. The fuck."

"So what. I did out of the kindness of my heart, and you ate that shit."

"I wasn't going to let it go to waste. You're tripping right now," she laughed nervously and looked toward the door.

"Go head'. I ain't gone chase you girl," he laughed.

Eyeing him suspiciously, Kolbee slowly moved from around the desk, grabbed her phone and took one step. When Denali didn't move, she high-tailed it toward the door. Just as she swung it open, Denali went after her. They both ran straight into Brittany who was coming to tell her that her presence was needed out front. Kolbee pushed Brittany in front of her and laughed.

"Liar!" she hissed with laughter.

Denali licked his lips coolly. "Whatever."

The three walked up to the front, and Kolbee's brows

furrowed at the sight of Sir standing at the counter. When he saw her face, he grinned, but it fell when he saw Denali walk up behind them. He and Kolbee had been keeping in contact and had lunch once since they exchanged numbers at the studio, but it wasn't anything more than that. Not on Kolbee's end at least. Sir was feeling her and felt a way about her coming out the back with some buff ass nigga. He had no clue who Denali was, but it didn't matter who he was. He was trying to make Kolbee his; add her to his roster of females anyway. Maybe move her to the number one spot.

"Sir, hey," Kolbee spoke and Denali's top lip curled in annoyance.

How she know this nigga? He thought and stood off to the side.

"What's going on, ma. You the boss lady around here?"

Kolbee nodded. "At the moment, yes. What's going on?"

"Small world. I been coming to this mufucka for a while and never saw you," Sir stated, and when Kolbee didn't reply to his statement he continued. "I brought some jeans in here yesterday, and I think I left some money in them."

Kolbee grabbed the sign-in sheet for her employees to see who was working yesterday. Logan had been by for a few hours, but she wasn't aware of some money being found. Seeing Josh's name, one of her newer workers having signed-in right after Logan left caused alarms to go off in her head. Kolbee didn't want to blame him, but he was the only one there until Logan came back two hours later.

"What time did you drop them off?" she asked.

"Shit. A little after three," Sir answered.

Josh had clocked in at two-thirty, right before Logan left

at three. Unless Sir was lying, she had an idea of where his money may be. Closing the book, she slid it back under the desk.

"No one turned any money in. You sure you left it in your pockets?"

"Damn. Yeah, I'm sure. It's all good though. I'll just have to take that L."

Kolbee shook her head vehemently. "No, no. I'll check with other staff later on this week, and let you know. Is that cool?"

Sir nodded. "Yeah, just shoot me a text on that. What you got going on this weekend? My partna's having a little welcome home party for his folks. You and yo sis should slide through."

Denali had heard enough. The fact that he knew of Logan pissed him off. *How close is she and this sucka ass nigga? Leaving money in his pockets like a little ass boy.* Grabbing Kolbee's elbow, she turned Denali's way with questioning eyes.

"I'm bout' to head out," he told her.

"Okay. Have a good day and thank you."

Denali gave her a head nod. "It ain't nothing."

Walking out, Sir glanced his way and chuckled. He confirmed right then that Denali wasn't her man, so Kolbee was really free game now. Even if Denali was her man, Sir wasn't going to stop perusing her. She had already shown him too much interest. Kolbee watched Denali's back until he climbed into his car and pulled off. She felt his mood change and knew it was because Sir was there. But, why? He was a paying customer; not her man. Brushing it off, she focused her attention back on Sir.

He was looking nice today with his dreads pulled into a bun. They were messier than the last time she saw him, but it didn't take away from his charming looks.

"What were you saying about this welcome home party?" Kolbee asked.

She figured she'd get out this weekend and enjoy her off day. Logan was covering the cleaners on Saturday, so she was already planning to hit the mall and bust down the stores with her sidekick Jordyn. After confirming plans with Sir for the weekend, he left out feeling like his position in her life had elevated.

"Kolbee," Brittany called out.

"Hmm," she hummed feeling mixed emotions.

"You got your hands full, girl."

Brittany chuckled, but Kolbee didn't see a damn thing funny. She indeed had her hands full, but one was lighter than the other. Since Denali wanted to continue playing games with her, Kolbee chucked it up as him not wanting to be involved with her on a serious level. She couldn't argue with him on that or change his mind, and at this point, she was just going to try to distance herself. At least that's what she told herself. Actually following through was going to be the issue.

"How shit been going at the cleaners?"

Logan thought of the friendly workers Kolbee and she

had been blessed with having, and she smiled.

"Things have been going well. Everyone is really nice, and so far we haven't had any issues."

"That's what's up. Well I'm headed your way now. Did your daughter come back with you?"

Logan glanced over at Jordyn and smiled. She'd spent a week in Detroit filing papers on Rome and was now back in Atlanta with her daughter. While Jordyn played with her new purse courtesy of her auntie, Logan talked with Bezo on the phone.

"Yes, she's back and ready to go," Logan replied, and Jordyn giggled.

"Is that the ice cream man mommy?"

Bezo chuckled. He'd talked to her a few times while chatting with Logan and she was smart as hell for her age.

"His name is Bellamy, sweetie," Logan said, and Jordyn glanced back at her.

Her thin brows bunched together as she frowned.

"That's a girl name mommy!" Jordyn shrieked before falling into a fit of giggles. She glanced over at Logan and smiled. "Maybe he could be my new daddy," she said and went back to looking at herself.

Logan stopped smiling and swallowed hard. Kids. They didn't know how serious their words were. They only knew to speak the truth, and once again Jordyn had absentmindedly said something that hurt her mother.

Bezo cleared his throat.

"When I was a kid my mom's met this old nigga that used to own this barbershop. He would always come around and be nice to my sister and me. I hated his ass for some reason, so

I used to give him a hard time. Because me and my sister clowned on him so much my mom stopped seeing him. After that life got bad for us. She had to get two jobs and still almost lost the house if it hadn't been for your pops. Now what she had going on with him wasn't my business. What I do know is when he came into my life taking on responsibilities that my father should have been doing this time around I was smart enough to accept them. I accepted him. Change isn't always bad Logan. You don't talk to a nigga about shit, but I can see your baby daddy isn't on his job. God has a way of giving us the things we need, and it's not always from the people we want it to be from. Don't let what that hoe ass nigga is doing get you down. He'll get his and I'm on my way," Bezo said and ended the call.

Logan sat her phone down and closed her eyes. Before she could open them, it was ringing again. She glanced down at the screen and shook her head.

"Yes," she said quietly with her eyes on her daughter.

"So now you think I'm about to give you money? What the fuck kind of games is you playing! Your pops left you all types of money, and you want a nigga to go broke behind you. You's a dirty ass bitch for this one,'" Rome vented so upset he was foaming at the mouth.

Logan nodded. She slowly eased off her bed and quickly exited the room. She stepped into the hall and licked her lips. She was *so* tired of fighting with Rome.

"Rome...she's your daughter. I just want you to do your part. Can you please just be there for her? Please?" She asked with her eyes watering.

Rome chuckled.

"Be there for her? Bitch if I have to pay you money that's gone take me working more fucking hours. Then you moving so I'm gone have to catch a flight too. What the fuck I'm not rich! You know what if you drop this I will make a schedule on getting her, how does that sound?" He asked.

Logan sighed. Kolbee stepped into the hall and eyed her. After noticing the frown on Logan's face, she decided to give her some privacy and go check on Jordyn.

"Rome you've told me before that you would get her, and you didn't. She doesn't deserve this. It's not about the money, but it's not right for you to choose when you want to be a parent. I don't have that option."

Logan could hear glass breaking in Rome's background, and she shook her head. He was angry with her for having to provide financially for a kid that he helped create. It was baffling to her.

"Wow. You so fucking selfish this shit is crazy yo. I wish I would have let off on your ass instead of in your pussy. I'm not paying you and if I do you might as well forget a niggas number because I won't, want shit to do with your grimy ass," he said vehemently and ended the call.

Logan walked to the steps and sat down. She hugged her knees while Kolbee played with Jordyn in the room. Before long Bezo was at the front door and ringing the bell. Jordyn whizzed past Logan excited to see him and darted down the stairs in her blue jean skirt with her pink top and leather slides. Her hair was in bouncy curls from her bantu set Kolbee had given her, and she looked like she should have been gracing a Gucci kids ad.

"You good?"

Logan looked up at her baby sister and nodded. Kolbee sat down beside her and pulled her to her side. It was crazy because just months ago she hadn't felt comfortable writing Kolbee on Facebook let alone having a conversation with her. Now they were living together. Running a business and building a bond that couldn't be broken. Logan thought of all the things Bezo had spoken about change being good, and she smiled weakly.

"I'm sorry. I don't think I ever said that to you, but I am Kolbee. I think in this whole situation with our dad you suffered the most. I do love you, and I'm thankful to have you back in my life," Logan told her.

Kolbee's eyes watered.

"You gone make a "g" cry," she joked and let Logan go. "But seriously the feelings are mutual. I see what he's putting you through and it's not right. You have to stop letting him control your emotions. Okay?"

Logan nodded. They stood up and began to walk down the steps together.

"I'm going to just block him for a while. I'll have my mom call his mom, and we can talk through them. He's thirty-two and acts like a child."

Kolbee snarled at the thought of Rome. She had never met him, and already she hated him.

"A grown ass boy is what he is," Kolbee mumbled.

"Mommy look! I got flowers and candy from Bellamy!" Jordyn said excitedly running up to Logan with her small arms full of gifts.

Bezo stood by the door in black jeans with a short sleeved collared Polo on and his gold wired Bugatti 508 frames. He looked so handsome it was insane. His mocha skin held a natural shine to it as his fresh cut stared back at you tauntingly. Even the line cut into his fade caught her eye. He smirked at Logan taking in her beautiful presence as she walked towards him.

"For you baby," he said and passed her a bouquet of a dozen red roses.

Logan smiled while Kolbee stood back watching the exchange. Kolbee was a bit skeptical of Bezo after finding out about the shooting incident at the club. However, after seeing him at the studio and watching how he stared at Logan like she was the only woman in the world her worries were slowly fizzling away. Bezo was a rapper, and she knew he had fans, but so far, he'd proved that he was into her sister and looking to treat her right. That was all Kolbee required of him.

"Jordyn remember what auntie said. He opens all the doors, he cuts the check, and he makes you smile. Okay?"

Jordyn looked up at her auntie and nodded. Her smile was so big it could be seen a mile away. Jordyn had never done anything classy with Rome outside of Logan. Once Logan left him it was as if Rome decided to place his parental duties on the back burner while trying to make his ex-pay.

"Got it! Make him cut the check," Jordyn said sounding a little too much like Nicki Minaj.

Kolbee giggled, Bezo even chuckled, but Logan cut her eyes at her baby sister.

"Okay, when she asking to go to prom in a Bentley I'ma have her call her auntie. You are turning her into a little monster sis," Logan said, and Bezo walked over to Jordyn.

Bezo dropped down to his knees and smiled at her.

"Call auntie? Jordyn who gone get you that Bentley for prom?"

Jordyn's small eyes wandered around the room slowly before falling onto him.

"You are silly," Jordyn replied, and she sounded so cute that even Logan had to laugh at it.

Bezo nodded, and they both slapped hands.

"I'ma make sure it's pink and purple too," he said and rose to his feet. "Let me put your flowers up," Bezo said and grabbed the flowers he'd given them before taking everything to the kitchen.

Kolbee noticed the uneasy look sitting on Logan's pretty face, and she frowned at her.

"What's wrong?" She asked quietly.

Logan shrugged. She watched her daughter stare down the hall anxiously waiting for Bezo to return and it made her nervous.

"I don't know about this. Maybe this was a mistake letting her come with us."

Kolbee smacked her lips.

"If you don't stop worrying so much. That could be your husband in that damn kitchen putting away them overpriced ass flowers. Rome not acting right. Looks like God is sending you someone that will," Kolbee replied and walked over to Jordyn.

After leaving the house, Bezo took Logan and Jordyn to the Georgia Aquarium as promised. Bezo booked the VIP tour and they were given the star treatment. Logan strolled behind Bezo and Jordyn as they followed the tour advisor to the top side deck of the Ocean Voyager.

Logan couldn't help but snap photos of the two. She even posted a picture of Jordyn and Bezo from the back and added it to her Instagram account with the caption *Day out with these two. Lucky me!* Because of Bezo's popularity, she chose not to tag him.

"I wanna see the dolphins!" Jordyn said excitedly as Logan caught up to them.

The advisor shook his head while smiling.

"You have to be at least seven. I could take you all back to the sea otters but to get up close you have to be seven for that as well," he replied, and Jordyn started to cry.

In her young mind being told no was, of course, the end of the world. Bezo looked at the advisor and cleared his throat. He dropped over $600 and he was pissed to see that Jordyn was on restrictions.

"Nah we good, you can go," he told him, and the advisor gave them one last apologetic smile before walking away. "We still going to them damn dolphins," Bezo said not giving a fuck about restrictions, and Logan shook her head.

"Yes!" Jordyn said and grabbed his hand. "Let's go, Bellamy," she said grinning up at him.

Logan looked at the two-people willing to risk being kicked out just to see some dolphins and she smiled.

"Um, you two both heard that man say no. Plus we've been here for over an hour. Let's go eat. I'm hungry."

Logan's words made Bezo think of sex. Bezo's eyes slowly scanned up and down her body, and he swallowed hard. Logan and Jordyn were both going for the bohemian look. While Jordyn looked like a flower child with her curls and fringe sandals, Logan wore wild wavy hair to match. She too had on a jean mini skirt with an off the shoulder mustard colored top and Jeffery Campbell platforms. Logan also wore large hoops with her freshly done nose piercing that was a thin gold hoop going through her left nostril. She'd seen a photo of Kevin's Hart wife rocking it and instantly fell in love. It was simplistic yet still eye-catching. The moment they'd exited the car at the aquarium people had been staring at the striking couple with the adorable little girl, and that whole time Bezo had been staring at Logan. She was just too damn beautiful to him.

He wanted to kiss her, slap her on the ass and yank her by the hair but with Jordyn around, he was on his absolute best behavior.

"Yeah let's be out. I got somewhere we can go eat," Bezo said forcing himself to look away from Logan.

Together they exited the Aquarium. As Bezo drove to Decatur, Jordyn decided to hit him with some questions.

"What kind of car is this? Why didn't we see the dolphins? Will we go back and where are we going?" She asked making Bezo and Logan laugh.

Bezo had decided to drive his black Quattroporte. It was more lowkey than his red truck, and the windows were tinted out. Bezo wasn't worried about Yung Cho or the niggas he ran with, but if something were to happen to Logan or her daughter, he wouldn't be able to live with himself. For them, he was being all the way careful.

"This is a Maserati and we'll catch the dolphins next time. I'm taking y'all to my moms to eat. You like soul food?" He asked making Logan glance over at him.

"Your moms, huh?"

Bezo squeezed Logan's hand choosing to ignore her, and his eyes shifted to the backseat briefly.

"What's soul food?" Jordyn asked frowning.

"It's that type of food that feeds your soul. Gives you the itis," he replied.

Jordyn frowned. She had no idea what Bezo was talking about.

"What's that?"

Logan cracked up laughing while Bezo chuckled.

"It's just this thing we get from time to time. You'll get hit with it after you eat but do you like to dance? My sister owns a dance studio that teaches girls how to," Bezo said, and Jordyn nodded.

She loved dancing and had been in ballet for two years.

"Yes! Can I go, mommy?"

Logan nodded while silently praying this situation with Bezo didn't bring any more pain in young Jordyn's life.

"Sure sweetie."

Jordyn smiled happy with her reply and pulled out her tablet.

"Don't be mad. She really wants to meet y'all," Bezo said glancing over at Logan.

Logan looked at him and admired his handsome good looks. From the color of his skin to the shape of his lips she was extremely attracted to him.

"It's fine. I'd like to meet her as well," she replied surprising the hell out of Bezo.

"Oh yeah?"

Logan smiled. She lightly squeezed his hand.

"I'm walking out on faith," she replied before quickly looking out of the window.

Her words relaxed Bezo. He felt like he could really have a chance with her now that she was open to being with him.

"You won't regret it beautiful," he promised.

After thirty minutes of driving Bezo was pulling up to his mother's two-story home off Ansley street. He pulled into her driveway and parked behind her SUV. While Logan re-applied her Saw-C matte lipstick Bezo stared at her.

"Did I tell you how sexy you look?"

Logan's face stretched into a smile. She noticed Jordyn was asleep while turning to face Bezo.

"No, you didn't, but you can tell me now."

Bezo leaned towards Logan. His warm minty breath fanned against her neck as he whispered in her ear. "You so sexy baby the minute I saw you I wanted to do all kind of nasty shit to you. You keep saying all the right shit and you gone watch me *really* change your life. I can't wait to be up inside of you," he told her then placed a sensual kiss on her neck.

Logan was positive that had she been Kolbee she would have been completely red in the face. She dropped her head smiling to herself as Bezo got out of his car and grabbed a sleeping Jordyn. They walked up the steps to his mother's large home, and she opened the door before they could knock.

"You made it! I didn't think you was coming Bellamy and oh my God she's so beautiful. They both are," Audra said and pulled Logan into a hug.

Logan smiled as she hugged her back. Audra looked like she

could have been Bezo's older sister surely not his mom, but she wasn't surprised. *Black don't crack.* Logan thought as Audra let her go and she saw Audra had a slimmer waistline than she did.

"I know he's scared to bring his friends around here," Logan said admiring Audra's youthful beauty.

"You know he is. I wouldn't mind getting my groove back either. Have one of them take me to a Jeezy concert or whatever it is these young men do nowadays," Audra spoke up and shared a laugh with Logan while Bezo frowned at them.

"Yeah okay," he mumbled not finding his mom's jokes funny.

Audra pushed his arm before smiling at him. She was the same complexion as her son only she was curvaceous and short with long hair that had been pulled up into a sleek ponytail. Audra also smelled divine and had a calming nature to her that made Logan less nervous.

"And who do we have here?" Audra asked turning her attention to Jordyn.

Jordyn slowly rubbed her eyes as she woke up. Bezo sat her down, and she hugged his leg while staring up at his mom. Logan stood the side almost like she was the third wheel imposing on a family moment and she watched Audra stare down at Jordyn.

"Hi, I'm Audra. Bellamy's mother. Who might you be?"

Jordyn looked at Audra and hugged Bezo's leg tighter.

"Jordyn," she replied quietly.

Audra nodded.

"Well, I have some food and desserts and even some goodies for you. Would you like to come in?"

Jordyn looked to Bezo for permission and Logan smacked her lips.

"I'm your mother little girl you look at me," she snapped playfully.

Jordyn smiled at Logan, and they all went in. Audra had a beautiful modernistic home that Logan immediately fell in love with. Everyone prayed and ate the dinner she'd cooked and soon Bezo's sister was coming over with her kids. Logan watched Jordyn stick to Bezo like glue while she helped his mother put away the food in the kitchen. Logan was beyond stuffed from scarfing down turkey legs, greens, sweet potato cornbread amongst other things.

"Your food was so good. I haven't eaten like that since I've been down here. It makes me miss my mom," she admitted looking Audra's way.

Audra smiled.

"Thank you. I was waiting for us to be alone to let you know how sorry I am about Deron. Despite what Bellamy thinks your father and I was always just friends. He was the type of person that you gravitated to. God has pushed you and my son together, and I couldn't be happier," she said as Logan's cell phone started to ring.

Logan noticed the ringtone. It was the only number in her phone that possessed one, and she looked at Audra.

"Thank you, and this is my mom. I'll be right back."

The minute Logan answered the call she could hear her mother cursing. Her brows furrowed as she stepped into the hallway.

"Ma, what's wrong?" She asked quietly.

"Rome has pissed me off for the last fucking time!"

Megan vented still breathing hard. "Do you know his little dumb ass came over here with all of Jordyn's things that she had at his place which wasn't much might I add and dropped them off on the doorstep. He wrote this note that said something about letting you go for good. I was so angry that I went over to his mother's house and that Chalmers and Harper came up out of me baby. Jocelyn said the wrong thing and before I thought about it I started beating her ass. I think she called the cops on me," Megan replied.

Logan gasped not believing what she was hearing, and Bezo stepped into the hallway. He walked over to her and grabbed her hand. Silently he took her upstairs to the room his mom had reserved for him, and Logan sat on his king-sized bed.

"Momma really? You fought Rome's mother?"

Megan laughed. Now that she thought about her actions she could take the time to laugh at them. When it had all happened, she'd been so angry she'd resorted to violence. Megan had called up her best friend Mary, and like the old days they'd rode down on Rome's family. Jordyn was her grandbaby, and she refused to let Rome toss her to the side as if she was yesterday's trash.

"Mom I don't know what to say and you're too old to be fighting someone," Logan admitted.

Megan rolled her eyes.

"Old? I'm far from old Logan. Don't try me," Megan said sounding much younger that what she actually was.

Logan smiled until she thought of Rome. She knew that filing for child support would get Rome's attention, but she had no idea that it would be so extreme. He'd completely made himself the victim and was now cutting off his daughter. That was the craziest thing she'd ever heard of someone doing.

"Why wouldn't he want to be in her life momma? Like I feel like a failure because I chose to have a kid with someone that's so sorry. She's suffering behind it, and I don't know what to do," Logan said quietly.

The pain in Logan's voice angered Bezo and saddened Megan. Megan's eyes watered as she shook her head.

"You can't control what he does. You had no clue that he would be this selfish. No matter what happened between me and your dad he always loved you. Rome isn't like that, and all we can do is give her double the love. If he doesn't need her, then she doesn't need him. I need to make a few calls to ensure those motherfuckas don't try to send the cops my way. I'll call you back baby," Megan said before ending the call.

Logan sat her phone down and glanced up at Bezo. He leaned against the desk in his room with his hooded eyes on her.

"He back at it huh?"

Logan gave him a weak smile. She wanted to cry, but she was so tired of doing that. She had to be strong for her daughter. She had no choice but to. Maybe once she was alone, and the world was sleeping she'd spill a few tears, but until then she'd hold her own.

"He dropped off all of Jordyn's belongings on my mom's doorstep and left a note saying that he was basically done with us. My mom found them and got so mad she went and fought his mom."

Bezo stared at Logan until they both cracked a smile.

Bezo walked over to Logan and bent down. His hands rubbed up and down her legs as he gazed up into her eyes.

"Fuck him. It's clearly his loss baby. This nigga acting out like a fucking child and cutting off his own seed. No real man would ever do some shit like that."

Logan nodded. She understood what he was saying but still his words did nothing to change the fact that her daughter was a fatherless child.

"I just don't want this to affect her later in life. When I was younger, and even up until he passed I questioned my dad's love for me. That led to me having issues with men. I would wonder if I was enough for them. I mean I couldn't even keep my father in the same city. He had a new family, a new child and while now I see that his love was there back then I didn't. It fucked me up Bellamy, and I don't want Jordyn going through that. That generational curse shit is real you know? She could easily fall into that role of being lost behind this mess with Rome."

Bezo grabbed Logan's face and pulled her close to him. The intensity in his eyes made her start to breathe harder. No man had ever stared at her that way before.

"Shit will work out how it is supposed to. You gotta relax beautiful. I got you," he promised her meaning every word he spoke.

Logan closed her eyes, and Bezo pressed his lips against her's. She pushed away all of the doubt and the fears plaguing her mind and kissed him back passionately. She could see the blessing in her lesson, and it was Bezo. Like her mom often told her, there was always a rainbow waiting at the end of the storm.

11

♪ *She's a stripper, naked dancer but she's begging me to wife her*
When the first time I met lil' mama, she was a one-nighter
Hell no, I don't love nothing but my money and my rifle
At the top like Eiffel Tower, I told her to beat it
You woulda' thought she was Michael ♪

Kolbee's gaze was fixated on the stripper who just graced the stage, but her mind wasn't physically there. Onyx Strip Club was live on a Saturday night, and as she chilled with Sir and his people, Kolbee realized this wasn't her scene. At least not with him. She was more of the laid-back type, but he had invited her. When they first arrived, Kolbee was having fun in their section, but after an hour the number of females who began to crowd it annoyed her. They were acting like they had never been around a group of men in their life.

"You're killing my mood, girl," Brittany, the worker from Flint Cleaners whispered in Kolbee's ear.

Kolbee wouldn't dare go to the strip club with them alone. She and Brittany had developed a cool business relationship though she was technically her boss. Kolbee didn't mind though. Until Brittany fucked up on the job, they'd be straight. When Sir invited her out, she asked her if she wanted to tag along with her and Brittany was down.

"Sorry, girl. This nigga Sir invited me, and he's only been over here twice to check on us. Such a fucking gentleman," Kolbee said with a roll of her eyes.

Across from the sectional she was sitting crossed leg on, Sir had his frame pushed up against one of the strippers in six-inch pumps. He was whispering in her ear and puffing on a blunt acting like he was trying to cuff her. Unbeknownst to Kolbee, the stripper was his ex-girlfriend. Drunk and in his feelings, Sir had some shit to get off his chest and apparently thought the time for that was now.

"At least we got free drinks," Brittany shrugged and drank from her cup. Kolbee would have easily bought her own bottle or two, but there was no need in wasting her funds. Plus, Brittany was diluting the Ciroc with so much juice, she was wasting the shit.

"Right. I'm about to go to the restroom. You coming with me?"

Brittany nodded her head and took another sip of her cup before sitting it on the table. Standing to her feet, Kolbee adjusted the custom-made army fatigued skirt with chains holding it together at the sides. The red mesh bralette matched perfectly with her Rudy Woo lips, and on her feet were a pair of black pointed toe stilettos. The added inches had her ass sitting up more than it already was, and the men who caught her walking by was wishing she was the one on stage shaking her derriere for the George Washington's in their hands.

While in the short line for the restroom, Brittany ran into a friend from college. Kolbee then realized how she hadn't made any female friends since moving to Atlanta. Her best friend Alaia was making plans to fly down next month, but Kolbee missed their closeness. Besides Logan, she had no one to share things with. There was Denali, but she needed a female companion to gossip with. Especially when it came to talking shit about him.

After relieving her bladder, Kolbee washed her hands and walked out. As she waited for Brittany her phone vibrated. It was damn near one in the morning, and she couldn't believe her phone was even going off. Logan had long ago told her good night, and Bryson was back on the block list. Her screen immediately unlocked once she placed her thumb on the home button. Kolbee's eyes read over the text contents, before shooting upward. Letting them roam the packed vicinity, she couldn't locate Denali.

Tucked in the corner of the club with a few of his boys, Denali smirked with low eyes as he watched Kolbee and Brittany reappear from the restroom. He saw her when she left the section she was in but wanted to wait until she was headed back to let her know he was there.

Come here before you go back over there with that sucka ass nigga.

"You okay?" Brittany asked when they stopped walking.

Kolbee was trying to figure out where he was at. "Yeah. You can go back up there. I'll be back in a second."

"No, girl. I don't know them niggas," she laughed. "Who you just get a text from?"

Kolbee grinned. Denali had just texted her where he was sitting. "You'll see," she replied.

Relaxed on the couch in their section, Denali drank in Kolbee's being as she stepped into their section. He had seen her legs plenty of times, but tonight they looked luscious stacked on top of her heels. Her beauty was illuminating. Captivating, and had his boys faces bunched in confusion when Denali stood to his feet to greet her. A few of them had seen her at the gym but didn't think anything of it. He trained beautiful women every day.

Kolbee didn't have a chance to admire his attire. Gripping her around the waist, she melted into his massive frame. His Sauvage cologne made her knees weak and mouth water. Denali finally got the hug he wanted from her before letting her go. Breathless, Kolbee gave him a shy smile though she was far from that. It was only when she got around him did these types of characteristics surface.

"Hi," she spoke.

"What's up. You looking good."

She blushed. "Thank you. This is Brittany," she said grabbing Brittany's attention.

Denali gave her a head nod. "What's good, Brittany. You can sit wherever. Make one of them niggas get up," he said, and his boys chuckled. One did move over for her to sit down and made her a drink.

When Denali sat down and pulled Kolbee onto his lap, she knew then that he must have been drunk. That, or he was feeling bold as hell tonight. It was both. That brown had him feeling frisky, and Kolbee was looking too damn good to be anywhere else except for on his lap.

"What you been drinking?" she asked, adjusting some so she could face him.

Denali's low eyes scanned the table. "Shit. Everything."

Kolbee shook her head and picked up the cup she figured was his. When he nodded his head in conformation, she sipped from it, and the Hennessey burned like shit going down.

"Ugh! That shit is strong," she complained and placed the cup down.

"Didn't nobody tell you to drink it."

"Shut up. You having a good time?"

He nodded his head. "I am now. Where you get this little shit from?" He tugged on one of the chains on her skirt, before settling his hand on the inside of her thigh. Kolbee's stomach caved. His touch was warm and setting her skin ablaze. She was certain if he removed his hand there'd be a hand print on her light skin. That's how hot he had her.

"I ordered it." She answered admiring his handsome face.

Denali's facial features were sharp and distinct. Kolbee meant to ask him his facial routine because his skin was gorgeous. It was chocolate and framed by a neatly trimmed beard and a thin mustache that she wanted to leave her scent on. Every time he licked his lips her pussy thumped in anticipation. She couldn't wait until that time came. She wasn't sure when it would go down, but it was on her list of things to-do in Atlanta. It was right at the top of her notes and marked with the emoji sticking his tongue out.

"Don't wear this shit anymore," he whispered while pulling her closer to him. Her scent was driving him insane. The perfume she was wearing was light and flowery. He wasn't sure if it was her body wash he was also smelling or her natural aroma that had him in a daze. But, he loved it.

"Why not?" she asked pulling away from him and his brow lifted.

"Don't pull away from me, and because. I know you ain't wearing any panties with this shit," he whispered the last part in her ear and slid his hand further up her thigh.

Kolbee inhaled sharply and tucked her head into the crook of his neck. She didn't even want to look and see who was staring at them. Her cheeks flushed as his thumb strummed over her swollen lips.

"Denali," she breathed out.

He kissed her neck. Moved to her ear and kissed behind it where she had a tattoo of a bumble bee. It was so tiny no one could hardly see it, but he knew it was there. Heat crept up Kolbee's spine, and she tried crossing her legs, but he forced them back a part.

"Denali," she hissed out when he bit her earlobe.

"I love the way you say my name with your proper ass."

She enunciated every syllable, but that didn't deter him.

Kolbee had no regrets about not wearing underwear with her skirt until now. She was getting more aroused by the second, and wetness only stemmed from that. Her pebbled nipples were already straining against the mesh material driving her nuts. The friction of him playing her with clitoris had her losing her cool.

Denali collected some of her juices and stroked her growing bud. "Give me a kiss, Busy Bee," he demanded when he heard Kolbee moaning lowly in his ear.

She shook her head no, so Denali pushed his middle finger inside of her gushy walls. Grabbing his chin, Kolbee kissed him hard and moaned inside his mouth. Her body was on fire, and Denali's long finger tickling her insides had her creaming up. Sucking on his tongue, she felt him thicken up underneath her. His Balmain jeans couldn't contain the erection he had if they tried. Moving his thumb quicker, Kolbee rocked her body to the beat of whatever song was playing. She couldn't hear the lyrics because her ears were filled with the angel on her shoulder telling her to stop.

You forgot you came here with Sir?

When that thought entered her mine, she broke their kiss. Denali used his free hand to grab her face. It was just enough roughness to let her know that he was done playing with her.

"Did I tell you to stop kissing me?" he asked while sliding in another finger. He needed her to come.

"Oh, my gosh," she whimpered and shook her head no. She didn't resume kissing him though.

Denali made her stare him in the eyes as her pussy muscles tightened around his fingers. He was challenging her to keep her eyes open as she came hard. As her body shuddered, Kolbee couldn't help but plant her face into his chest. She didn't know what the hell had come over Denali, hell, her too, but there was no turning back from here.

"You good, love?" he asked once his fingers were wiped off and Kolbee was sitting up straight. She was so glad he was sitting on the couch away from everyone. Her cheeks were flushed as ever. Denali had asked the question as if he hadn't just made her climax inside a club. A damn strip club at that.

A lazy grin crossed her face. "You were wrong for that."

"There ain't shit wrong with making you cum. You just looking to discredit my skills," he smirked.

"Not at all. But, just know this means war. Look at my face."

Denali smirked and ran his thumb over her bottom lip, making her smell her alluring scent on his hand. "You look like a fucking masterpiece. Just wait until I slide this dick up inside you. You gon' really look beautiful, then."

Kolbee choked. His nasty banter had her reconsidering leaving him, but she knew she had to. Denali was going to have her in the club giving the people a better show than the ones on stage. Standing to her feet, Kolbee took the damp paper towels he gave her and wiped the inside of her thighs.

"I hate to cum and run, but I should get back to our section," she said, and Denali didn't bother to keep a straight face.

"Your section or the nigga you met up with section?"

"You know what I mean, Denali."

He nodded his head. "Aight. Be safe. Let me know when ya'll leave out, too."

"I will. Don't be over here with no other females."

Kolbee's brow lifted, and Denali licked his lips. "You can't tell me shit when you're about to go chill with another nigga."

"Whatever. He and I are just friends."

"So are we."

His reply shouldn't have stunned her, but it did. *Friends? Yeah okay, nigga.* She said to herself. It lowkey hurt her feelings, but she wouldn't show him that.

Nodding her head, Kolbee smirked. "Bet."

She and Brittany walked back to Sir's section, and he immediately walked up to them. Kolbee was annoyed as fuck and had no interest in Sir at the moment. While she texted Alaia about what she just went down, Brittany made herself comfortable by grabbing another drink and standing up to dance.

"Where'd ya'll go?" Sir leaned down and spoke in Kolbee's ear.

"To the restroom," she replied evenly without giving him a glance.

He was so caught up in his ex, that he hadn't realized they both went missing. Nodding his head, he stood up and looked towards Brittany. One of his boys could tell she was on go and wanted to see what she was about, so he told Sir to check her out. She yawned just as he walked up on her from behind.

"You tired?" he asked.

She giggled. "A little. I worked all day."

"The cleaners open all day?"

"Not the cleaners. I have two jobs."

"That's what's up. You off work tomorrow? My boy trying to get up with you once we leave here."

Brittany rolled her eyes. "Your boy? He ain't man enough to step to me?"

"Shit, you'll have to take that up with him, shawty," Sir laughed. "So, what's up? You free?"

"Yeah. I should be. Let me check with Kolbee to see if she needs me to come in tomorrow."

Sir's interest was piqued hearing that. "She your boss for real? I just thought she was the manager on duty that day."

Brittany shook her head no. "Nah. She and her sister own it. I'll be right back."

That was news to Sir. He and Kolbee discussed a few things, but she didn't mention that. He figured she just didn't want to tell him, but it honestly slipped her mind. Glancing her way as the two women talked, Sir found Kolbee even more attractive than before. While his interest was beyond piqued, Kolbee was thinking of a way to ignore him, now. She didn't want any other mans attention except for Denali's. After the stunt he pulled, Kolbee felt like she deserved that plus more from him. Whatever games he was on, she was not with.

"Who presses charges on someone's mom?" Jerricka questioned.

Bezo chuckled. He blew smoke from his mouth as they pulled away from the Ocean Prime in Troy. Logan was back home for a few days. She'd packed up her place with the help of Jerricka and Bezo. She'd also attended court with her mom because Rome's mother was pressing assault charges.

"A bitch made motherfucka," Bezo replied as he drove down Big Beaver road like he was from the D.

Logan sat in the passenger side of the rental with her eyes closed. Having Bezo in her hometown with her, she felt good. It felt right, and she was happy she'd decided to embrace them being together. They didn't have a title, but Bezo made sure to spend all of his free time with Logan and Jordyn and even found himself turning down out of town gigs just so he could be up under them. Bezo had some serious shit he wanted to lay on her but was waiting for the right time.

"Not to be messy but Rome just posted his location on Instagram. We should go pull up on his ass how your mama and auntie Mary did," Jerricka suggested high off the weed Bezo was puffing on and tipsy from her drinks at the bar.

Bezo nodded liking that idea while Logan shook her head.

"No, it's clear they like to press charges and shit. He'll get his," Logan replied.

"Bezo get your girl. You know you wanna beat his ass. Shit I know I do," Jerricka instigated.

Bezo laughed, and she joined in with him. He fucked with Jerricka. She was cool and always looking to have a good time.

"Nah my baby right. I don't wanna do some shit that can look bad on her. Trust. I'ma get that nigga together, and he won't even see the shit coming. You got my word sis," he assured Jerricka.

Jerricka nodded. She was so damn happy to see her girl with someone that was good for her. Jerricka partied with Logan, but they prayed together as well. Logan's pain was her's and vice versa, so she was thankful to see one of their prayers coming to light. For years she'd been praying for her best friend to find a real man. One that could be a good man to her and a grand father to Jordyn. Jerricka had never liked Rome's lame ass. He was a fraud to her, and she'd seen it from the start.

"Good. I don't give a damn if it happens two years from now. Just make sure you fuck that nigga up good," Jerricka said in her outside voice sounding nothing like the nurse that worked around predominately white people.

Bezo smirked.

"Oh, I will sis."

After taking Jerricka to her man's club so that she could spend the rest of her night chilling with him, Bezo and Logan retired to her nearly empty apartment. Bezo had been approached by people at the resturant and while they were out in the city and Logan was smitten with him. He was so down to earth that it was easy for her to forget he was a rapper. She stood near the doorway in the only piece of lingerie that she hadn't packed up staring at him.

The white, lace crotchless bodysuit fitted Logan like a glove. Her long tresses were still wet from the shower she'd taken. She eyed him while he sipped on his drink. It was dark of course. She was drunk on him. Turned on by his tattoos, the rips, and cuts in his physique and his masculine beauty had her ready to pounce on him.

Bezo sat at the foot of her bed in his black Ethika boxers with a lazy grin on his face. He was kind of turnt. Detroit always showed him love so while Logan had been out earlier with her best friend and mom; he'd hooked up with his Detroit niggas. Some were hustlers, and some were rappers.

They'd popped shit and relaxed and even had him lay a few tracks. He was feeling good and to be with Logan made it a thousand times better. She was everything to him.

"Look at you," he said looking her over in her get-up that she'd finished off with stilettoes. "Come here, let me see you up close," he demanded.

Logan slowly walked over to him, and Bezo sat his glass down on the floor. He grabbed her waist and gazed up into her eyes. Music played from Logan's phone, but all Bezo could contrate on was her. She smelled like fresh flowers. Her pussy was freshly waxed, and the outfit she wore had his dick hard as a brick.

"You are the sexiest woman I have ever seen. Give me and princess a little boy that looks like me, and I swear I'll love you forever," he said lowly.

Logan slightly taken aback by his words, smiled. She tried to step back, and Bezo shook his head. Shit, he was thirty-one. Half the people he'd grown up with hadn't lived past twenty-one. Tomorrow wasn't promised, and the last thing he planned on doing was prolonging his plans for himself and Logan.

"Here you go. You sound so sure of us," she said with her heart pounding.

Bezo lustfully looked up at her. He knew that she could feel the strong connection that they shared.

"I am. I'm not letting your lil sexy ass get away," he murmured freeing his dick. His thick, long erection sprang forward as it stood at attention. Bezo pulled Logan onto his lap and slowly she slid onto him.

The things her body felt as he entered her made her

moan. Her head fell back, and she whimpered as she stretched around his member. Molding to his dick like she'd been made personally for him.

"Bellamy," Logan whispered holding onto him tightly.

Bezo slapped her ass. Logan was so warm and tight that no words could escape him. He needed to use all his energy on not letting loose too soon. His strong hands slowly raised Logan up and down onto his shaft as he stared at her pretty face.

"You feel so fucking good baby. This pussy is dripping," he said and started sucking on her bottom lip.

Logan whimpered again and moved faster. Her body had been begging for a release while she'd been fantasizing about Bezo. He was more than she imagined he would be. Logan was receiving so much pleasure that it took no time for her walls to cream up. She gripped Bezo tighter and he stood up. He tossed her onto the bed and climbed ontop of her. With both of her legs in the crook of his arms he slid fully inside of Logan.

The deep stroke damn near made her faint.

"Oh shit! Your too deep," she whined staring up at him.

Bezo shook his head.

"Relax baby. Stop fighting it and let me get all the way up in this pussy. Okay?"

Logan's body shook. Pleasure took over and all she could do was cry out his name as she erupted all over him.

Hours later Bezo could hear a loud banging noise coming from the front of Logan's apartment. He sat up on the bed as she rolled over to gaze at him. Her red hair that he loved so much was all over her damn head, and she wore a satisfied smile on her pretty face.

"You okay?" He asked.

Bam!

Bam!

Bam!

The noise was louder and made both Logan and Bezo hop up from the bed. Bezo tossed on his sweats and grabbed his gun. He wasn't in the streets, but he chose to stay safe at all times. Of course, being extra careful with his weapon around Jordyn who knew nothing about him even carrying it.

"Who the fuck at your door?" he asked leaving out of the room.

Logan frowned as she rushed to get dressed. Uriah didn't know where she lived, and she hadn't spoken to him in months. It was only one other person, and Logan was terrified to see her past and her present collide.

"Wait, baby! Let me call the cops!" she yelled running after him.

Bezo snatched Logan's front door open not trying to hear shit Logan was saying. Rome stood on the other side of the door with three of his boys. He'd heard from a few people that Logan was back in town with her rapper boyfriend and he was so hurt. She'd left him, moved to another state, then tried to move on with some rapping ass nigga. He was very offended and ready to beat some ass.

"Nigga what the fuck you doing here and where my baby momma at?" Rome questioned hype as hell.

Bezo looked at Rome who was as tall as him then pass

him at the group of scary ass niggas he brought with him. He chuckled before stepping outside. Logan tried to grab his arm, but he brushed her off. Rome wasn't quick enough to evade the ass whooping he had coming his way. Bezo used the butt of his pistol to bust Rome's nose open. The blood poured from it immediately as Rome staggered back. Bezo then passed his gun to Logan and chose to box with him instead. His skills were taught to him by the late Deron who'd taken him to the gym regularly.

Rome tried to keep up but failed miserably. His boys stood by quietly as Bezo beat his ass like he'd stolen something from him. With every punch Bezo landed on Rome's face he thought of Jordyn. How Rome was playing her and how sorry he was. As Bezo hemmed Rome up squeezing his neck with all the strength he had, he decided to give him some parting words.

"Only a boy runs from his responsibilities. Your daughter is still gone be good though cause' I'm gone make sure of that shit nigga. You gone have your scary ass momma drop them charges, and you gone stop causing problems for my baby. If you wanna fuck with somebody come at me nigga. I ain't hard to find, and I'll be waiting every time to beat yo ass," he told him before letting Rome fall to the ground.

Logan stood by with her mouth hanging wide. Rome who was always dressed to the nines was bleeding from his nose and his mouth. His left eye was closed shut, and his front tooth was missing. His Balmain shirt was completely ripped while his jeans hung loosely from his narrow waist. Bezo had even beat him up out of one of his Giuseppe sneakers.

Logan shook her head as his boys rushed to get him away from Bezo.

"Bellamy, oh my god," she said quietly.

Bezo grabbed his pistol and watched Rome's Camero speed away. He laughed hard as hell as he shook his right hand that was swelling up.

"Baby, call up your girl and tell her that shit came sooner than we thought it would. I'm hungry as fuck though. Come make me something to eat bae," he said and walked into the apartment.

Logan stared down at the ground noticing Rome had left his cellphone along with a few traces of his blood, and she smiled to herself.

"Daddy this man is as crazy as you," she said quietly before going back into her place.

An hour later while cooking the only thing she had in her refrigerator which was breakfast foods Jerricka laughed as Logan told her about how Rome got his ass handed to him. Jerricka's ex stood against the wall sharing a blunt with Bezo engaging in small talk with him.

"So that nigga actually left his fucking phone over here?" Jerricka asked.

Logan nodded while smiling. She'd called up her friend to tell her what happened and Jerricka had burned rubber to make it to her.

"Yes, he fucked him up bad. I was scared he was going to kill him," Logan replied quietly.

Jerricka laughed harder.

"I would have paid to see that shit, honey. He deserved that plus more. That was the perfect way for you to officially say goodbye to Detroit. I'm gonna miss you and my Jordyn," Jerricka said staring at Logan.

Logan walked around to her bestfriend and pulled her into a hug. She would miss her too, but it was nothing left for her in the city and the reality was Atlanta was her new home.

12

LEANING UPWARD, KOLBEE TURNED THE VOLUME DOWN on Bezo's latest mixtape. She and Denali's conversation was starting to get serious, and his rapping was throwing her off.

"What happened to your dad?" Kolbee asked him softly.

She knew Andre had been in Denali's life forever, but she was curious as to where his real dad was. The two were nine hours into their twelve-hour drive to Kansas City, and their conversations were flowing smoothly. Kolbee was missing home something terribly and invited Denali home with her. He was still a little upset about her choosing to hang with Sir at the strip club, but he didn't let that be the reason she visited alone. The fact that she even wanted him to tag along meant more to him than she knew. The truth was, she had never driven by herself for more than seven hours and knew he'd be willing to help her out.

"Can we even consider that nigga that?" he asked with a

chuckle, trying to control his temper. "Your guess is as good as mine, baby."

The endearing word melted Kolbee's heart. She was well aware of what went down at the strip club, and she was hoping Denali wasn't just calling her the pet name because it was a figure of speech.

"He never once tried to reach out to you or anything?"

Denali shook his head. "He did probably once or twice, but by then it was too late. He had already shown me what type of nigga he was, and I was good with that. We didn't need a relationship at that point."

"Do you have a close relationship with his other kids? I know that must be tough," she said feeling the mood shift inside the car.

Not too long ago had she been on the receiving end of that question. Though different circumstances, it was mind boggling to Kolbee how a man could just leave the mother of his child, a four-month old at that, and go start a family with someone else years later. Denali's sperm donor, Canan's excuse for leaving was that he wasn't ready for kids. But, years down the line he had created three with a woman who was deemed a side-chick in his eyes.

The love for her son was the reason why Shareese didn't fight or argue with him about up and leaving. It was the only reason she needed; fuck being heartbroken. In her eyes, if a man could put a woman before his kids, she didn't need him. What was even more disgusting was his wife. Shareese couldn't believe she had condoned his deadbeat ways. There was no way in hell she'd lay up with a man who didn't claim nor take care of his seed. It was the most trifling thing a woman, a mother, could do in her eyes. Fuck whatever excuses were made.

"Not for real. They hit me up sometimes, but I don't really have much to say to em'. I ain't too much pressed to have a relationship with none of them either. My mama used to try and have us connect but stopped once I let it be known it was a waste of time."

Kolbee nodded her head in deep thought. She wondered had Deron ever thought about not being there for her. It did take him months to tell Megan, Megan found out rather, about she and Tasia, and that was only because he loved them both too much. One of them was bound to get their heart broken.

"I'm glad Logan and I met. I couldn't stand her ass at first, but that was because I didn't really know her and was hurt. I wanted that happy family life with my daddy, and she got that, while my mama basically played both roles as my parent. I mean, he called and visited, but it's not the same as having your father's presence in the house, you know?"

Kolbee was in her feelings tough. Denali reached over, grabbed her hand and caressed it softly while she sulked. She and Denali had more in common than she thought. The outcome of their dad's decisions was just different. Denali knew exactly what she meant. Seeing his sister Shareese and Andre interact was a connection he wanted with his daughter one day. He and Andre had a bond out of this world, and he appreciated him for being a real man in the midst of his mother's storm. So often society looked down on black men for not being provider's or protectors, but Andre had been everything Shareese needed back then.

She thanked God for him walking into her life, and so did he.

"Let's change the subject. You got it all serious in here," Denali joked and kissed the back of her hand. "On the real, just know you were loved by that nigga Deron for sure. He may not have always been there physically, but you can't tell me he didn't come through whenever you needed him."

Kolbee shook her head. "I'd be lying if I said he didn't. I honestly wanted for nothing but him, which I guess I had to sacrifice. It's life. I'm happy for the times we did share though. He laced me with love and knowledge, so I can't really complain."

"Shit. You sure about that last part? I'm still trying to figure out why you wanted to drive to this hick ass town when we could have easily caught a flight and been there hours ago," Denali huffed out.

"First off, let's not get out of hand by disrespecting my city. It's not some hick ass town. We may not be as big as bumper-to bumper traffic Atlanta, but we're big enough. Secondly, how you know I just didn't want to spend time with you?"

His eyes widened in surprise at her admission. "Twelve hours? Shit, we go together now. If I survive this trip with you, you are mine. Fuck what you talkin' 'bout," he laughed but was slightly serious. Road tripping with just anyone wasn't the wave. He had enjoyed this one with Kolbee though.

"Whatever. You know you're not trying to make me yours. Mr. *I'm trying to respect your daddy*, head ass. If my daddy knew how you were playing games with his baby girl, he'd talk bad to your ass," she replied, and Denali broke out laughing.

It was so contagious, Kolbee just grinned and admired his profile from the side. She was never a fan of chocolate because it used to break her skin out horribly as a teenager, but she'd suffer for a taste of Denali again. She knew he tasted as good as he looked because he didn't put trash ass food into his body, and he took damn good care of it. Every time he switched hands on the steering his muscles flexed, and Kolbee sighed. She just wanted to be wrapped up inside of them.

"Aye. You funny, man. I am trying to be respectful, though. Andre already warned me about pursuing you."

That was news to Kolbee, but she should have known he would. She was like a daughter in his eyes. Denali didn't care about any of that shit. He and Kolbee didn't have a drop of the same blood running through their veins, so she was fair game in his eyes.

"I should have known. What did he say?"

"I can't go against the code; you know that. Just know the reason why I was checking on you in the beginning was because of him."

"And, now?" Kolbee asked lowly. Afraid of his answer.

Denali licked his lips, glanced her way and grabbed her hand. "Cause' you're mine to look after now. On some real shit, we're grown Kolbee. I fuck with you on a level I've never given any woman the opportunity to make it to. Not because they couldn't, but because I knew they weren't the one for me. They weren't capable of accepting me and my potential to be the man they claimed to need. I really think I was meant for you. It's weird, but I go off vibes. We've been vibin' since we were youngin's, so that gotta mean something."

Kolbee was losing her shit. She wanted to cry, kiss him, and have him pull his truck the hell over so she could make love to him, but instead, she just leaned over and kissed his cheek. Holding his head in her hands, she bit his cheek for getting her so worked up.

"Boy," she breathed out flopping back into her seat. "You can't be saying that type of shit to me in this car. I'm over here hot as hell," she fussed, placing her face in front of the vents.

Laughing, Denali shook his head at her craziness. He loved that she could freely be herself around him. The words he spoke weren't expected, but Kolbee had him in an element where being vulnerable to admit how he felt was okay. He had to tell her how he felt since he couldn't touch her right now. Their connection through words was deep, but whenever they touched she could literally feel him in her soul. Knocking at the door of her heart to be let in. Whatever shield she had guarding it was let down. She just hoped Denali wasn't just saying these things because they sounded good.

Three hours and seat positions later, Kolbee was pulling up in front of the home she used to share with her mama and younger brother. The Lee's Summit neighborhood was quiet for a Tuesday, just how it had always been when growing up. Denali had just woken up from the quickest nap in his life with a scowl on his face. He was most definitely not the most pleasant when he didn't receive enough sleep. Kolbee glanced his way and handed him a stick of gum.

"Here. My mama will clown you if you walk up in there with stank breath."

"I'ma clown her ass right back," he replied before popping the gum in his mouth.

Undoing her seatbelt, Kolbee let out a yawn and let her eyes roam the streets. The neighbor from up the street was walking her big ass pit bull dog, and Kolbee rolled her eyes. She'd never forget the day that damn dog chased her and Latrell home. She wanted to shoot that mufucka so bad but knew she'd probably be doing jail time. It was absurd how the life of a dog meant more than humans nowadays.

"Shit's crazy," she mumbled.

"What?" Denali asked following her gaze while standing next to her. He had just grabbed their bags out the car and was wondering what had her occupied.

"Nothing. Let's get in here. I need a shower, some food, and a nap."

Playfully, Denali wrapped his arms around her waist and kissed her neck. He had been waiting twelve long hours to feel her against him.

"Can I take a nap with you."

Kolbee giggled like a school girl. "Mhm. I'ma warn you now; I sleep wild."

"I'ma just have to fuck you real good so you can't move then."

She clamped a hand over her mouth and Denali smacked her ass just as the front door opened.

"Oh my gosh, bitch!" Alaia screamed and rushed toward her. "I missed you so much."

Kolbee couldn't talk. She was still stuck on Denali's

choice of words from a few seconds ago. Finding her voice and strength, she hugged her best friend back.

"I missed you, too, honey. I thought you didn't get off work until six?"

Alaia waved her hand. "Girl. Fuck them. They knew today was my off day and wanted to call me in. I gave them their little six hours and shook."

"I hear that. Alaia, this is Denali. Denali, this is my best friend Alaia," Kolbee introduced the two.

Pursing her lips together, Alaia looked him over and smirked. "Hmm. I see why she's been up there acting like she didn't want to come home. Let me find out."

Denali smirked. "I ain't got nothing to do with that. What's up, though. Nice to meet you."

"Likewise. I've heard nothing but good things about you," she said, and Denali looked Kolbee's way. She shook her head and walked in the house.

"I ain't tell your ass shit else. Watch," she hissed, and Alaia laughed.

"I love you, too, boo."

Denali followed the duo into the immaculate home and was immediately greeted by the smell of fresh linen. Tasia had fallen in love with the smell when she was pregnant with Latrell and couldn't let the damn scent go. The only time she changed it was during the Christmas season, and it was changed right back come January.

Walking from the laundry room with the phone to her ear, Tasia told her mama she'd call her back when Kolbee rushed her. Pulling her into a hug only a daughter could give a mother, Tasia accepted it all. She missed her baby girl.

"Okay, Kolbee. I know you've been working out, but loosen up some," Tasia laughed.

"Sorry, mama. I missed you. Look at your hair!"

Kolbee was so used to seeing her mother with long hair; she couldn't believe how good she looked with the pixie cut. The front was longer than the back and brought out Tasia's facial features even more. At this point, Kolbee was sure her fine ass mama could rock any hairstyle and pull it off. She looked ten years younger. Her melanin skin was glowing under the bright kitchen lights, and Denali then knew why Deron had stepped out on Megan. Though she was fine too, Tasia didn't slack at all in the looks department. Now that he was up close and personal, the body either.

"Damn, she looks Kolbee's age," he said to himself.

"I know. You like it?" Tasia asked.

"I love it. You look so young."

She smacked her lips. "Girl, I am young. What you mean?" She laughed and peeked her eyes at Denali. "I know you better stop staring and come give me a hug."

Stepping into the kitchen, Denali gave her a hug and Tasia squeezed his arm. "Who you think you are with all these damn muscles? Walking up in here looking like my daughter's body guard," she joked.

"Mama," Kolbee groaned.

Denali just smirked. "Hey to you, too. You already clowning, and we just got here."

"You know I'm just messing with you. Thank you for getting my baby here safely," she said kissing Kolbee's forehead.

"You're welcome. We're flying next time. She was tripping wanting to drive all this way."

"We made it though... right?" Kolbee sassed and he gave her a simple head nod. He had something for her smart mouth.

"Right, and we need to plan the rest of your week out. When are you going back?" Alaia asked as Denali and Tasia fell into a comfortable conversation.

Kolbee watched them with appreciative eyes and smiled. She knew if her mama liked him, then Denali was a keeper. Tasia didn't think any nigga was good enough for her baby. Not even Bryson's lying ass before he got caught up. She had told Kolbee to be careful with him, and Kolbee had tried to be. But, she learned her lesson for sure. Never catch feelings when it was just sex.

"Probably Saturday or Sunday. I'll have to check with Denali. What you trying to get into?" Kolbee asked, squinting her eyes at her best friend. She was always up to something.

"Nah. It's more like *who's* trying to get up in you," she whispered with a grin.

Kolbee's face flushed with a red hue. "Shut up. I'd never disrespect my mama's house like that."

"Shit. What she can't hear won't hurt her," Alaia laughed but quickly stopped when Tasia looked their way.

"What ya'll over there cackling about?"

The friends looked at one another. "Oh, nothing. You know us," Alaia replied.

"Mhm. Too well. Don't get embarrassed in front of company."

They laughed. "Where's Latrell?" Kolbee asked.

"Staying after school for a play. He should be home in a few hours. I know ya'll are hungry, but I do not feel like cooking. Where ya'll trying to get some food from?" she asked.

"I'm more tired than anything. I need a nap first; then we can discuss dinner plans," Kolbee answered.

"Denali?" Tasia quizzed.

"A nap does sound good as hell. Your daughter here made me drive the entire way."

Kolbee gasped. "How dare you."

"I know I raised you better than that, Kolbee," Tasia said with a shake of her head, feigning disappointment. "Had this poor man driving for twelve hours. You owe him an apology."

Laughing, Kolbee started to walk out of the kitchen. Yeah, she owed him alright. "After the lie he just told? I think not. Come on Denali so I can show you where you'll be sleeping at."

"And it's not in your old room. Don't try to play me," Tasia yelled out as he followed behind Kolbee.

"My old room? Dang, just move me out."

Tasia was only joking; somewhat. Kolbee's room was still the same as she left it minus her belongings. Her move to Atlanta was going to be permanent for a while, so hoarding things at her mama's crib was no use. Walking pass her bedroom door, she stopped at the door down the hallway where the guestroom was located and opened it. Inside there was a queen-sized bed made up with a cream comforter set, matching window drapes, and a furniture set that Kolbee knew was brand new. A bathroom with a tub and shower was off to the left connected to it.

"Ya'll crib nice as hell," Denali complimented.

"Thank you. My mama swears she needs all this space like she has company over."

"Don't be a hater."

Dropping his bag into the chair positioned in the corner, Denali walked up on Kolbee from behind while she looked in the mirror hanging on the wall. The sight of them together made Kolbee's heart race. His chocolate skin against her light caramel color was beautiful. Massaging her shoulders, Kolbee's eyes closed in appreciation. Though she had only tackled three hours of the drive, her body was tense as hell.

"We look good together," Denali confessed loving the reflection staring back at him.

"Mhm. Damn, I need a full back massage now."

"That ain't gone turn into nothing but me massaging yo ass before I get real nasty and have your mama trying to beat my ass up in here," he said and humped her booty from behind.

Laughing, Kolbee broke their embrace to turn around and face him. Without thinking, she wrapped her arms around his neck. "Why you always talking so freaky to me? Say something nice."

Denali licked his lips and grinned. "I love the color of your eyes. Especially when you stare at me like this. Shit makes a nigga feel all funny inside."

Kolbee smiled wide. "What do my eyes look like?"

"The color?" She nodded.

"Sure. Describe them."

"You are so fucking mushy, man."

"Just do it," she whined, and he continued.

"Like honey. The sweet kind bee's produce that hasn't

been tampered with. Straight out the honeycombs, oozing with thickness. They're intense though. Like you're always searching for the right words to hear through your eyes. I see unspoken pain, too. That glows the most when you open up to me about your life. About Deron." Kolbee squeezed them shut.

She was not expecting him to do all of this, but Denali could never just give her a short answer. He wanted her to know exactly what he saw when he looked at her. He placed a soft kiss on her cheek where a tear had landed.

"More than pain, I see a longingness. The gentle look of wanting to be loved, and the hopeful glint of needing to be loved properly. Even when you're angry, your eyes twinkle with understanding. You get that it may not happen when you want it to, but you'll be ready when it does."

Hiding in his chest, Kolbee shook her head. She didn't know what in the world she had gotten herself into with Denali Westin, but she wanted more. More of him, his tender words, and more of his touch. He was doing and saying the right things at the most perfect time; when she needed to hear and feel them the most.

"What you hiding for?" he asked.

"I can't believe you just said all of that. I'm scared to look at your ass."

Denali chuckled and lifted her head. "Don't be. That's how we'll always connect. Now, your turn."

Kolbee's perfectly arched brows pinched together. "You want me to describe your eyes? How they look?"

He nodded.

"Hell. Like you want to fuck the hell out of me and pull my hair from the back if I had some."

Denali laughed so loud, Kolbee hurriedly threw a hand over his mouth. "Hush. I don't want my mama to know I'm in here."

He continued to laugh, but finally got himself together and said, "Man. I love your crazy ass."

Kolbee gasped, as her eyes watered. "W-What?"

Denali's face went serious, and he realized how natural it felt to tell her he loved her. He didn't even catch the words slip from his lips. It was as if he had said them a thousand times before. Grabbing her face, Denali pecked her juicy, pink lips.

"I love you, Busy Bee. Is that okay with you, baby?"

Kolbee started crying hard, and Denali looked alarmed. "Sssh. What the hell you crying for? You gone get us caught in this mufucka."

She choked on a laugh and a cry at the same time. "I love you, too. I have since you cut my fucking ponytail when we were kids. I hated you but loved you so much."

He chuckled and ran his fingers through her curls that had grown out, before massaging her scalp. "Is that why you never grew your hair back out?"

She nodded. "Yes. I thought you liked girls with short hair, so I never wanted to grow it out just in case you did," she laughed realizing how silly she sounded. Denali felt honored, and the erection he was rocking was appreciative of her gesture as well.

"I *love* short hair on you. I don't give a fuck about what

these other females do with their shit," he hissed before attacking her lips.

Kissing him back like it would be her last time, Kolbee hungrily accepted his lips. Sliding his warm tongue into her mouth, she groaned and fisted the t-shirt he was wearing. Dipping low, Denali picked Kolbee up, and she wrapped her long legs around his waist. The thin leggings she was wearing were suddenly ripped, as he savagely tore them at the middle of her ass cheeks. Fuck taking them off.

"The door," Kolbee groaned out.

He had the right mind to leave it open and let Tasia hear exactly why her daughter had been up in Atlanta not wanting to come home, but he knew his baby wasn't having that. He was surprised she was letting him take it this far. But, it was what Kolbee asked for. She wanted Denali to get disrespectful, and there wasn't anything more disrespectful than fucking a mother's daughter while they were under the same roof.

After closing and locking the door, Denali laid back on the bed with Kolbee straddling his lap. With all that ass she had, he needed her to bounce it all on his nine-inch dick like she owned the mufucka. Pulling his shorts and boxers down, Kolbee reached beneath her, lifted some, and sank onto his bulbous head. Her breath got caught in her chest at his width. Not only was he long, but the thickness had Kolbee trying to straddle him on her tippy toes.

Smacking her ass, Denali thrusted his hips upward and slid all the way into her. Kolbee fell to her knees. "Nah. You gone take all this dick. Don't run now."

"Sss, fuck. I'm not running," she hissed.

It was a lie, but he'd make her learn how to take all of him real soon. Denali was much more blessed than Bryson, but even then, that didn't matter. It was the connection she felt with him that had her never wanting to give her pussy up to another nigga ever again.

Grinding into her, Denali gripped the front of her neck while she road him slowly. Rubbing on his face, neck, and chest once she lifted his shirt, Kolbee stared him in the eyes. Everything he had said to her earlier rocked her soul to the core. She couldn't believe how in tune he was with her. She wasn't even that in tune with herself.

Pulling her close, Denali kissed her lips as her tears fell. "I love you, Bee."

Kolbee's body trembled as he rolled her over onto her back without missing a stroke. He needed to handle his pussy and really give her a reason to cry. Tossing her torn leggings to the side, Denali placed kisses up her calf, the back of her thighs, and pushed her legs back toward her head. Dipping into her honey pot, he grunted as he fucked her slowly. With every stroke, he went deeper; searching for the spot to make her come undone.

"Denaliii," she cried out, biting her bottom lip.

Pulling out, Denali slapped his dick coated with her juices against her swollen lips. The way she moaned his name had him ready to nut so fast. Dropping his head, he parted her lips and admired her pink center. He rubbed her pearl, before snaking his tongue inside to taste her. He stretched it and poked as far as her tight hole would let him. With precision, he attacked her clitoris. Sucking on it had Kolbee ready to cry to the Lord above.

"Aaagh! Shit! Shit! Shit!" she panted loudly while rotating her hips.

Stopping his assault, Denali captured her cries while shoving his dick back inside her. He slid in with ease thanks to her wetness. Kolbee clawed at his back when he found her spot. Repeatedly, he tapped on it before breaking their kiss.

"You gotta quiet this juicy pussy down. She talkin' back like a mufucka," he hissed and pinned her legs back. He was over the gentle strokes.

The loud sounds of their skin slapping echoed throughout the room. Kolbee was biting down on her bottom lips so hard; she was sure she'd have a bruise when they finished. Staring down at her sexy body, Denali shook his head. Her skin was red as ever and as bad as he wanted to hit her pussy from the back he knew it'd be too much noise. He wanted to leave a print on her juicy ass cheeks.

"This my shit," he said, more than asked.

Kolbee nodded.

"You ain't gotta ever worry about another mufucka taking care of it, cause' she belongs to me," he hissed out.

"Yes," she spat back while throwing it back at him from the bottom.

Denali grinned, and she smiled. "Yeah... that's it. Make this pretty pussy cream all over this dick. That's what you been wanting to do ain't it?"

He gripped her neck, and Kolbee's eyes twinkled. She loved that rough shit. "Make me."

Denali loved a challenge. She knew that. Relocating her spot, he didn't let up from it until Kolbee had coated his pole in her juices and creamy nectar. She was so wet there was a puddle in the sheets and dripping down Denali's thighs. Squeezing her muscles, she gave him a wicked grin while tracing his abs with her nails.

"You gone come for Bee? You gotta hurry before we get caught," she teased.

"I don't even care. This pussy so good, I'll fuck around and cuss your mama out she come knockin' on this door."

She laughed but cried out when he hit her with five deep, lethal, toe curling, eye rolling strokes. Withdrawing quickly from her warm center that damn near had a vice grip on him, Denali's thick nut shot out on Kolbee's stomach, with some almost landing on her chin. It was so much she just knew Denali hadn't been having sex with anyone else. And, she was correct. If it wasn't her, he was sliding his dick in anything but his hand and boxers.

"Shit, girl," he huffed out finally catching his breath. "I'm about to pass the hell out."

He didn't even finish his sentence before dropping beside her on the bed. Kolbee couldn't move. She was so sexually satisfied that the grin on her face might as well have been permanent.

"You good, baby?" Denali asked with heavy eyelids.

"Mhm. Can I ask you something?"

"Anything."

Kolbee hesitated with her question. She didn't want to make it seem like it was the sex that was clouding her judgement, and it wasn't, but she just had to know. For her sanity alone, at least for the moment, she needed some reassurance.

"Do you really love me?"

He opened his eyes and looked her way. "Is your

head big?"

She smiled and shook her head. "For real, Denali. It's a serious question."

"Yes, I love you. Kolbee Janelle Flint."

She sighed. "Okay."

"Why? You don't think I do. I can show you my other moves once I recuperate."

Kolbee chuckled and shook her head. "Hush, silly. I just... I don't know. I used to feel like I wasn't good enough to be. Competing with Logan for something she had first."

Her eyes flashed a sense guilt, and hot tears welled in them. Turning her face to look at him, Denali ran his fingertips over her jawline before softly gripping her chin.

"You don't have to compete for my love, you hear me? You've always gotten it first, and I'll prove it to you everyday if need be. Fuck thinking you weren't good enough. A person would be a fool not to love you. You're more than enough, Bee. Whoever couldn't love you, just meant they didn't love themselves."

Kolbee's mind instantly went to Deron, and she blinked back tears.

"That, or they loved you so much it weighed you down with doubt making you think it wasn't real or that they didn't. You just couldn't balance it all."

She liked that example more, but his first one made her smile as well. Denali sure had a way with his words, and every time he spoke Kolbee understood why Andre had warned him about pursuing her. If she wasn't careful, their love could turn into something far beyond her wildest day dreams. Smiling, Kolbee climbed from the bed. Now that it had been confessed; she felt better. As long as Denali kept it real with her, they'd be good.

After a much-needed shower and nap, Kolbee and Denali both were up and energized by ten that night. With their stomachs growling and everyone in the house sleep, the two decided to step out and grab some food. Denali knew he shouldn't have been eating so late, but Kolbee convinced him that they'd just work it off that night. Round one of them having sex was so damn good, she was tempted to cop a hotel room during her visit just so she could be as loud as she wanted to be.

"Why they holler at you as soon as you walk in?" Denali whispered in Kolbee's ear, and she laughed. They were at Gates Bar-B-Q in the city, and she was ready to go in on a mixed plate.

"That's just how they greet you. They've been doing it for years."

"They wild for that. Made a nigga feel like he was in trouble just for walking through the door. Talkin' bout some *"How may I help you?!"* Like, damn, Bernice. Let me look at the menu first," Denali chuckled in disbelief.

Kolbee held back her laugh as best as she could. She couldn't take Denali anywhere. He stayed making jokes and talking shit about people. It was his thing. Their thing, and truthfully, he just loved to see Kolbee smile.

"Will you stop," she laughed and slapped his arm. "Her name is not Bernice."

"Shit, that's what she looked like. Somebody's old ass auntie who yelled at you for coming through her front door instead of the side one as a kid."

She shook her head and slid into the opposite side of the booth he had chosen to sit at. "You say anything. Dang. I forgot to get some hot sauce."

Denali frowned. "Hot sauce on barbecue? You trash."

"Not the real hot sauce, fool. The barbecue kind. I'll be back. You want some?"

He looked down at his plate. "Yeah, mild. And, grab me some ketchup."

"Ugh. Ketchup and fries are disgusting."

"You'd eat it if I fed it to you," he smirked, and she smirked back.

"Yeah...so would you."

Her innuendo made him grin. "Hurry up, girl."

When she made it back, their booth was quiet except for the sound of them chewing. With each bite, Kolbee felt herself getting sleepier. Denali, on the other hand, had got his second wind.

"You not gone eat your pickles?" he asked her.

"I save them for last. You wanna taste these beans?

He nodded his head, and Kolbee fed him some from her spoon. The gesture was simple, but Kolbee knew shit was getting real if she shared her food.

"You like em'?"

"Yeah, they straight. Imagine them hoes on a hotdog. It'd be straight hitting," he chuckled, and she agreed.

"Hell yeah. You need to fire up the grill when we-"

"Kolbee?"

She hadn't heard his voice in a minute, but not long enough to forget it. Turning her frame in the booth, Kolbee looked Bryson and the girl standing beside him over with a smug expression on her face before smiling.

"Bryson," she replied sarcastically. "And, company."

"Don't get cute," the girl sassed, and Kolbee chuckled.

"No. That would be something you need to do, rather than sending messages to me through my DM, sweetie."

Kolbee couldn't stand females like the one standing before her. She was the same girl that had messaged her some months back about leaving Bryson, "her man," alone. Kolbee had done just that, and the girl was still pressed.

"Girl. Ain't nobody sending you messages."

Kolbee's eyebrow lifted in amusement. "Shall I pull up the receipts?"

"Ain't need for all that, Bee. My man, you and yours gone head about yall's night and stop interrupting ours," Denali spoke calmly.

Ignoring what he said, Bryson mugged Kolbee as she ate one of her fries. "So, this the nigga you been parlaying around Atlanta with? Now you all in our hometown on some disrespectful shit?"

"Boy. If you don't leave me the hell alone," Kolbee spat. "I haven't talked to you in how long? What I do is no longer your concern. It honestly never was. And, this the nigga you told me to leave alone?" Kolbee laughed at the girl. "With pleasure."

Bryson was fuming on the inside and wanted to snatch Kolbee the fuck up out of her seat, but he'd never go there with her. With any female for that matter. His ego was bruised, and as heartless as she used to be Kolbee didn't give a fuck about him or his feelings.

"Aight, Kolbee. I see how it is," Bryson replied.

"You gone see how it feels to have a broken jaw you say shit else to her, nigga," Denali replied. The nigga was doing too much. He had already let him talk too much to begin with.

Not wanting no smoke, Bryson walked out of their section with his date trying to catch up with him. Being the childish person she is, Kolbee cracked up laughing before they were even out of the door.

"What the hell is wrong with people?" she asked and shook her head.

"I don't know. But, you got me fucked up, too."

She stopped laughing. "Me? What the hell did I do?"

"Fuck with that lame ass dude. Up here begging you to explain yourself. You a lame too for even messing with him," Denali said and shook his head as of he was disappointed.

Kolbee sucked her teeth. "Whatever. Don't be mad at me cause my old niggas got feelings for the girl."

Looking up from his plate, Denali gave her a mean glare. "Aight. Keep on with that trying to be funny shit. You ain't gon get no mo dick."

Denali was imitating the comedian Desi Banks, and Kolbee broke out laughing. The skits he and B. Simone put together stayed having her scroll their Instagram accounts just to get a laugh. She should have known Denali had been doing the same.

Once Kolbee caught her breath she said, "But I didn't-"

"No mo' dick, Bee."

Pouting, she stood from her seat and walked over to his side. Denali kept right on eating his food and ignoring her. Thankful for them being the only customers in their section, Kolbee placed her hand in his lap and caressed his dick. He was trying his best to keep a straight face, but it was everything about Kolbee that had him struggling to do so.

"No more what, Mr. Westin," she whispered seductively in his ear and kissing on his neck.

"Aye, excuse me! Can I get a to-go box?" he yelled out.

Kolbee pulled away and laughed. "That's what I thought, nigga. This my dick."

Grabbing her face softly, he brought their foreheads together and said, "Keep that mentality when we get back to the crib. You bet not run from it this time."

Denali pecked her lips and lightly pushed her out of his side of the booth. "Now, go find somebody to give us some boxes for this food."

Standing completely to her feet, the emotions coursing through Kolbee's body warmed it all over. It was foreign, but she welcomed it. A somber feeling came over her when she realized Denali was the type of man Deron spoke about that day in the car. A man who respected Kolbee's demands. The demands she had and hadn't set yet. Denali just knew how to care for her without a manuscript. He was versed in being a man of his word. He wasn't just showing but proving to her just how much she was worth. Just how much she meant to him, and how much he could smother her with love and admiration.

Kolbee sighed with a heavy heart as she walked back to their table. "Damn, I can't wait to talk to Logan."

13

Two weeks later Logan sat on the lounger naked as the sun beamed down on her body. Her long hair was in two braids to the back while oversized pink shades covered her eyes from the bright sun. She was a day into her weekend vacation with Bezo and was thoroughly enjoying herself. She missed Jordyn and Logan and was catching up with her sister. They both had so many things transpiring in their life, and at times it had been overwhelming to them.

"Has Rome given you any issues since he got his ass beat?"

Logan laughed. She smoked on the hookah and slowly blew the smoke from between her mouth. Bezo had treated her to a shopping spree and a spa date. She was the happiest she'd ever been with a man and prayed the feeling lasted.

"No, he even had his mom drop them charges. I guess

Bellamy really put the fear of God in his ass," Logan replied and laughed.

Kolbee laughed with her.

"Yes, a good ass whooping will do that to a person. How is Cali?"

Logan glanced around at the palm trees and sighed. It was so peaceful and relaxing. The AcquaSanta Lofts hotel was a dream. The staff was friendly, and the hotel itself was set up as a resort. They had their own back patio that gave them complete privacy.

"It's really nice, and I can't wait for all of us to come back out here. I'ma tell you now the men love them some red hair. Bezo had to check niggas all night when we hit up the clubs."

Kolbee laughed.

"Oh gosh, thanks for the warning. I don't want Denali catching a case. He gets enough heat about my ass," she said and laughed.

Logan's eyes met with Bezo as he stepped outside, and she licked her lips.

"I bet he does. You shaped like a Coca-Cola bottle but let me hit you back. My baby is back."

Kolbee grinned at the happiness that could be heard in Logan's light voice.

"You do that and have fun. We deserve this, and the business is good so don't worry. I love you."

Logan's heart warmed like it always did when she heard her sister say those words.

"I love you too. Be safe and call me if you need me."

Logan ended the call and sat her phone down. Bezo

walked over to her in his blue jean shorts with his green Supreme t-shirt on, and he admired her shiny naked body.

"Damn a nigga feel like it's his birthday and shit," he joked sitting at the foot of the lounge facing Logan. He made Logan open her soft thighs, and his hands gently slid up and down them until he was pushing his long fingers against her silky folds. Logan's breathing picked up as she stared into his eyes.

"How did your meeting go?"

Bezo shrugged. His irritation with his earlier meetings washed over his handsome face as he sighed. His cut was thicker than usual making his regular waves curl up however he was still lined to perfection. He smelled divine, and the way his long pink tongue swiped against his bottom lip was enough to make Logan cream herself.

"What's wrong?" She asked noticing his worried disposition.

Bezo slowly slid two fingers inside of Logan and pressed them as deep into her as he could making her body shudder.

"Bunch of bullshit. Niggas trying to give me some slave ass deal that I'm not signing. I did see Cho's bitch ass up there going through with the shit though. He ain't shit but a house nigga," Bezo replied.

Yung Cho's name made Logan fall out of her lust haze Bezo had put her in.

"Chauncey?"

Bezo pulled his fingers out of Logan and frowned at her. No man wanted their woman to say another niggas name while he was bringing her pleasure.

"Don't say that shit like that and we know a lot of the

same people, so I wasn't surprised to see him. Lay back," he said and took his shirt off.

Logan quickly did as instructed and Bezo rested his head between her thighs. His tongue eagerly smothered her pussy with slow licks before he pulled her clit into his mouth. Logan moaned and grabbed his head as he feasted on her.

"Bellamy...that's it. I can feel it," she admitted with a whimper, and before the words were fully out of Logan's mouth, she released on his tongue.

Bezo not giving Logan anytime to recover pulled her up and took her into the suite. He took Logan to the mirror and slid back inside of her. Bezo had Logan rest one knee on the dresser the mirror was connected to as he pounded into her. He had so much on his mind, and the only thing that made sense was Logan and his time with her.

"You so wet. Why this pussy leaking bae?" He asked burying his face into her neck.

The position was awkward as fuck for Logan, but Bezo felt so good that she made the shit work. Her body trembled as he fucked her.

"You know why. Just thinking about you makes me wet baby."

Bezo grunted. He sucked on Logan's neck while fucking her a little harder. Logan yelped, cried out and soon came all over his member again only this time it was creaming up. Bezo loved when her pussy got real nasty with him like that. He wrapped his arms around her waist and drove his dick so deep into her that he started to climb up the dresser knocking over everything that she'd placed on it earlier.

"Baby!!! Got damn," Logan said breathlessly.

Bezo grunted. He couldn't get enough of her.

"Stop running. Take your dick," he said before his back stiffened. His balls tightened, and the best pleasure known to man came over him. He unloaded into Logan until he was empty. Tired and feeling sleepy as fuck Bezo pulled out of Logan and walked over to the bed. He fell on his back while Logan rested on the dresser with her face pushed against the mirror. She had been fucked so good she felt like paying his ass for the sex.

"Bellamy I'm stuck," she finally said, and Bezo chuckled.

His legs felt like noodles, and he was so tired he couldn't even open his eyes.

"Just stay like that bae, and when I get up I'll slide back in it," he promised her.

Logan sore from the sex quickly peeled herself away from the mirror and joined him on the bed. Bezo slid up behind her, and she sighed as his arm went around her waist.

"You make me happy Bellamy," Logan said quietly before closing her eyes.

Bezo smiled with his own eyes closed.

"That's all I wanted to do baby."

Hours later after getting in a good nap and taking a hot shower Logan and Bezo were en-route to a club with his people. The music world called them his entourage, but they were his family. While Bezo wore all white with his white Bally high top sneakers, Logan wore red. Her mini dress hugged her body. Already her hips were spreading, and even her ass looked slightly bigger. The red bottoms she wore gave her three inches while the messy waves gave her an exotic look. Bezo couldn't stop staring at how beautiful she was, and the Bezo diamond chain that hung from her neck looked sexy as shit on her making him want to fuck her in every position imaginable.

"You so fucking beautiful baby," He said glancing over at her.

Logan smiled loving the affection he pushed her way.

"Thank you," she said and licked her lips.

Bezo continued to stare at her thinking of all the nasty things he wanted to do to her when his cousin glanced his way.

"Cho gone be there," Jefe said with a frown.

Logan pretended to not pay any attention as she looked out of the window. They were in the back of the Bentley truck that Jefe was driving.

"I know. I told the crew to fall back. Shit different now and like I said before I care more about Logan then that old ass beef. I already let the OG's know what's up and they cool with it."

Jefe nodded while staring straight ahead.

"Just letting you know nigga. Just because you dropped a beef don't mean he will. We still need to be on guard and did you think about the tour yet? That could be big for you."

Bezo placed his hand on Logan's thigh while glaring at his cousin. Audra was his manager not Jefe, so he wasn't sure why his cousin was all up in his business like that.

"I got time. A year is a long time to be touring nigga. I'm good on money, and I'm good right now," he replied.

Logan sighed feeling guilty because she knew why Bezo didn't want to tour.

"You independent though nigga. Auntie said that this

could gain you some big ass offers. Don't let it pass you by," Jefe replied before turning on the radio.

Bezo pulled a blunt out that he'd pre-rolled and lit it up. He was stressed and upset with everyone trying to control his life. For that reason alone, was why he was still independent.

"Baby. Jordyn and I would love to see you go on tour," Logan said once he'd lit his weed up.

Bezo rolled down the window and blew the smoke from between his thick lips.

"That's a long ass time to be on the road. I pull in good money baby, and I'm not hurting for fans. I'll be good," he assured her.

Logan leaned over to him and kissed his cheek. If Bezo was to miss out on a blessing because of her, she would feel like shit.

"Jordyn would love to see you at an arena. She'd be telling everyone at her new school about you. I wanna see you win baby. You're so talented, and you deserve the fame. You have to do the tour for us," she told him.

Bezo nodded. Logan kissed him again, and he smirked at her.

"Would y'all tour with me?"

Logan smiled at him. Kolbee already did so much at the cleaners. She knew that she couldn't possibly put it off on her for a whole year. That would be just selfish. She also wanted to enjoy that part of his life with him.

"Maybe not the whole year but Jordyn and I would find ways to sneak off to see you."

Bezo nodded not quite satisfied with that reply. He knew she had her own things going on, but he wanted her with him.

He was addicted to seeing Logan and being up in her space. He didn't wanna lose that, and to him, her presence was worth losing out on a tour. He was confident in his rapping abilities and knew his fans would be good with the small tours he did. He wasn't one of those people that felt you had to bury yourself in your work. People like that were often lonely and ended up being slaves to their passion. For him, if he couldn't have the people he loved with him enjoying the shit, then it wasn't that big of a deal. He wanted to do his thing at his own pace because it worked for him. That way he rapped. Put out good ass music and still enjoyed life.

"We'll see," he murmured knowing that if she couldn't commit to a year, then he wasn't doing no funky ass tour. He didn't give a damn who it was with.

Logan's eyes connected with Jefe as he glanced back at them in the mirror and she shook her head. Jefe chuckled.

"He stubborn as fuck cuz," he said making Bezo wave him off.

The nightclub that Bezo had been invited to was off Hollywood Boulevard. Foreign cars lined the streets, and because of his status, they were allowed to valet. Logan spotted Yung Cho a few feet behind them as they entered the club and she squeezed Bezo's hand. He glanced down at her as people called out his name trying to get his attention.

"You good baby?"

Logan smiled.

"Yes, just please don't be on no rowdy stuff. You said you let the beef go right?"

Bezo pulled her close to him, and a few people snapped photos of them.

"I wouldn't put you in harm's way. That shit from the strip club won't happen ever again. I promise. Come on," he said and pulled Logan away.

Logan shy because of all the attention that was on them held onto Bezo tightly. They were taken up to the VIP section designated for him, and it happened to be next to Yung Cho's section. Bottles were brought out while the DJ shouted out Bezo and Cho. Logan made herself a drink praying Bezo, and Yung Cho kept shit civil.

"I made sure everybody got patted down for guns so relax. I told that nigga to let this shit go, and I hope for his sake he listens," Bezo said rolling up a blunt.

A football player that Bezo had grown up with stepped into the section and Logan immediately noticed him. Ra'Son Jones was a football phenom that had given California two super bowl rings.

Bezo jumped up and quickly dapped up his friend that was like his family before introducing him to Logan.

"This Logan. She's Deron's daughter. I told you about her," he said, and Logan did her best to not come off as a fan.

She stood to her feet and gave the handsome Ra'Son a quick hug.

"Damn he speaks highly of you so welcome to the family. My daughter always looking for a new playmate and he mentioned you had a daughter. I'll make sure to send him an invite for her birthday party. I'm renting out Disney world for her spoiled ass," Ra'Son said, and Logan nodded.

"That would be nice," Logan mumbled still star struck by Ra'Son.

Bezo and his friend began to talk while Logan tossed back

a few drinks. Time seemed to fly by and around the fourth drink Logan was buzzing. As she leaned on Bezo sucking on his neck, Yung Cho took the mic. Because the DJ played most of Bezo's song only two of his tracks had been cut and his ego was once again bruised cause of Bezo.

"I just wanna shout out my nigga Bezo! He been lighting the club up all night with his new cd and that shit hitting. I also wanna shout out his bitch Logan that knows how to give some superb sloppy toppy," Yung Cho said, and the club fell silent.

All eyes went to Bezo as he stared at Yung Cho calmly. Bezo raised his glass and saluted him. Yung Cho saluted him back satisfied with all he'd done, and he stepped away from the Dj's booth. The Dj frowned at Yung Cho as he went back to his seat.

"Ol' hating ass nigga," the Dj mumbled putting on another Bezo song just to piss Yung Cho off.

Logan's face was covered in embarrassment. She buried her face into Bezo's neck as Ra'Son looked Bezo's way.

"You wanna handle this nigga?" He asked not giving a fuck about his status. For his family, he was always down to ride.

Bezo shook his head. His beef with Yung Cho went back ten years. Yung Cho was related to a slew of Crips from the southside. Bezo had gotten into an altercation one night with Yung Cho's older brother. Things quickly escalated, and everybody began to fight. In the middle of the mayhem, Cho's brother was shot and killed. Bezo hadn't been the only person fighting but because he was the most known everyone blamed him including Cho. Regardless of what the world or Yung

Cho thought Bezo had never even killed anyone. He'd never had to and was hoping the day would never come. However, as Bezo sat in the booth with Cho's disrespectful ass words running through his mind, he felt like that day might have arrived.

Bezo sat up and kissed Logan on the cheek.

"Let's go sexy," he whispered in Logan's ear.

Cho was back in his seat and smirking Bezo's way wanting him to react. The fact that Bezo was keeping his cool was angering Yung Cho even more.

"Okay."

Bezo and his people stood up, and everyone started to exit the section. Yung Cho laughed at how pussy he felt Bezo was being.

"Scared ass boyyy. Fuck you going with that hoe? Hope you know she a bust it down already! Yet you wifed this bitch," he said loudly making a few people laugh.

Bezo nodded not bothering to acknowledge him, and they soon left the club. After dapping up his boy Ra'Son, Bezo and Logan climbed into the Bentley truck. As his cousin pulled away from the club, he glanced back at them.

"You must really be feeling her," he said before looking straight ahead.

Logan looked at Bezo and smiled at him. The calmness on his face masked the storm that was brewing inside of him.

"You good?" He asked her.

His maturity with the situation was turning Logan the fuck on. She hugged him and kissed his cheek. Once they arrived at the hotel, Jefe went to his room while his people that had been following them in another SUV went to their own suites. Bezo smoked on the balcony as Logan sat next to him. They both had so many things to look forward to, and she didn't want him losing it all behind some bullshit.

"Don't do anything crazy to him, baby," Logan said quietly.

She was now wearing her underwear with her hair in a sloppy bun. Bezo was in his underwear with his socks on. Still, hood as fuck at the end of the day but Logan liked that about him. He was who he was, and she wouldn't dare ask him to change.

"I won't. People like Cho fuck up their own life. Now I'm not saying that I won't knock his ass out if I see him again, but I won't go looking for him. Like I told you before I'm serious about us. When I told my Og's that I was done with gangbanging, I meant that and that includes that hoe ass nigga Cho. People like him self-destruct, so I don't have to do shit but sit back and watch. We both know you not a hoe, and that nigga wish he got some head from you," he replied.

Logan eased off the lounger and dropped to her knees in front of him. She was nervous, but for Bezo she would try new things.

"You will though baby and be patient with me. I've never done this before," she said nervously.

Bezo nodded as he watched her pull his half erect penis from his boxers. Logan kissed the head of it before pulling it into her warm mouth. Bezo groaned as he puffed on his blunt.

"Damn baby I'm honored. Take your time and watch them fucking teeth sexy," he coached her.

Logan smiled. She'd seen plenty of porn. She mimicked what she remembered and allowed Bezo's groans to guide her.

When she realized that she didn't possess a gag reflex she quickly took his whole dick into her mouth. Bezo grabbed her head, being done with his blunt and he looked down into Logan's eyes. She was making his toes curl with her mouth game.

"You so perfect with that pretty little mouth. I want you to swallow it all, okay? Drink that down for me," he said and licked his lips.

Logan moaned. She was breathing through her nose as he pumped into her mouth. She nodded, and Bezo closed his eyes. He shot off into Logan's mouth and as promised she swallowed it all. Logan leaned up when he was done cumming, and she kissed him passionately. She refused to let Yung Cho or anyone else ruin the happiness that they had.

14

S‍ITTING IN HER OFFICE AT THE CLEANERS ON A F‍RIDAY night, Kolbee listened to Logan with a frown on her face. She couldn't believe the audacity of these niggas in Atlanta. Yung Cho especially.

"Girl, niggas are disgusting," Kolbee hissed. "With his ugly ass."

"Who you telling," Logan added.

The sisters snickered. They both knew Young Cho was far from ugly, but his personality definitely was. The stunt he pulled in Cali had Kolbee ready to find him herself. A man who harassed women was a pussy in their book. Especially one who couldn't take no for an answer. Those were the worst.

"Speaking of which, did you know Sir was cool with him?" Kolbee asked.

"Your Sir?"

Kolbee rolled her eyes. "He's not mine, but yeah, him. I saw them in a picture together on his Instagram looking like the best of friend's girl."

"I thought he was cool with Bezo's people?" Logan asked.

"I did, too. I guess not. You know how niggas be switching up," she said while going through her emails really quick. She had stopped by to pick up that week's sales to drop at the bank tomorrow morning because Logan forgot to do so earlier that day. It was past six, and she had no plans to get up super earlier, drive an hour across town, just to come back to their bank. It made no sense, so she dropped by tonight.

"You're right. Well, be careful. I'll see you when you get back or are you staying at Denali's this weekend," Logan cooed being funny. She loved the connection the two shared.

"His place. I just talked to him right before I called you."

"Okay. Well, tell him I said hi."

Kolbee let her know she would and began packing up her belongings. Her quick stop turned into her being there for an hour more than she anticipated. No more than a minute of hanging up with Logan, her phone was vibrating again. Thinking it was her calling back Kolbee pressed the green phone icon without reading her screen.

"Hello."

"What's good, Kolbee," Sir said, and she sucked her teeth.

Speak of the damn devil, she thought. "What's up, Sir?"

"Shit. I'm trying to see what's good with you. You been dodging a nigga like we got an issue or somethin'," he spoke with a little too much bass and grit in his tone.

She looked at her screen like he lost his mind. "And, nigga. If we did? I'm not your girl. Don't be calling my phone on no tough shit. I texted you and told you I think it's best we chill out on whatever it was you were trying to build with me anyway."

Kolbee heard snickering in the background and rolled her eyes. It was just like a nigga to front in front of his boys, when she had already told him what was up. Sir was in a car with a few people who had their eyes set on Kolbee from when they first saw her at the studio but didn't approach her. They couldn't believe she was talking to their boy like that.

Feeling played, Sir showed his true colors. "Bitch wasn't nobody trying to build with you. I was just trying to fuck your bald-headed ass and pass you around to my niggas. I heard how you Kansas City hoes get down. You ain't nothing special."

Kolbee chuckled, and that pissed him off even more. "Yeah? Well, why you on my line trying to plead a case with your broke ass? You hang around a bunch of get money niggas, but you the brokest one. How's that? All you're doing is looking for a come up off your homeboys, you bum. And, you ain't gotta ever worry about wanting to fuck my bald-headed ass. This pussy belongs to one nigga, and his name isn't Sir. Good day."

With a mug on her face, Kolbee hung up in his face before blocking his number. Sir had her fucked up. She was so glad all she did was kick it with him at the studio a few times, instead of taking things further. Between him and Bryson, Kolbee didn't know who disgusted her the most. Replying back to an email Denali had carbon copied her on, she sent it off and closed down the screen. She had somehow become his assistant when he needed a hand around the office, but she didn't mind.

Gathering her things, Kolbee slipped her phone into her back pocket and closed the office door. It was bright out when she first got inside and now nightfall. She shook her head at how fast time went by when she didn't need it to. Just as she was making sure things were in place for the staff in the morning, Denali sent her a text.

I know it doesn't take that long to pick up some money.

It doesn't. I'm on my way now. Be there in twenty minutes.

Aight. Call me when you get in the car.

Nope. She replied with a smirk.

You know what happened the last time you said no to me.

Kolbee bit her bottom lip. Just the thought of how Denali had her spread eagle on the desk inside his office earlier that week when she told him no had her ready to break the speed limit to get to him. He had eaten her pussy so good; she curled up at his desk and took a nap.

"That's that hypnotizing head game," she snickered.

Double checking to make sure she had the money, car keys and purse, she made her way toward the font door but stopped when she heard something coming from the back of the cleaners. Standing still, she stared in the direction she heard the noise come from. When she heard it again, Kolbee thought maybe it was the wind forcing the security screen open again. It had happened earlier that week, and she meant to call someone out to exchange it, but it slipped her mind.

Smacking her lips, she huffed and walked toward the back to close it. When she turned the corner, she damn near peed her pants at the sight of black masks. Thinking they didn't see her, she tried scurrying away without being noticed but bumped into a clothing rack before running as fast as she could toward the front door.

"Bring your ass here," one masked man gritted chasing after her.

Kolbee felt like she was in a horror movie, and the first black person to get killed when he snatched her up by her purse. She let the purse go, not giving a fuck about the money. Her life was much more important. She wanted to cry when she realized her keys to get out the front door was in her purse.

"Ugh!" she gritted once snatched away from the door. Her heart fell to her stomach when the cold steel of a gun was shoved into the side of her neck.

"Thought you were getting away, huh," he snickered sinisterly.

"Fuck you!"

"Now is that how you talk to the man who has a gun to your throat, bitch?"

He asked the question, and shoved Kolbee away from him with so much force, she tripped and hit her head with a bang against one of the chairs nearby. Collapsing to the ground, she cringed in pain while holding her tears back. She hated that she didn't have her gun on her. The one time she forgot to have it on her after Deron took them to the shooting range, she was now regretting it.

With three guns pointed at her, Kolbee was at a disadvantage. Not understanding why three men came to rob a cleaners, she sniffled and went to ask what the fuck they wanted, but one answered her question.

"I'ma only ask you once, and if it's not the right answer; my mans here gets to decide what body part of yours to put a bullet in," the tallest one spoke, and Kolbee swallowed hard.

"Where's his safe?"

"Whose safe?" Kolbee asked with squeezed eyes. Her head was killing her.

"Yo, shoot her ass."

"Wait!" she screamed. "I don't know who you're talking about. This is a cleaners. Does it look like we bring in that type of money to be robbing?"

The guys looked at each other and laughed. "Bitch. Does it look like we're stupid? We know what the fuck kind of money is coming through here. Now, you got one more chance and he gone let loose on your ass."

Kolbee's entire body was trembling. She had no idea what he was talking about. Instead of crying like she wanted to do, she just pointed to her purse that was on the ground.

"What? In your purse?" he asked, and she nodded.

The guy who held the gun to her neck grabbed the purse and snatched the bag of money from it. Hardly ever did their customers pay cash, so they waited until it hit a certain amount to take it plus any donations that were still coming in.

The bag was small but held some cash and at least fifteen checks from the older customers who liked to still pay by those.

"Man. This ain't no fucking money," he gritted and aimed the gun at her head. Kolbee jumped and scooted away from him.

"Please! I swear that's all I have on me. I don't know what fucking safe you're talking about." She began to cry for real because she was all out of chances.

The two men who had only spoke whispered between one another, while the other had his gun trained on Kolbee. He hated flunky missions, but most of all he hated when they didn't fall through. He was told this lick was a guaranteed come up, but it was proving to be a lie.

"Fuck, man! This bitch doesn't have a clue," one hissed.

"We can't let her walk up out of here, though."

"Killing her wasn't apart of the plan nigga," he hissed, and Kolbee's eyes widened going from being scared to fucking terrified for her life.

"And neither was leaving out of here with this punk ass bag of money. Shoot her ass, bruh."

The gunman looked his way as if he were questioning him. and Kolbee yelled out for him to please not shoot her, but it fell on deaf ears.

"Shoot her ass, nigga!"

Hearing that, Kolbee got up and began to take off toward the hall where her office was located, but before she could turn, the gunman sent a bullet flying straight through Kolbee's back. In shock, her eyes widened, mouth fell open, and a hand shot to her chest as she turned around tumbled onto the ground. As tears rolled down the side of her face, warm blood oozed from the gunshot wound. Her breathing became much more like wheezing, but she was still conscious for now. Thoughts flooded her mind as the robbers ransacked the building while she was left to bleed out.

Her first thought was of her mama and how sad she'd be having to bury her daughter the same year she had to bury her baby daddy. Next was her Daddy. She loved him. She hated that he left her here in this cold world, but they'd meet again soon. Kolbee knew it. They then drifted to Logan and her baby Jordyn. They had just come into each other's lives, and now she was being taken away. Lastly was Denali. More tears fell as her eyes fluttered. Her chest seemed to ache even more thinking of how hurt he'd be once he lost her. The love they shared was so short-lived, but she cherished every moment.

"Aye, she gone bleed to death," one called out as if he had somehow gotten sympathy.

"Shoot her ass again just to make sure she's dead."

Kolbee could faintly hear them, and though it was a bad time, she couldn't help but think about the meme that had social media in stiches. Imagine her hanging onto her life by a thread, and then... BOOM! They shoot and end her life immediately. She wanted to cry out, but even that was tough to do.

"Nah. Fuck her. Let her folks find her body," the gunman spoke before they scurried out the same way they came.

In agonizing pain, Kolbee used all the strength she could possibly muster up to pull her cell from her phone. Her hands were covered in blood, so none of her fingerprints were unlocking it, but that was okay. The emergency icon in the bottom left corner was what she needed. Dialing 911, she wheezed and said, "I've been shot, before passing out. Had she known moving to Atlanta was going to cost her her life, Kolbee would have gladly stayed in Kansas City.

Standing at the foot of Kolbee's bed, Logan wiped the lone tear that slid down her cheek. She couldn't believe all the bullshit that had transpired in both of their lives. Between the street war Bezo was in and her sister being laid up in the bed on medication for her pain; Logan was losing her mind. She needed another miracle to happen because she needed it more than ever right now.

Surviving a gunshot wound to the chest is a miracle indeed. The bullet had entered her chest cavity through her right shoulder region at the back and exited through her right upper chest at the front. Though a clean shot, she passed out from shock and the amount of blood she had loss so quickly. Deron had truly been her angel that night.

After the paramedics arrived, Denali wasn't too far behind them. Once twenty minutes passed and Kolbee hadn't called him, he knew something wasn't right. He couldn't believe some punk mufuckas robbed his baby, shot her, and left her for dead. A week had gone by, and Denali wasn't a killer, but he was ready to knock a nigga out and do damage for his.

"She still sleeping?" he asked once Logan walked out of her bedroom.

"Yes. She looks so peaceful, but I can only imagine how much pain she's in. I hate this," Logan cried before rushing away down the hall.

She was so fucking sick of crying it didn't make sense. In her head, she was thinking their move to Atlanta had been nothing but heartbreak since arriving. The only sure thing out of them moving was she and Kolbee's sprouting relationship, and her love for Bezo. Any and everything else had caused nothing but grief.

Sighing, Denali rubbed a hand down his untamed hair and walked into Kolbee's bedroom. He hadn't gotten a cut in weeks. His gym was still up and operating, but he had taken a step back to ensure Kolbee's healing process wasn't done alone. Staring down at her, Denali's chest ached, and hands tightened into fists. Muthafuckas were going to pay. Kolbee stirred out of her sleep, feeling his presence. When her eyes opened, her hand immediately went to her chest out of habit. It'd take a while for her to get used to the bandages and scar there.

"Hey," she said in her raspy tone.

"Hey."

"Sit down. I need to feel you near me. Something's wrong."

Denali closed his eyes. He hated and loved how she could sense things. He used to be so in tune with her, but now they were on one accord. Doing as she said, he sat at the spot she patted next to her and rubbed his back.

"Talk to me. What's the matter?"

"You. Seeing you in this bed like this is fucking up my

head, baby," he grimaced, and Kolbee went to sit up, but he stopped her.

"Nah, nah. Lay down. You ain't gotta sit up to talk to me."

"Well, lay down then. I'm not about to talk to your back."

She was still putting her foot down even while injured. Denali slipped his shoes off, swung his legs onto the bed and Kolbee lay on his chest. His heartbeat was irregular, but the more she rubbed up and down his abs, it slowed down.

"You smell good," she complimented.

"Thank you. I wore it just so you can sniff me," he joked, making her grin. "How you feeling?"

Kolbee sighed. She had a ton of emotions floating through her body. One minute she was sad and talked down on herself, the next she was angry and wanted to choke the living shit out of the niggas who had her going through the motions. Laying up in the bed on bed rest was not how she envisioned spending any of her days until she was pregnant, and that wasn't happening anytime soon if she could help it.

"I feel... I feel confused more than anything. Why would he want to rob a cleaners, bae? Did I tell you they kept asking about a safe?"

Denali stayed quiet. She did tell him after she came to at the hospital, but his mind was everywhere else. Mainly on who could the robbers be? Now that he knew, or had an idea of who, Denali was trying to come up with a plan to not go to jail for murder. That was the only option in his mind unless someone wanted to suggest a lesser punishment. It was sad that a man couldn't handle a woman telling him she wasn't interested, andthought the only option to get over it was by taking her life. It happened every day by jealous, psychotic men; only Kolbee survived to tell who her attempted murderer was.

When she was still faintly conscious, hearing Sir's voice is where the jolt of strength she got to call for help came from. He hadn't said two words the entire time they were there, just following instructions like the puppet he was, but when he did Kolbee couldn't be happier to hear his voice. Though she didn't think she'd survive, she thanked God she had. When detectives came doing their job, she didn't tell them a thing. Him going to jail before he got what was coming to him wasn't what she had in mind at all.

"Denali," Kolbee called out.

"Yeah?"

"Did you hear me?"

"I heard you. Did Deron tell ya'll there was a safe in there?"

This time Kolbee sat up in the bed. "Inside the cleaners? No. Why would there be a safe in there? Especially one that niggas wanted to rob the place for?"

Denali lowered his head and shook it. He couldn't believe this shit. "So he ain't tell ya'll?"

"Tell us what! You're about to piss me off, for real," Kolbee spat with the meanest glare on her face. "Just say what you're trying to say. I'm a big girl. I can handle it."

"He gave ya'll a letter. You and Logan, right?" he asked, staring at her with his sepia colored, questioning eyes.

"Yeah. I told you I was reading that one day, remember and I kept crying."

"But, did you finish reading it?"

Kolbee scratched her scalp and shook her head no. "No. I

got a headache and just put it away. I planned to read through it when the pain wasn't so fresh, but I forgot. Why? Was there something in there I should've known."

Denali nodded his head and told her to call Logan into the room. For the life of him, he didn't understand why Deron wanted to reveal yet another secret to them in death. They had to learn about his illness through paperwork, and the reading of the will took the cake for Logan. She honestly didn't want to move but had no reason not to.

When Logan came into the room, Tasia and Megan followed behind her. They had come down to somewhat restore order in their late baby's father's home and figured they'd do it together. They weren't friends, and never would be, but for their daughters and sanity, they'd go to war with whoever. Both Logan and Kolbee had gotten into some shit they thought had been left in the past. The past when Deron was living a totally different life.

Once Kolbee told Logan about the letter they were given at the attorney's office, she went to retrieve hers that had never been open and Kolbee's from her nightstand. Logan was far too hurt to read a letter from Deron. He used to write her all the time once he moved out of the house, and it brought back too many bad memories for her. She hated reading them because he should have never had to write them in her eyes.

"Do ya'll have a clue of what this may say before I start?" Kolbee asked and looked at her mama before her eyes skirted over to Megan. Logan looked up at her mama, too.

They both released heavy sighs, and Logan sucked her teeth while Kolbee rolled her eyes. She was so sick of everyone being secretive she didn't know what to do. As the two read silently, Megan and Tasia were both nervous. They had an idea of what Deron may have written to them, but they could never be too sure with him.

"Wait. What?" Logan said to herself. The passage she just read over had her face frowned completely up.

"Right. What the hell does he mean '*I was into some illegal stuff, baby girl,*" Kolbee mocked.

She and Logan both shot daggers at their moms. Tasia shook her head. "I thought that part of his lifestyle was over a long time ago. I guess it wasn't."

"Girls," Megan started, taking the motherly approach.

"No. Fuck that," Logan hissed, and Megan reached back and was ready to snap the freckles from her skin, but Tasia stopped her.

"You better watch who you're talking to, Logan Flint. You done lost your damn mind," Megan hissed on the verge of angry tears.

"Sooo," Kolbee dragged. "What is it? I'm probably laid up in this bed with a gunshot wound over some mess he had going on before dying." When neither of them said a word, Kolbee started crying. "Oh my gosh. I can't believe this!"

Denali went to console her, but she pushed him away. "No! Don't try to hug on me. You knew about this shit, too, huh? That's why you got the stupid look on your face."

"I knew to a certain extent, but it wasn't my place to tell," Denali said in his defense.

"Can one of ya'll please just tell us what he was into. I'm stressed out enough," Logan said in a much calmer tone.

"Fraud embezzlement," Tasia answered, and Kolbee tossed her letter to the ground.

"A thief. Wow. Great, Deron. Because you wanted to steal shit that didn't belong to you, I have to suffer. Like always. After cheating on you, he should have known that his decisions would come back to haunt him," Kolbee told Megan who had tears in her eyes.

"Kolbee," Tasia called out, and she shook her head no. She wasn't trying to here anything her mama had to say.

Logan was stuck. She didn't know how to feel right now. Yet again, Deron had lied. All this time she thought he had been a successful businessman, making an honest living. And, he may have once opening Flint Cleaners, but before that, he had two feet planted into almost anything that brought in cash. Legally, and most definitely illegally.

Before he and Megan's relationship, Deron was fooling around with an accountant named Liana. She considered it much more, and Deron let her think it was but played her in the end. Maybe that was why so much bad karma had come his way and was being passed down to his children.

Being the accountant over a fortune-five-hundred-company had its perks. Especially being the daughter of the owner. Liana's father, Shelton of Lockridge Financial, was beyond wealthy. He had raised his daughter to know numbers backward, forward, upside down, and anyway her brain could obtain them. What Shelton didn't instill in his daughter was trusting him. So, she placed that in the palms of someone else; Deron.

Shelton cheated on her mama for as long as Liana could remember. It started off with her best friend, then the choir lady at church, the mail lady, even his assistant. Liana witnessed all of her father's affairs but turned a blind eye. It was hard to still treat him like the King she once thought he was, but she did it for the sake of her and her mother, Leela. She had a plan to get them as far away from him as she could, but "love" blindsided her mission.

While they dated, Liana would confide in Deron about her dad's infidelity, and she told him how she was going to hurt him where she knew it'd hurt the worst; his pockets. At the time, Deron was just getting his feet wet in the drug game. He had a little money to his name but needed some real funds to make a major move. For weeks, he listened to Liana complain until one day they both came up with a plan. Having access to so much money as her father's accountant, Liana knew it'd be easy to embezzle money from his clients.

She started off small with the accounts she knew no one would think twice about checking. Once that worked, she got greedy. Her father had to pay. She'd have the money sent to separate accounts and then almost always give Deron a cut for being her confidant. By the time six months passed, she was madly in love, Deron was getting drug money hand over fist, and it was because of her scamming ways that it was capable.

Things were going smoothly for a good two years until Leela got fed up with his cheating, Deron starting publicly dating Megan, and Liana wasn't feeling any gratification anymore from the money. She wanted Deron to herself. One evening, Shelton and Leela got into a big argument, and she didn't just threaten to leave and divorce him, but she already had the papers for him to sign. Shelton was a mess as if he hadn't brought all of this upon himself. In the heat of their argument, Leela let it be known that Liana always had her back. She mentioned the money she had tucked away for her and was walking out the door but Shelton shot and killed her. Not believing what he had done, he turned the gun on himself, taking both their lives right in front of Liana.

Depression sank in immediately for Liana, and the one person she wanted to console her was heavily in the streets with a new woman. Deron appreciated Liana for sure, but she was just a pawn in his game to get to the next level. He never loved her, but always gave her the impression that he did. When Liana found out about Megan and that she was pregnant, she tried to take her own life but failed. In her eyes, there was no reason to live anymore. She was parentless, the man she loved no longer needed her, and she was heartbroken.

When the first attempt failed, she was placed in a psych ward, and the medications turned her for the worst. Liana was never herself after that, but she never once gave Deron up. In her mind, he still loved her and would come for her when the time was right. That time never came. Deron got heavy in the streets, created two children, moved to Atlanta, and started over after a few years of hustling in his new city.

Megan knew all of this. Tasia knew some of it, but not all the details, and Denali only knew about Deron having been in the drug game. Once Megan was finished giving them the details, leaving out a few because she hated to relive them, everyone in the room was left in shock. When Sir and his boys came masked up into the cleaners, they had the intentions of getting their hands on a safe. A safe Deron had buried with Flint Cleaners on top of it. No one was ever bold enough to run up in there while he was alive but instead waited until he was dead and gone.

Rumors of a safe being inside had circulated, but whoever started it waswrong. Deron had never told anyone where the safe was until he wrote Logan and Kolbee in their letters. He had taken that secret to his grave, but now that they were owners of the shop, he felt it needed to be revealed.

Kolbee sat in disbelief, feeling the need to pop another pain pill. Her daddy had yet again proved to her that love really did hurt. Liana was living proof of that.

"I can't... I don't even know what to say. This is unbelievable," Kolbee said lowly while Denali helped her get back comfortable in the bed.

Logan couldn't speak. Her soul was shaken, and all she wanted to do was hug on Kolbee. They were all still getting backlash for Deron's reckless behavior from years ago, but Kolbee had almost lost her life. Logan didn't think he could do something more idiotic than cheating on her mama, but this topped everything in the book. She didn't even know what secret to expect next with him.

Once everyone came to terms with what and who was the cause of Kolbee being robbed and shot, Andre was called over. He was staying away because seeing Kolbee laid up like that had his trigger finger itching. He was no longer in the streets and hadn't been for years, but he'd be lying if he didn't want to lay hands on Sir. He wasn't a killer, but he sure was going to wish he had finished Kolbee off once he got to him. It wasn't going to be shit nice.

"So, you mad at me? I didn't know any of that," Denali told Kolbee.

She was staring up at the ceiling with tears in her eyes. "Can you just get out," she said lowly.

"No."

His stern answer made Kolbee break her concentration with the white paint. "No?"

Denali didn't answer. Instead, he pulled the covers back on the queen-sized bed, got comfortable and stared at the ceiling. "I'm not leaving you to get through this shit alone, so let that be the last time you ask me to get out. Don't think you running shit cause you done took a bullet, gangster."

Blinking back tears was no use. A few slid down her face, and Kolbee leaned over to kiss his cheek. "Thank you, Denali River."

"Mhm. You better thank me."

Kolbee smiled. It was the first time she had all day, and after the shit she just heard, it made her feel good knowing Denali wasn't going anywhere. His words were so reassuring and therapeutic; she just wanted to lay in solitude with him until all her worries of the world erased. *Doesn't hurt to think positively,* she thought before staring back at the ceiling. Their heartbeats fell in sync on one accord.

15

A week later Logan walked outside of the doctor's office with her mind all over the place. She hit the locks on her car, a shiny black Audi truck and grabbed the handle.

"Aye hold up!" Yung Cho yelled running over to her with his little sister following closely behind him.

Logan glared at him as her eyes looked his way. She was dealing with a lot and Yung Cho was only making it worse.

"What the fuck could you possibly want from me?"

Yung Cho shook his head. He was in basketball shorts with a beater while his sister wore her dance uniform. He felt fucked up behind Logan getting caught up in his beef with Bezo, and after spotting her leaving the doctor's office, he decided to speak to her.

"I'm sorry. That was some hoe ass shit and..."

"Chauncy I'm getting in the car," his little sister said

tiredly. She'd gotten her first checkup as a teenager and was drained from the whole process.

"Aight," Yung Cho said and hit the locks on his old school.

Logan tried to get in her truck, and he grabbed her arm gently. Logan was looking sexy as hell in her blue leggings with a mustard colored half shirt that read Honey going across the chest. She'd paired the outfit with her Yeezy's and was wearing her hair in a low ponytail.

"Don't fucking grab on me," she said and snatched away from him.

While Logan begged Bezo to leave Yung Cho alone, she had no problem shooting his ass with her gun that was registered.

Yung Cho nodded and let her go. He took a step back and looked down at her.

"I'm sorry beautiful. You didn't deserve that. It's just after a while a nigga gets tired of shit always being about Bezo. Even when we were younger, he was always that nigga."

Logan sighed and licked her lips. She was under the weather and looking to climb into her bed.

"Chauncey, I don't accept your apology. Sorry doesn't make what you did okay. You were wrong, but that's something you have to live with. If you want to live to take care of your sister and watch her grow old, you need to change your attitude," Logan told him.

Yung Cho nodded. She wasn't telling him things that he didn't already know.

"I hear you shawty. I am who I am though. If it's meant for me to die, then the shit gone happen regardless. I just wanted to speak my peace. I see he hit a home run like I would have," Yung Cho said and gave Logan a knowing smile before walking away.

Logan got into her truck and pulled away. After picking up Jordyn from school, she took her back to Bezo's West Midtown place. Logan and Kolbee had been discussing giving Deron's house to Deena but after the robbery and Kolbee getting shot they'd hadn't spoken about it.

While Jordyn rested in Bezo's extra room that he'd turned into her palace, Logan attempted to cook. With her baby sister getting shot then learning about her father's shady past she was spent. Logan was knocked off her feet by her latest news and wondering if she could handle it all?

"Hey baby I'm finally home," Megan said answering her phone.

Logan relaxed once she heard her mother's sweet voice. Now that she was with child it made her miss her father even more. With so much going on she'd been forced to move past it, but now with life in her precious womb, she was hormonal. Her emotions were on overload, and she was a mess.

"Mom I miss my dad," she quietly admitted. Logan closed her eyes. She willed, herself to not cry and Megan sighed on the other end of the phone.

"I know you do baby. I miss him too."

Logan got up to cut off the stove and stirred her spaghetti. She did a taste test and was happy with the outcome, so she sat back down at the table in Bezo's dining room.

"I do momma. For the longest, I couldn't even take hearing people talk about him. He made me so angry. I was so mad with him dying. I guess blaming him made it easier for me to cope with him being gone. It's just now with me being pregnant I can't ignore the fact that my father is dead."

Megan gasped. Jordyn was five and as far as she knew her daughter wasn't looking to have any more kids. To know that she was now carrying another life inside of her excited Megan.

"A baby. Wow, thank you Lord," Megan said with happy tears streaming down her face.

Logan smiled.

"I just found out I was twelve weeks. I usually have irregular periods, so I didn't think anything of missing one. I was extremely sick last week though, so I made an appointment. It's like I can't keep anything down and I have the worse migraines," she replied still shocked at being pregnant.

"I'm so happy baby. Bellamy is good to you and Jordyn and as long as that doesn't change he's a winner in my book. It's a plus that Deron already knew him too. Like maybe he was prepping him for you," Megan told her.

Minutes later Bezo stepped into the townhome dead ass tired with his traveling bags. He'd just flown in from doing two out of town shows in New York and Memphis. He dropped his luggage's at the door and stepped out of his sneakers as Logan approached him.

"Bellamy's back ma so I'll call you later," Logan said and ended the call with Megan. She looked Bezo over and smiled. She was so happy to see him. "Hey baby," Logan said walking up on him.

Bezo hugged her and groped her ass. Like always she smelled so good and had his place smelling right as well.

"I missed your pretty ass. Miss Jordyn where you at!" He called out.

Jordyn emerged from the room and ran as fast as she could towards Bezo. She hugged Bezo's leg, and he ruffled the curly hair on her head. It had been an adjustment having a kid around. Jordyn seemed to have hundreds of toys and had managed to waste chocolate milk in his living room in various spots but like all things he was getting more and more used to her as time went on. She wasn't bad she was just a kid. He knew Logan was a package deal from the start and he was cool with that.

As Logan looked down at Jordyn, a wave of nausea fell over her. She rushed out of the room but wasn't successful in making it to the hallway bathroom before the contents of her stomach expelled from her mouth.

"Mommy, what's wrong?" Jordyn asked worriedly as she rushed over to Logan with Bezo behind her.

Bezo grabbed Jordyn's arm, and she glanced up at him.

"Let me take care of your moms then we can go over your homework. Okay?"

Jordyn nodded. Bezo was great with helping her do her homework, and Jordyn loved spending the quality time with him.

"Okay, will you make my mommy feel better? I heard her telling grandma something about a baby," Jordyn told him.

Bezo's smile quickly fell on his face.

"Yeah, I got her. Matter of fact go wash your hands, and I'll fix your plate."

Jordyn did as he requested and Bezo cleaned up the hallway floor before running Logan a bath in his bedroom.

His mom had passed down a lot of remedies to him, and he knew that ginger cured nausea so while Logan rested in the tub, he made her some lemon and ginger tea. Bezo then fixed Jordyn a plate and sat with her while she ate. He was tired but having them at his place was what he wanted.

"How was school? Was everybody nice to you?" He asked Jordyn.

Jordyn swallowed down her food and nodded. She thought of the boy that had picked on her during recess, and she frowned.

"It was this one boy that was mean. His name is Randy. He kept pushing me down," she remembered. She'd forgotten to tell Logan but now that Bezo knew he planned on taking her to the overpriced ass private school and getting little Randy's ass together. He didn't play that pushing bullshit and Randy or his people was gone have to answer to him for that.

"Oh yeah? And what you do?" He asked her trying to remain calm.

"Ummm," Jordyn looked up at the ceiling before looking back at Bezo. "I kicked his leg and told him my daddy was gone get him. You will, won't you?"

Bezo could have fallen out of his chair. He'd gotten used to the idea of having a little family. So naturally his parental instincts were kicking in. Still in the back of his mind he wondered if he was doing the shit right. To hear Jordyn call him her dad was humbling to him. Especially since he wanted nothing but the best for her.

"You called me your dad?"

Jordyn smiled at him in a way that made his heart pump faster.

"Yes silly. Now can I go watch tv?" She asked.

Bezo stood up from his seat and went to Jordyn's side. He gave her a quick hug and looked at her.

"I'm honored that you would give me that title. We gone get Randy together tomorrow okay?"

Jordyn giggled. She loved the sound of that.

"Okay, daddy."

Bezo let Jordyn go, and she ran out of the room. After he cleared the table, he found Logan laying down in the bed with the lights off. Beside her was the empty cup his special tea had been in. Bezo joined her on the bed, and she looked at him. Her throat was raw from vomiting, and she was sleepy, but her stomach didn't hurt any longer, and she was thankful for that.

"Guess what," Bezo said looking at Logan.

Logan smiled at him weakly. "What?"

Bezo rubbed her stomach as he thought of what Jordyn had said to him.

"Jordyn called me her dad and shit a second ago," he replied.

Logan smiled at him. She wasn't expecting for him to say that and was watching him intently to see how he felt about it.

"And what did you say?"

Bezo smiled.

"I told her I was honored for her to call me that. Shit warmed my heart up," he replied making Logan grin at him.

"I'm twelve weeks," she whispered.

Bezo sighed. He pulled Logan close to him, and he tenderly kissed her on the lips.

"I love you, Logan. When we first met, you said it was lust and you was right. I was so caught off guard by how fine you are, but then I got to see you beyond your looks. I wanted all of you, and the best thing you did was give it to me. Thank you for giving me another child," he told her.

Logan closed her eyes soaking in his words, and he kissed her again. Bezo was so happy, and he couldn't wait to call up his mom and tell her the big news.

"You love me, Logan?"

Logan nodded. How could she not?

"Of course, I do. I love you so much Bellamy, and I can't wait to give you a baby," she replied before kissing him again.

Back in Detroit Logan stood patiently inside of the courtroom. To her left was Rome. He was back to his old self-looking handsome in his black suit with his thousand-dollar loafers on as he stood next to his lawyer. Logan felt like her head was on the verge of exploding as she stood next to her own lawyer. For twenty minutes she'd debated with Rome about his job, his pay and the time he spent with Jordyn. Once it was confirmed that Jordyn was spending no nights with him, the referee was ready to set a price.

"You currently spend no nights with your child. You said that you have no interest in changing that and when you do you will have to contact the courts. It is ordered that you pay six hundred and eighty dollars a month in child support for Jordyn Flint along with two twenty-one in expenses that will go towards her health care and after-school activities. You have twenty-one days to object, and the court is adjourned."

Logan quickly exited the room so that she could take some medicine. As she swallowed a pill that she'd received from her gynecologist in the hallway Rome advanced on her. Bezo wanted to come along, but Logan begged him to stay back wanting to keep the drama levels down. Jordyn was with Megan, so Jerricka had shown up in support of Logan and had been waiting for her in the seating area.

"I see you got what you wanted. You just want all my fucking money," Rome said walking up.

Logan wiped her mouth, and Jerricka walked over to her with Logan's lawyer.

"Any threats will be reported to the proper authorities," Logan's lawyer told Rome before telling Logan goodbye.

Rome waited until the lawyer was out of earshot before he looked back at Logan. He hated her. She was so selfish, and he regretted the day he slid deep inside of her.

"You got money and so do that nigga. Why the fuck you need mines? I don't even see her, and now I'm supposed to pay for her," he said angrily.

Jerricka held Logan's hand as they both glared at him.

"Don't forget you're pregnant," Jerricka told Logan wanting to piss Rome off even more.

"Damn," Rome chuckled. He nodded his head as he looked up and down the hallway. "I see you about to hit that niggas pockets too. I out of beat that baby up out of your hoe ass but I won't. I'll just quit that job and find something that pays under the table. Have a good day ladies," he said before walking away.

Logan looked at Jerricka and before she could break down her best friend pulled her into a hug. Jerricka rubbed her back and recited her most favorite verse out of the bible. *The Lord is my strength and my shield. My heart trusted in him, and I am helped. Therefore, my heart greatly rejoices, and with my song, I will praise him."*

Jerricka hugged her friend tightly, and they gave Rome to the Lord. They had no interest in trying to fix him and knew that if anyone could, it was God.

16

"You sure you're okay with doing this?" Kolbee asked her best friend.

Alaia had flown in town after hearing the news about Kolbee being shot but could only stay for a few days. Thankfully, she was relocating to another job but didn't start until next month. It had been over a month since the terrifying night Kolbee thought she was going home to meet her maker, and she was more than grateful to be alive. God was surely looking out for her that night.

Still in a bit of pain when she did certain activities, Alaia had come to relieve some of her stress. Sir had been hitting her up still even after everything that had gone down. Denali wanted to beat his ass so bad, but Kolbee told him to wait it out. The time to get his was coming soon. The audacity for him to text Kolbee's phone from a different number like shit was cool between them made her sick to her stomach. There were really some sick individuals roaming this world, especially to commit such a crime and act like it never happened.

Kolbee had something for his ass though. While on bed rest, she was able to sit and plot her revenge. Though death would have been the easy route to take, especially with Andre's attempt to jump headfirst back into the streets, she didn't want that for him. Doing her research, Kolbee was made aware that all the things she said about Sir were true. She knew them to be somewhat but didn't think he was really broke like that. But, he was.

Sir was a leech. Anything he could sink his fingers into to bring him money, he did. That included people as well. He stayed in the clubs flexing with money he nine times out of ten gotten illegally, belonged to someone else, or was money he owed. The nigga couldn't hustle on his own to come up, so he tried to come up off everyone else.

"I'm sure," Alaia replied. "I'm glad he's somewhat okay to look at. His ass has been getting on my nerves all week."

"Trust me. I can only imagine. He still calls my phone from all these different numbers. I swear I'm getting my number changed once this is all over."

"You should have been got your number changed like I told you to," Denali added in as he walked into Kolbee's bedroom.

Her stomach fluttered at the sight of him. Anytime Denali wore jeans; it turned Kolbee on to the highest degree. She was used to seeing him in sweats and basketball shorts, but it was just something about him in a pair of designer jeans. It could have been because of the way they fell at his waist, showing off his perfect v-cut abs. Or, the way he was standing with his hands in his pocket like he was ready to punish her.

Smirking, she motioned for him to come to her. "You did tell me that, didn't you?"

"You always playing. That's yo problem now."

Alaia giggled. "Ya'll are so cute. When's the wedding?"

"When she starts doing what I say," Denali replied and leaned over the bed to kiss her lips.

Kolbee melted. He was so in charge all the time, mainly when she was being stubborn, and she loved it. He wasn't controlling but didn't let her handle him any type of way. That's why she and Bryson didn't last. A man that let Kolbee walk all over them wasn't the man for her. At least not the one to settle down with.

"Welp," Kolbee laughed. "We're never getting married."

"Yeah aight. What's up, though. What ya'll in here doing?" he asked taking a seat on the bed.

"She's meeting up with Sir, tonight," Kolbee answered.

"This what, the third date?"

Alaia nodded. "Yeah. And I hope this nigga finally take me to his crib. He still hasn't told me what he does for a living, so I know he must be a scamming ass nigga. He has to be."

"I told you he was," Kolbee said with disgust laced in her tone.

"Where ya'll going? To the strip club?" Denali asked, and they all laughed. Just like when he asked Kolbee to come out for a gathering, he had asked Alaia the same thing, and they ended up at the strip club. If he thought that was a date, he had a lot to learn.

"I think out to eat. I'm not sure yet. I have a feeling he's just going to talk my head off like he always does. For a nigga who doesn't have much going for himself; he sure does talk about himself more than I care to hear."

In Kolbee's attempt to seek revenge, setting Sir up was the best option. He was attracted to pretty girls who looked like they had money and had smart mouths. Alaia possessed all of those qualities, plus more. Her skin complexion wasn't as light as Kolbee, but that didn't matter. Her brown skin was gorgeous, with an arm full of beautifully inked designs. She loved tattoos and, in another life, could have been a model had she wanted to pursue that field. While Sir was so hell bent on setting folks up, he was unaware of the pretty grim reaper headed his way.

"You tired?" Denali asked Kolbee. The three of them were sitting around talking until it was time for Alaia to get dressed.

"No. I wish I could go with her tonight. I really don't trust that nigga."

"Neither do I; that's why I'll be there until they leave.," Denali reassured.

Kolbee's shoulders deflated in appreciation. "Good. I'd hate to have to really kill this nigga."

Tackling her onto the bed, Denali tickled her sides. "You ain't no mufuckin' killer, girl."

"Oh, my gosh! Stooop," she squealed trying to get away from his assault.

"Nah. Call me Daddy Denali first."

Kolbee really cried laughing at that. She was laughing so hard she could hardly breathe. "D-Denali. I-I can't-."

She didn't even finish her sentence before Denali hopped up from the bed in a panic. "Damn, baby My fault." Standing at the side of the bed she was lying on with his hands intertwined behind his head, Denali's face was masked with concern.

Kolbee's eyes were closed and hand still on her chest, but a smirk teased the corner of her mouth. Peeking her eyes open she said, "I'm just playing. I could breathe."

Denali sucked his teeth and shook his head. "Childish. I was trying to get a quickie in before I left and you wanna play games."

"What! You the one came over here tickling me," Kolbee pouted.

"And, then you pulled this. I'm going to the living room."

She climbed from the bed. "And, I'm going with you."

Denali looked at her and laughed. "For what? Don't follow me now. Stay yo childish ass in the bed."

"Nope. I'm following you wherever you go in this house. If we not fucking in here, you gone give me that dick somewhere in this house before you leave. You got me messed up."

Slick talking, Kolbee tried to walk past him, but Denali stopped her. Grabbing her by the back of the shorts she was wearing, he pulled her into his chest and slipped his hand in the front of them. Massaging her mound, Kolbee bit her bottom lip as he guided her toward the edge of the bed.

"Bend yo ass over, and you better tell me when it starts hurting," he gritted out, undid his jeans and dropped them to the floor before sliding into her. She didn't even realize he had yanked her shorts down that quickly.

Kolbee held the comforter between her fists as Denali

long stroked her pulsating walls. Her thick ass slapped against his thighs as he fucked her like he was trying to write his name on her pussy. He wanted to be gentle, but Kolbee needed some act right.

"Fuck, I wish I had some hair you could pull on!" she hissed loudly, and Denali stopped to crack up midstroke.

"What the hell is wrong with you, girl?"

Kolbee continued throwing her ass back. "I want you to grip my hair, but I don't have any," she whined.

"It's okay, bae. We gone get you a wig, aight?" Denali smacked her ass and lifted her leg so he could stroke at a different angle.

"Oooh, fuck. Okay, baby. Okay. We gotta make sure it's a good kind. Not no synthetic shit."

Denali chuckled and gripped the back of her neck just how she liked it. He kissed down her back and went deeper. "Aight, Bee. I hear you, baby."

The thought of strapping up crossed his mind for a millisecond, but as quickly as it entered, it was gone. On the real, Denali was ready to settle down, have a couple of auburn haired babies, and put a rock on Kolbee's hand that weighed it down. He'd wait though. At least on the babies. He knew Kolbee had a few goals to accomplish before she'd be walking around barefoot and pregnant. With the way Denali was tossing dick in her stomach, she'd better hope like hell he was a pro at the pull-out method still.

"So, you got any brothers or sisters?" Sir asked Alaia as he smacked on a shrimp.

He decided to take her to Pappadeaux, and she was praying he'd hurry up and finish his meal. She loved their food, and their drinks were her favorite, but she opted for lemonade for the night. Sir, on the other hand, was getting a good buzz off the drinks he kept requesting. He was stunting, as usual, trying to impress Alaia, and the whole time she was annoyed.

"No. I'm an only child," she replied. It was a lie. She had three older brothers and a younger sister.

"So, you spoiled and shit?" he grinned. "I can tell. It ain't shit, though. I'm the nigga you want to spoil you."

"Is that right?" Alaia asked and licked her lips so she wouldn't roll her eyes. *This nigga is so fucking lame.*

"It is. Matter fact. If you play your cards right, I may just wife you. The last little bitch who got that privilege from me lost it with her stuck up ass. Tried to talk bad about a nigga, but it's all good though. I can tell you not that type. You want anything else fore' we head out?"

Underneath the table, Alaia's foot was bouncing so hard she had to hold her knee to not shake the table. Sir was the worst kind of nigga ever; a pillow talker. How dare he sit up and discuss the next female, one whom he tried to kill, with her. Her appetite was ruined more than it had been when they sat down.

"Dang. That's crazy," she mumbled. If Alaia said anything else, she was going to snap.

"It is, but that's the past. I'm trying to make you my future," he grinned, reaching across the table for her hand.

Alaia's skin crawled at the gesture, but she played her role. Holding his pinky, she said, "I'd like that, Sir."

His grin went even wider before he got their waiters attention for the bill. Peeking at the time on her phone, she frowned when she realized how long they had been dining. Denali was frowning the same way parked outside. Seeing his text, Alaia excused herself and headed for the restroom.

What ya'll in there doing? Buying the entire menu...

No. I told ya'll this nigga likes to talk. I'm so annoyed.

Just another hour or so, and you'll be good. Kolbee texted.

I hope so, she thought before using the restroom, washing her hands and walking out. Sir was at the table bagging up all the food he hadn't eaten, while the waiter assisted him. Alaia was so over this setup, and if it wasn't for her love for Kolbee, she'd walk the hell out.

"You're going to eat all that later?" she had to ask.

Sir looked at her like she was crazy. "Hell yeah. All that money I spent... that's leftovers like a mufucka. I got yours in here too. Shit be hitting late at night."

"Right. You don't want to waste money." She gave him a smile as the waiter brought the bill back over.

Alaia held her breath, and thankfully whatever he gave her for payment had gone through. Sir placed his hand on the small of her back as they walked out of the restaurant. With all the drinks in his system, she was tempted to ask him could she drive, but she had no clue where he was trying to go. Instead of meeting him, Alaia got dropped off at one of Denali's cousin's house where Sir picked her up. She told him she was from New York when they first met and was only staying in Atlanta with her cousin for a few weeks. He fell for it, and the plan to set him up had been in motion since.

"You sure you okay to drive?" Alaia asked once they reached his car. "I don't mind driving."

Sir didn't even think twice before handing her the keys. "Shit. Go 'head. Don't wreck and we good."

She rolled her eyes as he walked around to the passenger side and mumbled, "This probably ain't yours anyway. Bum ass nigga."

Denali couldn't believe his eyes when he saw Alaia climb into the driver's seat. If he knew it was going to be this easy to get to this nigga, he would have had his cousins in on the plan weeks ago. He waited a few seconds after they pulled out to follow behind them.

"Sooo, where am I driving to?" Alaia asked after he told her to hop on the highway.

"Shit. We can stop by my crib real quick. I gotta get some money. You trying to go to the strip club?"

"That's cool with me. Just let me know where to go."

Knowing Denali was following her, Alaia tried to keep at a steady yet reasonable speed in the Atlanta night traffic. Since she'd been there, she had gotten somewhat used to the reckless driving. Kolbee was calling Denali's phone trying to see if things were going smooth, but he ignored the call. He was wishing there was a way he could get Alaia to follow him somewhere, but he'd just have to stick to the plan.

Alaia followed Sir's janky directions until she was pulling into some apartments that looked worn down. She peeped right away that there was only one way in and one way out. Taking note of that, she glanced in her side mirror to see Denali's Charger turning in after her.

"Aye," Sir called out. "Park right there."

"That's on the wrong side of the street."

"We in the hood. Don't nobody give a fuck about that. Just park there and come on. A nigga gotta piss," he griped.

Alaia parked the opposite direction of the way she should have, handed him the keys, and climbed out. Denali was parked at the top of the heel with his lights off, waiting for her to give him the go ahead. He had never set someone up before, so his adrenaline was pumping. If shit went wrong, things could end up worse than they already were.

"You walking all slow," Sir chuckled as Alaia sent Denali a text from behind him.

"These heels are killer," she faked complained.

It looks like they all have backdoors. She sent.

Yeah. I peeped that.

Once inside, Alaia assessed her surroundings. For Sir to be living in the projects, he had his place laid out lavish. A sixty-inch TV was mounted on the wall, with more than enough gaming systems underneath it. The living room was small, and he had it cluttered with unnecessary shit that he had either purchased or stolen. From where she was standing, Alaia noticed the back door inside the kitchen. There was an upstairs, and she assumed that's where his bedroom and bathroom were located.

"You wanna come upstairs?" Sir asked, turning some music on.

Alaia just knew this nigga had lost his marbles. He was trying to set the mood for no reason. This shit was about to end quicker than it began.

"Nah. I'll just wait for you down here."

"Aight. Get comfortable. I'll be right back."

Get comfortable my ass; she said to herself right before he skipped up the steps. She waited a few seconds after before cautiously moving towards the backdoor. Her heart was beating so fast she had to tell herself to calm down. To her surprise, Denali had already made his way to the backdoor. In the neighborhood Sir lived in, it wasn't suspicious for people to be roaming around at night. Many addicts got served through the backdoors of these same apartments every day.

Slowly, trying not to make too much noise, Alaia unlocked the door and opened it. The screen door had more than one lock, and she about pissed herself when Sir called out to her.

"Ma, what strip club you trying to go to?"

She rushed back into the living room. "Um, I don't know. Surprise me."

Denali sucked his teeth. "That's all she could come up with."

Alaia shrugged her shoulders once Sir said aight. Scurrying back to the kitchen, she undid the locks and stepped to the side as Denali stepped through the door. Not bothering the close the screen, he cracked the main door before grabbing Alaia's attention.

"What he doing?" he asked.

"Using the restroom," she whispered back.

Denali nodded his head. "Bet. Just chill in there, and I'ma stay right here until he comes down."

Nodding, Alaia went and sat in a fold up chair by the couch. Her leg was back bouncing as Sir shuffled around upstairs. He was changing into another fit and trying to sober himself up. He wasn't as drunk as Alaia thought he was, but high off coke. Before their date, he sniffed a few lines to calm his nerves. Ever since he supposedly killed Kolbee, he was fucked up behind it. He knew she was still alive, but with her not replying or reaching out to him, he figured she was still mad about their little argument. Kolbee was mad about way more than that.

Bringing his head up from the sink, Sir stared at himself in the mirror and blinked slowly. He was high as hell, but that one line had him feeling good. Slapping his face a few times, he grinned and wiped the residue away before hitting the lights.

"You okay up there?" Alaia called out.

"I'm good," Sir answered coming down the steps. Alaia stood to her feet with her clutch in her hand. "Let me grab a water and put this food up. You want something?"

He walked into the kitchen, and from where Denali was standing, Sir didn't see him at all. With his back turned and refrigerator door open, Denali made his move as soon as the door shut. Placing him in a chokehold, Sir's eyes stretched wide while snatching his gun from his hip. Denali grabbed his wrist damn near crushing his bones, causing the gun to fall to the ground. Kicking it her way, Alaia went to pick it up but stopped. Reaching into the pocket of her jeans, she pulled out a pair of gloves put them on, then picked it up. Aiming it straight at his head, she felt her blood boil with animosity.

"What the fuck!" Sir gritted out, struggling to breathe. "You setting me up, bitch!"

Alaia smirked. "Awww. You should be used to this. That's your thing, right?"

He tried going after her, but the pressure Denali was applying to his windpipe stopped him from doing so. Slamming him against the side of the fridge, Denali landed a vicious blow to his jaw, before reconnecting and breaking his nose. Blood spewed out, and Sir covered his face.

"C'mon man," he cried out. "Please don't kill me."

"Where the safe at, bitch?" Alaia hissed out, and Denali looked at her like she was crazy. *What you doing,* he mouthed.

"The safe? What safe man?" Sir was lifting back up, but the punch to his gut knocked the breath out of him.

Denali was sick of hearing his ass talk. Snatching him up, he tossed him effortlessly into the living room. Losing his balance, Sir fell onto his table, and that was all the ammunition Denali needed. The thought of Kolbee losing her life had him seeing red and delivering hits that shook Sir's brain. He was beating his ass to the point where he didn't want anyone to recognize him. Had he had it in him, a bullet would have been sent through his head once he finished his attack.

Breathing hard, Denali took a step back with low eyes.

He was happy with the work he had done, but Alaia wasn't. She needed Sir to feel how her best friend was feeling. Firing the gun – his gun – she sent a bullet to his thigh. Sir's jaw was broken, so the scream he was trying to let out only came out muffled.

"What the fuck," Denali hissed with wide eyes at Alaia.

She didn't feel any type of way. In fact, she smiled knowing he was going to be left there to bleed just like he had done Kolbee. After removing the bullets, Alaia placed the gun on top of the PS4 and sighed with content.

"Let's go," was all she said before walked toward the front door.

Being Denali, he punched Sir one more good time, knocking him unconscious before pulling the back door open. For as much shit as he stole from everyone else, he deserved to get the same treatment. The duo walked swiftly to Denali's ride and hopped in. Alaia was quiet as they pulled out of the complex, and when she started whistling, Denali chuckled and broke their silence with words.

"Aye. You crazy than a mufucka."

"So, I've been told," she replied. For Kolbee, she'd ride out on whomever. She was just glad her friend had a man who was willing to do the same.

No less than ten minutes after they left Sir's crib, the junkies who stayed out back came through and wiped him clean of every item worth value. Even some of the folks who he had robbed in the neighborhood came through to collect what belonged to them. A crackhead even pocketed the gun. He'd find someone to give it to for a quick hit.

Later that night once Sir came to, his entire apartment was empty. Even the table he had been laying on. They tossed his ass onto the floor. An anonymous tip was sent out to the police about some suspicious activity going on, and before he knew what was happening, police were rushing in and cuffing him. Sir's scheming ways had finally caught up with him. A few of the credit cards he had stolen, one's police found still in the home, were reported but they could never pin it on anyone. Unbeknownst to him, they had been watching him for a while now. Tonight, was just his luck to get caught slipping; twice.

"Auntie Deena," Kolbee stressed. "Please relax. I'll be fine."

"Are you sure? Because there are plenty of rooms in that house for us to stay together. You didn't have to move all the way over here," she fussed.

Kolbee had just moved to a chic two-bedroom, two bath, skyrise apartment on Peachtree St. After living with her mama, then living with Logan – which wasn't bad – Kolbee *had* to venture off and learn responsibility on her own. Her decision to move was made once the summer weather turned to fall. She'd be damned if she moved in one hundred degrees weather and faint.

With all things to consider, staying in the home Deron passed down to her was something Kolbee no longer had interest in. Though she didn't grow up in the home making tons of memories to share with her kids, the place was full of negative vibes. As hard as Deron tried to be the best father he could be, he fell short a few times. Those times causing the most damage to his daughter's adult lives.

Kolbee wasn't blaming him anymore. She had gotten over that stage. In fact, she was glad he had taken them through the storm. Had he not, she wouldn't have met Logan, built a sisterhood that no one could break between them, and gained an adorable niece. But, most importantly; met Denali Westin. His charming, irresistible personality and goofy laugh were what pushed Kolbee to move out as well.

Denali was a motivator given his profession, but he was selfless with it when it came to Kolbee. He encouraged her beyond her wildest dreams to go for what scared her. She was nervous about getting back into school, not having a clue as to what she was good at, but together they sat and wrote up her skills. He explained to her that getting a degree just to have one was a waste of money and time. If she decided it was something she was passionate about, then did he suggest for her to go.

She enjoyed being his assistant, and not just because she got to see his handsome face for the majority of the day and fuck him during random work hours in his office. Kolbee was growing to love the knack for being organized. Denali's clientele was growing every day, and though it may seem like running a business was easy; it wasn't. He was more than grateful for Kolbee's help.

"I'm sure. Plus, he'd be happy knowing you and the kids are somewhere comfortable. They can all have their own room now," Kolbee smiled.

Deena was so grateful for her nieces. With tears in her eyes, she hugged Kolbee tight. She could still remember the first time she held her. On one of his many trips to KC, Deena tagged along to visit some friends, and they stopped by Tasia's crib first. Kolbee's big, light brown eyes, toothless grin, and head full of hair immediately won the young auntie over. They hadn't been as close over the years, but they had the rest of their lives to share.

"Thank you, niecey pooh. Let me know if you need anything else. You know I'll come through for you."

Kolbee smiled softly. "I know. I appreciate you for making the transition down here a little easier. Even though you got on my nerves at first."

"I don't care. You act just like your daddy with that smart mouth. You and Logan. I pray my baby Jordyn doesn't take after you two," Deena said waving her off.

Kolbee laughed. She was more than positive Jordyn was going to have wit, and spunk like her. She could gain everything else from her mama.

"Mhm. We'll see. Tell the kids I said hi."

Deena said she would, and Kolbee closed the door once she left out. Sighing, the breath she released was one filled with happiness. All of her worries of the world had been eliminated, and she could hardly remember the last time she felt so at peace. Her debt was erased, the baggage with Bryson was dumped to the curb, and for once she felt genuinely loved by a man. It wasn't a necessity she had had been searching for, but love wasn't something on her agenda. If it happened, it happened. If I didn't, it didn't. That was her motto.

Warmth engulfed her frame as Denali hugged her waist from behind. He had just gotten in from work when Deena was leaving out and was now smelling like Dove men's body wash. The scent drove Kolbee nuts. *He* drove Kolbee nuts. Inhaling him, she turned her head to meet his gruffy beard.

"What you thinking about?" he asked.

"Nothing really. Just enjoying this space I'm in. Why'd you shower?" she questioned, maneuvering to face him.

"Did you not smell me when I came in? I ain't trying to stink your place up in the first week," he chuckled. "Have you gossiping to your sister and shit."

With a smirk, Kolbee traced his bulging abs. He had one of the best body's, and it all belonged to her. Sticking her hand in the band of his shorts, her eyebrow lifted when she saw he was free-balling. Tugging them down, she squatted and began to stroke his dick to its full potential.

"I like the taste of it after you work out. It gets me wetter."

Her words were low and sultry, making Denali's dick jump. With one hand holding onto his leg for support, Kolbee skillfully sucked him into her relaxed mouth. With each twirl of her tongue, her slurps got louder. She was so glad she could now be as loud and nasty as she wanted to be in the comfort of her own home.

Denali's eyes glossed in appreciation. After a long day of training, his limbs were sore, and there wasn't anything like a great blowjob to end the day with a smile. All he wanted to do was lay up inside Kolbee until she had to meet up with Jordyn for their playdate. Gripping the long, twenty-four-inch weave in her head, Kolbee deepthroated him, until he snatched his dick from her mouth with a mug on his face.

"Like that?" he hissed sexily.

She licked her lips before biting the bottom one. "Just like that."

Pulling her to her feet, Denali wasted no time bending her over the barstool and sliding into her. Dripping wet, Kolbee's tunnel sucked him in with ease. Finally getting the wig she wanted, Denali met her request by wrapping the curls around his fist and digging her guts out. The wig was cute, and the black looked amazing against her light skin, but Denali loved her with her signature short curls.

"Aaah, yes," Kolbee cried.

"You love this dick, Bee."

"Mhhhmmm. I love you."

Denali smirked. That may not have been the answer to his question, but he'd take it. Kolbee didn't willingly give up her love. It was earned, and he had earned every piece of it and gave her his in return. Even when she didn't feel as deserving, Denali made her feel like the luckiest woman in the world by his side. To receive his love unconditionally and without fault made Kolbee realize that Deron may not have been able to provide his all the time, but God created Denali for her. He was destined to be her soulmate from the day they met, and she was forever grateful for their paths crossing when they did.

17

"Are you happy with the manager's we chose?"

Kolbee nodded. They were seated in the back of the cleaners eating lunch. Kolbee was looking forward to finishing college and Logan was taking some time off to travel with Bezo. He'd decided to do his tour that started in the next four weeks, and he'd even hired a nanny and licensed teacher to travel with them. Musician kids did it all the time, and Logan was confident that Jordyn would be fine. She was also excited for her baby to travel the world. It was something she had done with Deron because he'd taken her and Logan to many vacation spots when they were kids.

"Yes, I like them, and they seem very responsible. Plus, you know I'll be able to check in on them along with auntie Deena," Kolbee replied.

Logan nodded. She rubbed her stomach that was slightly

upset at the burger she'd scarfed down, and Kolbee looked at her.

"You okay?"

Logan went into her Givenchy bag and pulled out her sonograms. She passed them to her sister, and Kolbee's eyes widened. She looked at Logan then at her flat stomach.

"Where the damn baby at?"

Logan laughed. Her breast was fuller and hypersensitive. Her hips were spreading, and she was always horny, but besides that, she hadn't changed any. Her stomach was still flat as ever.

"You sound like Bellamy. Sis, I swear every day he's looking for a baby bump. I think I need to be like five or six months to show. I'm only a hundred and forty-five pounds," she replied.

Kolbee gazed at the sonograms while smiling.

"I'm so excited! I can't wait to do the baby shower and tell Jerricka now that I'm running the show, so she needs to call me to see what the plans are."

Logan laughed. She was happy that her family had her back because she surely needed their support.

"Thank you. I'm scared, but he makes it easy. He's not perfect. He leaves the toilet seat up and irritates the fuck out of me when he wants to get high and discuss politics, but I love him. You know how you were saying you felt about Denali's fine ass?"

Kolbee was going along with Logan until she said the fine part. Kolbee's pretty face fell into a frown, and Logan laughed.

"I said that just to fuck with you but for real you know

how you were saying you loved him and how good it felt? Well, I know the feeling. It's scary, but you can't help but embrace it. It's so crazy too because with dad knowing both of them it was like it was meant to be. I do know I'm happy life got better for us," she admitted.

Kolbee smiled.

"Me too and it can only go up from here," she said making Logan nod in agreement with her.

After leaving the cleaners, Logan stopped for gas and ran into a familiar face. Yung Cho stood inside of the small gas station having a heated debate with a tall man that possessed grey eyes. He spotted Logan and quickly dropped the argument.

"You lucky I don't feel like hurting a nigga today," he told him.

The man waved him off while walking away and Yung Cho went over to Logan. He noticed how much bigger her ass was getting and he licked his lips. He still wanted her although he knew she was off limits.

"You been good?" he asked dropping a fifty down to pay for her gas.

Logan looked at him and nodded.

"Yes, and you didn't have to do that. I'm perfectly capable of filling up my own tank."

Yung Cho chuckled.

"I know that. Still, I wanted to do that. How is the baby?"

Logan exited the gas station with him on her heels.

"The baby is good," she replied watching the men Yung Cho had been arguing with glare their way. "You should leave. Let this drama shit go," she told him.

Yung Cho noticed the niggas staring at him too, and he smiled at them. He tapped Logan's arm, and she glanced over at him.

"You be good Logan," he told her before going over to his Infinity truck. He jumped in and pulled out of the lot.

Logan quickly got her gas and went back to Bezo's place. After taking a shower and eating she laid in bed with Bezo while he ran his fingers through her hair. Jordyn was spending the weekend with Kolbee and Logan planned on sleeping all Saturday to catch up on her rest. Her baby was taking all her energy.

"You okay?" Bezo asked her quietly.

Logan nodded with heavy lids.

"Yes, I'm kind of horny, but I'm too tired to even get naked so we can do it tomorrow," she mumbled.

Bezo chuckled as he turned to the news channel. Breaking News cut on with Yung Cho's face plastered across the screen. Bezo noticed him immediately and turned the volume up.

"Another life has been taken far too soon. Atlanta born and raised rapper Yung Cho whose real name is Chauncey Lewis was gunned down today inside of his truck while outside of his aunts East Atlanta home. Were told that dispute between him and a known gang member started at a gas station earlier in the evening. That escalated into him being followed, and once he parked his truck, the gunshots began. Forty bullets were placed into his SUV. He was pronounced dead at the scene. He leaves behind a little sister and two small kids ages three and five. He was only thirty and headed for Los Angeles next week to sign a million-dollar record

contract. It seems the street life got the best of him. It's back to you Clark."

"Wow," Logan said shocked by what she'd just seen.

Bezo cut on one of his favorite shows and nodded. Death wasn't new to him. He saw the shit all the time and was glad he'd left all that rowdy shit behind.

"Yeah, the streets ain't no joke. Its niggas that rap about it to sell records then its niggas that really live that life. Yung Cho was really living that life, and it caught up with his ass."

Logan rested her head on Bezo's chest as he started back massaging her scalp.

"I saw him arguing with someone earlier, and I told him to leave the drama alone. He'd apologized to me the day I found out I was pregnant but with so much going on I forgot to tell you. I hated how ignorant he was towards the situation with you but still its fucked up he's dead."

Bezo chewed on his bottom lip. Hanging with the wrong people was a sure-fire way to get yourself killed. Logan could have easily been catching a bullet today had the niggas started blasting at the gas station instead of at Yung Cho's aunts home.

"Baby you have to watch your surroundings at all times. You could have gotten hurt today then I would have been looking for that nigga. I can't lose you beautiful," Bezo told her.

Logan looked up at him, and she smiled.

"You won't, and I need you to make sure we don't lose you."

Bezo waved his head.

"You already know I'm here to stay."

Weeks later on a warm fall day Logan, Kolbee, and Jordyn followed by their mothers visited Deron's gravesite. It wasn't tears, it wasn't pain. On his birthday it was nothing but smiles for the king that had brought all of them together. They all wore black, and everyone sipped on his favorite drink except for Logan and Jordyn of course.

His gravesite was already decorated with flowers from many others that loved him, and the sisters were once again reminded of just who their father was.

Jordyn began to play with the bubbles Megan had given her while Logan and Kolbee sat down near the headstone. They held hands, and Kolbee rested her head on her sister's shoulder. Hard times had brought them together, and now they were as close as sisters could be with one another. They both had so many exciting things happening in their life, but they wouldn't dare let it stop them from being close. They talked regularly and made time to always hook up. They also ran the business together without any problems. Logan had now moved all of Jordyn and her things into Bezo's townhome while Kolbee had her own place. Deena was happy to move into her late brother's beautiful home.

"Daddy we made it," Kolbee said and smiled.

Logan nodded.

"Yes, we did, and we know you're so proud of us. We have been through some things daddy. Kolbee took a bullet, and I got knocked up. We also made a lot of good changes and finally know what it's like to have your sister in your life.

We're good to each other and we have you to thank for that. You are the reason why we are here," Logan spoke.

Tasia and Megan stood off to the side in their own world discussing life while Jordyn played around them with her bubbles.

"Yes, daddy we did good. Denali is so good to me. He treats me right and makes me feel like his queen. I know you had something to do with that up there. I miss you, and I love you, daddy. Happy birthday," Kolbee said before tearing up.

Logan's eyes watered.

"Happy birthday daddy. King Deron Flint. The man that created us. Today we celebrate you," Logan said and wiped her tears away.

The sisters could feel that their father was resting in peace because as the wind blew around them brushing against their skin, his spirt hugged them ever so gently. Deron was with them, and they could feel it. Just knowing he was there made everything all right.

EPILOGUE

Six Months Later

"Hey, my favorite sister in the whole wide world," Kolbee grinned into the screen.

Logan smirked. "I'm your only sister."

"Shit. As far as we know. We could have another sibling running around somewhere."

The sisters chuckled at that now that they could. Deron's death had taken a toll on them both, but with the support from one another, it made the days of living without him – permanently – manageable.

"Sooo, how's tour going baby mama. Is Bellamy treating you and my babies, good?"

Logan rotated her camera to a peacefully sleeping Jordyn and turned it back around.

"Of course, I am. What type of nigga you think I am," Bezo said, leaning into the screen. He shot Kolbee his infectious grin, and she knew that's how Logan ended up pregnant. The man was just too fine.

"Mhm," Kolbee replied. "I think you the type that's trying to take my sister from me. Let me find out you jealous of our bond."

Logan and Bezo laughed. Kolbee was a mess. "Never that. Can't be jealous of something I shared with her first."

"See. That's that slick, rico suave shit Logan likes. Bye, Bezo. Get out of our conversation."

"And, you get off the phone period. Ain't you supposed to be running," Denali butted in, walking over to Kolbee and smacking her on the ass.

She was supposed to be finishing up her two-mile run on the treadmill but got tired. Needing a distraction, she called her sister. Logan gave her a sneaky grin and waved in the camera.

"Hey, Denali."

"Whats up, Lo. You about to get your girl in trouble."

"Oooh," Kolbee cooed. "I like trouble. Bye, hoe. Tell Jordyn to call me when she wakes up."

Before Logan could get a word in, Denali hung up in her face. Placing his hands on the arms of the treadmill, he swung his legs upward and tried wrapping them around Kolbee's waist to climb on her back.

"Oh, my gosh! Denali! Get the hell down. You're too

heavy," Kolbee hollered out being dramatic as always. Denali hadn't even put all his weight on her.

"Come on, bae. I don't be complaining when you get on my back."

"That's cause you're stronger than me," she whined, and Denali laughed before placing his feet on the rubber.

Turning around, Kolbee glared at him with those eyes he loved staring into. "You done playing today?"

"Nope. Give me a kiss first, and then I'll be done."

She shook her head no.

"No?" He questioned, moving closer to her.

The sweaty, musky smell of him had Kolbee breathing hard. When she went to wrap her arms around his neck, Denali started tickling her. Panicking, because she knew he'd go too far with his shit, Kolbee ducked her head underneath the arm of the treadmill and took off running. Denali was chasing her until Kolbee tripped and fell, scraping her knee on the carpet in the process.

"Owww," she cried, cradling her leg.

Denali was laughing so hard he had tears in his eyes.

"It's not funny. Look at my knee. I'm too light to be having this ugly ass red bruise on me."

Wiping his face and breathing heavy, Denali flopped down beside her and grabbed her leg. Wincing, Kolbee punched him in the arm.

"I've given you worse marks than this. Stop crying," he shushed her and kissed her small carpet burn. His cool lips made her body shiver.

"If you hadn't been chasing me, I'd be okay."

"You're okay, now. With yo dramatic ass," he replied

falling onto her and bear hugging her. He was so touchy feely, and Kolbee loved it except now. She was mad at him.

"Move, Denali River. You play too much."

"Nope. We gone lay here until you lose that attitude."

They lay in silence, with Denali sprinkling kisses on her neck while Kolbee pouted. When he kissed behind her ear where her bumble bee was tattooed, she grinned.

"I can't stand you," she said rolling over to face him.

"Good thing you laying down then, huh?"

She chuckled but got serious. "You know I love you right?" He nodded, and she continued. "For real, though Denali. I do. And, I just want you to know that I thank you. I swear you're everything I didn't know I needed until I had you."

He wiped a fake tear and gave her a smirk that made her panties wet. "I love you, too, Busy Bee. That day at the cleaners when I said I needed a girl like you; I really wanted to say you. Can't no other girl compare to what we got."

"Ah yeah. So, you been comparing me to other girls?" she sassed, and he grabbed her by the neck softly. Her eyes fell into a lustful gaze.

"Never. You're in a league of your own. Now, open them legs so I can stretch you out since you couldn't finish your workout."

"Oooh, with pleasure," she cooed making him laugh.

Right there on the gym floor, Denali made love to Kolbee the way he only knew how to. He gave her all of him. All of what she deserved. All of what she had been missing her entire life. It was an indescribable feeling flowing through her veins at the genuine love she received not just from him, but from Logan, Deena, and even Megan. It wasn't forced either. It was just what Deron wanted for her. Especially knowing that one day his just wouldn't be enough.

The luxury tour bus that housed over twenty seats with two cabins and a slew of other amenities was temporarily Logan and Jordyn's home. Traveling with Bezo had been challenging in the beginning. His boys had to accept that he was a man with a family, so all the hardcore partying only happened off the bus. Between crazy fans and the media Logan was overwhelmed atfirst but as time went on she got used to it.

Bezo let it be known he was taken and the love he showed her was always real. As promised Rome disappeared on Logan and Jordyn. He cut off all communication with them and so did his family. Logan was more concerned for her daughter and whenever Jordyn brought him up she did her best to comfort her. Logan knew that years from now he would have to answer to Jordyn for all the wrong he'd done her, and she prayed that when it happened he was a better man.

"Baby slow down," Logan whispered.

With Jordyn asleep in the back Logan and Bezo were sneaking in some adult time in the front bathroom. Logan sat on the small sink with her legs wrapped his waist. Bezo gripped her sides tightly as he pounded into her.

"I'm trying. You so fucking wet. Give me a kiss," Bezo demanded and attacked her lips.

Logan moaned as his tongue went into her mouth. After Rome she hadn't envisioned herself being with anyone else let alone having another child. Sometimes when she thought about it she still laughed because it was crazy to her, but she didn't regret a thing. Rubbing on her stomach after they both climaxed, Bezo shot her a smirk.

"You look even better than when I met you. All that's me," he boasted and bit down on is bottom lip.

Logan rolled her eyes with a grin. Her hair was longer which meant she spent all damn day at the hair salon and her body was curvier. She wasn't on Kolbee's level, but she was a nice slim thick, and Bezo loved every second of it.

"This is all your son. He has me eating everything in sight Bellamy. Then, you got me eating all this unhealthy shit. It's going to be so hard for me to drop the baby weight," she fussed as he helped her off the sink.

Bezo shook his head. He would fuck it off her if that's what she wanted. If not, he'd love it the same way he loved her. He planted kisses all over Logan's neck until Jordyn came from the back room. She was rocking her hair straight for the first time in her life, and it made her look older than what she was. Bezo hated that and made Logan promise not to do that bullshit again until she was at least sixteen.

Logan agreed to shut him the hell up.

"I'm so hungry, lets go eat," Jordyn said, and Bezo chuckled.

"Yo mama trying to put us on a diet princess. We gone leave her here and hit us up this soul food spot. Did you sleep good?"

Jordyn found a seat next to Bezo, and she rested her head on his shoulder. Bezo had introduced her to what life would be like with a real man raising her. Jordyn loved him with all her little heart, and while sometimes she did still ask about Rome she was happy to have Bezo in his absence.

"Yes. I had a dream that the baby was born and we were on an island. In the dream auntie Kolbee was there, and she had a baby too mommy. My grandpa was there, and I was showing him that I could swim. You even had on a white dress," Jordyn said recalling the longest dream she'd ever had in her life.

Logan thought of her father and smiled. She often dreamed about him, and she knew it was his way of still being around.

"Was your daddy there?" She asked Jordyn.

"Of course! He was making sand castles with the baby. It was so nice mommy," Jordyn replied.

Logan kissed Bezo on the cheek and looked down at her beautiful daughter.

"That sounded like an amazing dream baby. I guess we can go eat since y'all determined to make me as big as a house."

Jordyn smiled happily ready to eat some food and stood up. As she walked away to put on her shoes, Bezo turned his attention to Logan.

"I love you, baby," he told her.

Logan leaned over and kissed his lips. She then kissed his chest that was decorated with a tattoo of her name in the most beautiful calligraphy style writing one could ever see, and Bezo pulled her face back up to his.

"No, like I love the fuck out of you baby. I woke up this morning so happy, and it was all because of you. I'm happy you gave us a chance," he said before kissing her again.

Logan closed her eyes and relished in the feeling of kissing the man she was madly in love with. She was happy she'd given them a chance as well. Letting go of all the pain, insecurities, and worries that she had turned out to be the best thing she could have ever done.

Her life was perfect. Rome had completely cut off all lines of communication with Jordyn including his family. He'd also quit his job and fell off the radar, but Logan didn't allow for it to get to her. She prayed about it and gave it to God. The things Rome did he would have to answer for. That person would more than likely be a beautiful young woman with red hair, freckled skin, and light eyes many years later and Logan hoped that by then he was a better man. If not, Jordyn would still have Bezo who was proving daily why he was the right man for the job.

The Flint women would be just fine because they had Deron's blood flowing through them. He was a fighter, and so was his girls. Not only that, but their mothers had raised them to be strong, black women regardless of their hardships. They cried, shouted to the heavens above for peace and answers, and still smiled when they had to. That was the strength God blessed them with, even when they didn't know they had it. Even when they didn't have love. Now, though? They'd gone from not feeling loved at all to having an abundance of it.

The End

OTHER BOOKS BY BRIANN DANAE

Speechless: When Love Hurts 1-3

I Was Never Supposed to Love You: Meechi & Erica's Story 1-3

Juvie & Solai: A Hood Love Story 1-4

She Used to Be the Sweetest Girl

He Want That Old Thang Back 1-2

Feenin' For a G 1-2

The D-Boy Type is What She Likes 1-2

Sen and Neicey: Life After Love

My Heart Is a Fool 1-2

My Heart Was A Fool: Esmin & Greigh's Story

A Senful Holiday

The Love

OTHER BOOKS BY DOMINIQUE THOMAS

I Only Wanna Be With You 1-2

Pray You Catch Me

Fallin' 4 The Bad Guy

Made in United States
Orlando, FL
06 March 2024

44482331R00183